The Keeala Series

Village Secrets

Kumari Gorman

By the same author

The Keeala Resort Series

Book 1 - The Last Resort

Book 3 - The Road Home

Book 4 - Crystal Clear

The Keeala Resort Series

Village Secrets

© Kumari Gorman 2014

National Library of Australia Cataloguing-in-Publication entry (pbk)

Author:	Gorman, Kumari, author.
Title:	Village Secrets / Kumari Gorman.
ISBN:	9780992388027 (paperback)
Series:	Gorman, Kumari. Keeala Resort Series
Subjects:	Resorts—Queensland--Fiction
Dewey Number:	A823.4

Published with the assistance by www.inhousepublishing.com.au

The Keeala Series

Village Secrets

Acknowledgements.

I would like to thank Ocean Reeve for his wonderful words of wisdom and his freely given support. He arrived at a time when I was about to give up. He guided me back on to the right track and I am very grateful that he inspired me to keep going. Thank you Ocean.

To my husband, John. Thank you so much. Thank you for your time, patience, advice and support.

Well, for some of your time and patience.

Well, perhaps tolerance is a better word.

Maybe I mean a bit of your time and occasional patience.

Definitely some tolerance and some occasional advice.

Whatever. You know what I mean.

Kumari Gorman

October 2014.

Chapter One

"Jessie, are you there? It's Diane, the manager."

The manager of Keeala Resort, Di Watersen, knocked loudly on the front door of Unit 27 and waited. Another woman stood behind her. There was no response. After a few seconds she knocked again, hesitated, and then, using her master key, unlocked the door and pushed it open. She stepped inside and a black miniature poodle welcomed her. There was no sign of the unit's occupant, no response to Di's shouted, 'Jessie, are you there? Jessie?' The dog jumped around the lounge room and then went to the front door, before he ran back down the short hallway. The dog disappeared through a doorway. The door was slightly ajar. Di pushed it open and looked in. The heavy brocade curtains dulled the bedroom to semi-darkness, but Di could see Jessie in bed, lying on her side and faced away from the door. A heavy doona scrunched up around her chin.

Di walked over, and bent close to the scruffy, grey head and said quietly, close to her ear, "Jessie?" then louder, "Jessie?"

The manager reached out and gently shook her shoulder. No response. She pulled the cover back a little and looked closely at the old woman's serene expression but was alarmed to see she was not breathing. Quickly, she pulled the bed cover and sheets off Jessie and turned her onto her back. She shook her firmly.

"Jessie!" she shouted at the pale, elfin features; so still, so cold, so lifeless.

"Miriam!"

The other woman was behind her in a moment.

"She's dead, Miriam."

******

At that same moment, a young man slipped through the gate at the rear of the old woman's tiny backyard. He took a tentative step into the adjoining community garden. His eyes darted from left to right as he scanned the area. He checked the windows of the four units overlooking the garden. Satisfied that no one was watching, he moved forward and used a hedge of camellias for cover. He kept his head down and made his way to a perimeter security gate where he punched in the code and let himself outside.

A lowered, double-cab ute was parked at the kerb. Its V8 motor idled, but throbbed intrusively. A younger man got out of the vehicle and asked, "G'day, mate, you Kevin?"

"Yeah." Kevin looked around. Checking that the street was deserted, he reached inside his shirt and pulled out a small plastic bag. He handed it over then stood with his hand out. He waited expectantly.

The youth from the ute opened the bag, raised it to his nose and sniffed. He wet his finger, dipped it in and tasted the contents.

"Okay?" Kevin asked.

"Sure." The youth handed over a small wad of money.

Kevin quickly counted the notes, gave a thumbs-up to the buyer and said, "Next week?"

"Yep. Same time, same place."

They both nodded and the young man turned and got into his tricked-up ute. Its ultra-low profile tyres squealed as he drove off, and the sports exhaust made far too much noise for Kevin's liking. He shook his head as he turned back to the gate.

"Dickhead," he muttered.

Chapter Two

Two weeks before the discovery of Jessie's body, Di Watersen had walked out on to the shaded, timber balcony of the manager's residence and joined her husband who stood leaning against the railing. She had a half-full bottle of Australian sparkling white wine in her hand. "How's your drink? Shall I freshen it up?"

"I'd love another. Thanks, darling." Jim Watersen drained his glass and gave a little belch, followed by a contented sigh, as Di refilled the champagne flute.

"I really love this veranda. This Poinciana tree is magnificent, isn't it? I've never seen one quite like it. Its shade makes this a perfect spot to unwind with an afternoon drink, doesn't it? If it wasn't for the mozzies, I'd be tempted to sleep out here."

Jim put his arm around his wife's waist and gave her a gentle squeeze.

"Yeah," he said, "it would be tempting, wouldn't it, but thank God the air-conditioning means we don't have to, eh? You know, Di, whoever designed this place did a really good job. Look at the beautiful curves they've used to soften the landscape." Jim pointed to the ornate security gate at the entrance with its discreet *Keeala Resort* sign, then swept his arm slowly around to his left.

Di followed his outstretched arm and could appreciate what Jim was saying. She saw how the driveway wound its way into the resort, past their residence to a graceful, circular sweep in front of the Clubhouse. It then meandered past a large, kidney-shaped swimming pool surrounded by Golden Cane Palms and other tropical shrubbery. Short side streets, also curved and with four or six, freestanding homes fronting them, branched off the main driveway at irregular intervals.

"I've had so little time in the past few months to really appreciate the gardens and all the exotic trees and shrubs. It's so well planned and it really is a credit to the gardeners," Jim said, as he sat down. "Speaking of gardeners, I had a talk with old Tom today and he reminded me of how the previous managers had left in such a hurry; he didn't even know they were gone until the area manager informed him, three days later."

"I don't think Allen Sinclaire is the type to worry about how he may treat any employee, including us," Di said.

She thought about the phone call they had received, nine months earlier, from the head office of their employers, The Sleighmen Group, based in South Australia. Even after many years in the business, this adaptable pair had been surprised when asked to take over the management of the Over 50's resort on the northern outskirts of Brisbane. They were on leave when they had received a somewhat curt telephone call from Norman Russell, head of human resources in Adelaide. He told them the managers of Keeala Resort in Brisbane had left without notice and he needed someone to take over immediately. He had assured them the area managers, Allen Sinclaire and Georgeina Bunning, would be there to introduce them around when they arrived.

Exactly one week later, Di and Jim Watersen had commenced duties, despite serious reservations about the pressure Russell had exerted with his insistence on their taking over within a week. They had also been less than impressed with Allen Sinclaire at their first meeting with him. Di remembered his reaction when she had asked him about the previous managers.

"They've gone and won't be back. Don't worry about them," was all Allen had said.

Georgeina Bunning was also present at that first meeting but had remained silent, Di recalled.

When Norman Russell advised Allen Sinclaire of the Watersen's appointment, Sinclaire remembered the pair from previous postings as being a competent couple with the skills and disposition to equip them to operate as an effective and resourceful team. He recalled that Jim's background was in real estate and business management and his wife, Di, was a registered nurse with more than thirty years' experience. Together, they had managed both retirement villages and Over 50's resorts for many years so he had no doubt they would adapt to their new situation quickly and efficiently.

******

Di sank into a deck chair, next to her husband. She tapped her foot as she thought over the day's work and took stock of chores still to be completed. Their nine months at Keeala Resort had been hectic and sometimes confusing. The pair sipped their drinks, each lost for the moment in their own thoughts of the recent events.

Jim looked up and noticed that the birds, which had entertained them for the last hour or so, had now quietened and the cicadas were giving their final, piercing choruses for the day. Motorway noise in the distance melted away and a small breeze lifted the leaves of the great Poinciana tree that hung over the balcony.

"It doesn't get any better than this does it," he said quietly.

"Oh, if only it was like this all the time," she answered. "I think we should try to take it easier, not rush around so much, and worry about every little thing. We should start to enjoy ourselves more. Don't you think, darling?"

Jim nodded. His expression softened as his eyes rested on Di's long brown hair. As always, it twisted up in a loose knot at the back of her head, and escaped in wisps around her neck and face. Jim loved the little creases around her eyes and mouth that gave her a constant smile and he was impressed that, although she was in her late fifties, she was as active and quick of movement as ever.

Jim towered over his wife, but he always saw her as larger than life, in that she often seemed to be everywhere at once. He had come to depend so much on his wife to organise and conduct events in all aspects of their partnership.

Jim snapped out of his reverie and said, "Yes, it would be nice if things just flowed along, wouldn't it? But it doesn't seem to matter how much you think you've got things running smoothly, something always crops up that makes you say to yourself, 'Uh oh, here we go again.' For instance, there's that couple in Unit 26, Richard and Beryl. I've come across this pair before – I think I may have mentioned them to you," said Jim. "They were having a dispute with the couple in Unit 28. I recall these four have had problems previously because they'd exchanged some personal insults. The old woman in Unit 27, you know, Jessie Thornton, complained about the noise and I had to intervene. In addition, yesterday afternoon as I walked back to the community centre from the pool, I interrupted an argument between Jessie and Kevin. It seems he kicked her dog and then she really let him have it. Verbally, I mean, but all the same, I wouldn't have liked to be on the receiving end of that tirade. She's a tough nut and with that poodle going for the gardener and everyone shouting, you could have been excused for thinking you were anywhere other than a retirement resort."

Jim stretched both arms out in front of him; he locked his fingers, turned his palms outward, and stretched his arms above his head. He turned his stiff neck from side to side and let out a long, relaxing sigh.

"Mind you," he continued, I don't know who was in the right, but if I'm to go by what the other three residents had to say about Kevin, I think I'm going to have to keep an eagle eye on him."

"Like, what did they say?" Di frowned, as she asked the question.

"They reckon he's always coming to work late, sneaking in through a security gate in one of the common areas, an hour or an hour and a half after he's supposed to start. It seems he spends half his day hiding in the little courtyards, smoking, if you can believe what they say. I don't know whether there was some implied criticism of me in their remarks, but hell, I can't be everywhere, especially at 6am. Even if I did go looking for him, this place is so big it could take me an hour to find him. It also appears there have been things going missing around the resort. According to those neighbours, he's the most likely culprit. I'm taking that with a grain of salt for the time being, though." Jim rested his head back on the chair. "All this is circumstantial, simply because the gardeners are the only ones who have access to the private courtyards at the back of the units – apart from us of course! It's easy to get caught up in the local rumour mill and, as we both know from previous experience, every place has some light-fingered residents."

"Same old, same old, sounds like to me," said Di.

"Yes," agreed Jim, as he closed his eyes and breathed in deeply.

He had taken no more than two breaths when the resident alarm buzzed loudly in the downstairs entrance hallway. *Damn, who could that be? I've just begun to relax.* Jim stood quickly, strode towards the stairs and took them two at a time.

He let himself into his office where a light flashed up on the board on No.18, *Simon Jessop* displayed under the insistent light. Jim picked up the internal phone and dialled his number. The call was answered almost immediately.

"Hello, Simon Jessop speaking."

"Yes, Mr. Jessop, this is the manager, Jim Watersen. You have an emergency?" Jim had learnt from bitter experience that it was always best to make phone contact first in these circumstances, before he ran all the way to a unit, only to find he needed to take either a tool, first-aid kit, or had to ring the ambulance immediately.

"It's not me that needs help, Jim, it's the lady opposite. There's smoke coming out her front doorway."

"Have you rung the fire brigade?"

"No, I haven't."

"Thanks, Mr Jessop!"

Jim pressed the master-fire alarm button in his office, rang Di at the residence to tell her he would need her assistance, then took his keys and phone and ran off in the direction of Unit 15.

He was breathing hard as he approached the doorway of the villa. He saw smoke curling out under the door. He paused for no more than a couple of seconds, used his key and pushed open the front door. Smoke billowed out. He gasped as his lungs filled with the acrid cloud. The heat from the fire shocked Jim and he covered his face with his hands and squinted. Barely discernible was a shape slumped in a recliner lounge chair; what looked like an arm hung over the side.

Jim hesitated, but instinct overrode his fear. In two strides, he was at the side of the chair. He leaned across, swung the chair around to face him, and scooped a woman's body into his arms. He turned to make their escape. At that moment, a blood-curdling scream rent the air. Jim looked down to see the woman, eyes flared, mouth open, frozen in a rictus of fear. She stared at him, then, with extraordinary force, she pounded on his chest and tried to push him away.

That was all it took to unbalance Jim. He bent backward, stumbled, and hit the burning carpet. He still clutched one of the woman's outstretched arms. Together, they rolled and wrestled until both contacted the floor-length, flaming curtains that billowed at the part-open window. They both rolled away, terrified of the flames that snaked up the fabric and raced towards the ceiling.

The smoke grew darker and filled the small room. Both gagged as they struggled to stand. Defeated, Jim fell to the floor, taking the old woman with him. He pulled her beside him and crawled towards the door.

The woman went limp in Jim's grasp. Though slight of build, the dead weight of her body was almost too great for Jim to move, but at that moment, two strong hands grabbed him by the shoulders.

"Let's get you out of here, mate!" said a voice above him. Just as Jim was yanked upright, he saw another shape enter the smoke-filled room.

"Behind me, behind me, there's a woman on the floor," Jim spluttered hoarsely, unable to shout. The dark form rushed past Jim's startled, watery eyes.

A firefighter, his face hidden by breathing apparatus, emerged through the doorway with Jim, whose gasping body passed to yet another pair of hands. His rescuer helped Jim down the small ramp on to the cool, green grass on the front lawn.

Simon Jessop's strobe light and siren, set off when he had activated the emergency alarm inside his unit, was still filling the air with its jarring visual and auditory warning. A crowd formed a semi-circle beyond the fire truck as another one pulled up in the driveway.

Jim sank to the soft grass in the arms of his wife as she lowered him onto her lap, then stretched him out and turned his head to the side.

"Take a good breath, Jim ... and again." She stroked his head as he sucked in the fresh air.

He coughed and struggled to sit up. "Is she out?"

"She is. It's all under control now. The firemen are in there with their hoses."

Jim turned to see the ambulance arrive and park behind the second fire truck. Two officers jumped out and ran towards the body of the woman, prone on a patch of lawn. A firefighter bent over her. The ambos took over. They knelt beside the woman and quickly placed an oxygen mask over her gasping mouth and nose.

A loud crack split the air as a window, hit by a stream of water, exploded. It showered the front garden with shards. A firefighter emerged from the entrance, quickly checked that the hail of glass had not struck anyone, and went back into the unit. Everyone watching backed away quickly. Jim grabbed Di's arm as she helped him to stand and he walked unsteadily to the grassed area across the driveway. Jim felt his heart racing as the chaotic scene ebbed and flowed around him. With Di's help, he lowered himself to the grass and sat with his head between his hands.

"G'day, sir. How are you feeling? Do you feel any burns?" said an ambulance officer, as he squatted on his haunches and shone a torch over Jim's body.

"No, I'm right, mate ... just a ... bit short of breath ... whew."

"Here, put this on. It'll help you breathe," said the ambo, as he slipped an oxygen mask over Jim's mouth and nose. "Are you okay to hold this for him, luv?" he asked, as he held the portable oxygen unit towards Di. "I just want to get back to my partner for a second – see how he's going with the lady."

A couple of minutes later, someone deactivated the alarm and the water pumps on the fire appliance droned to a stop. The firefighters came out, dragging their collapsing hoses behind them. The noise subsided but the red and blue emergency vehicle lights continued to stab at the encroaching darkness. A police officer moved the crowd back again, as the firefighters pulled their fire hoses along the driveway, prior to rolling them up and putting them back on the fire engines.

A tall firefighter approached Jim and Di. "I believe you're the manager, sir? How are you feeling now? Are you able talk?"

Jim looked up and nodded. He slipped the oxygen mask off. "Yes, Jim Watersen. My wife, Di." He pointed to the woman beside him. "We are joint managers. Thank God you guys came quickly. Is it all out now?"

"It is. We'll go back in a few minutes and give it a final check. Can you tell me what happened?"

Jim sat upright and coughed. Di patted him on the back and handed him a bottle of water.

"I had an emergency call from a neighbour who saw smoke coming out of the villa. I punched the alarm, and then raced up here. The door was locked, so I used my master key to get in. I saw the lounge room filling with smoke and the old woman slumped in her chair." Jim coughed again and cleared his throat. "When I went in to get her she fought me and we ended up on the floor. Just after that you guys arrived and you know the rest."

"Yeah, fair enough. Look, as I said, we'll give it a once over before we leave. We may be able to get some idea what caused it, but in any case, someone from our Fire Investigation Unit will attend the scene. I'll just need to confirm a few details before we go. Perhaps you could help me with that, Mrs. Watersen?"

"Sure. You okay to hold the cylinder, Jim? Maybe you could see Mrs. Dern when you feel up to it?"

Jim took a few more whiffs of the oxygen, removed the mask, and turned off the valve. He stood, took a couple of deep breaths, and walked over to the woman on the trolley. He could see bandages on her legs and assumed that she would probably go to hospital for further treatment and kept in for observation. He wanted to see how she was and to reassure her that he would look after everything while she was in hospital.

Jim put his hand on hers and said, "Hello, Lydia, how are ..."

"Get your bloody hands off me!"

"You ungrateful old bitch," Jim muttered under his breath, as he stood back and watched her trolley slide into the back of the ambulance. He shook his head and headed back to Di, who was still with the firefighter.

"Just about done," he said, as Jim arrived. "It looks like my police colleague is waiting to have a word with you, so

I'll get back to the cleaning up. Thanks for your help, Mrs. Watersen."

A police sergeant introduced himself and Jim went through his story again. It was past midnight when the exhausted managers walked back to their residence.

Quiet settled over the resort.

Chapter Three

All heads turned towards Di as she approached the small group gathered in front of the scene of the previous night's fire. She smiled as she drew level with them and a plump woman in a loose, floral dress asked, "Have you ever seen all the cigarette burns on the carpet in there?" She pointed to the burnt out lounge room, and said, "Well, you wouldn't have, would you, being new and all?"

"No, I've never been inside. Has this happened before?" queried Di.

"God no, not like this, but it was only a matter of time. Lydia Dern is a stubborn, rude, nasty old woman and she's always dropped cigarette butts on her carpet. There were burn marks all around her chair. This time it's gone beyond a burn mark, eh?"

Di raised her eyebrows, but was loathe to ask too many questions lest she become trapped in the group and waste half her morning having to listen to inane gossip.

"Yes, it was mostly left to her neighbour to keep an eye on her," said another woman, "but she's away right now and so we can all go to bed tonight and wonder if we'll be burnt alive in the middle of the night."

"What do you think, Mrs. Watersen?" said the plump woman as she grimaced and huffed from one foot to the other and looked to the other residents for support.

"It's early days yet and I'm sure we'll be able to implement a plan to prevent this sort of occurrence from being repeated." Di turned to get a closer look at the damage.

"How's the hubby and the old girl this morning, then?" asked another of the group.

"Jim's much better this morning, thank you, and I've contacted the hospital about Mrs. Dern. I'm happy to say she too, is doing well." Di stood there, nodded, and smiled.

An emergency call-out for a new manager presented a great opportunity to get to know people quickly and to spot others who would always play a significant role in resort affairs. It was also a good chance for the residents to form opinions about the managers.

Police tapes sealed off the fire-damaged unit that day, and Lydia moved into respite care while the repairs and refurbishment took place. It was becoming evident to Di and Jim that Lydia was at the point where independent living was probably not her best option. She was too big a risk, not just to herself, but also to her neighbours.

******

One person not taking an interest in Lydia's fire was Kevin, the young gardener. He opened his eyes when he heard his name called. He recognised the voice of Tom, his boss.

"Where the hell've you been, mate? I thought you were doing the lawns over the east boundary."

"Yeah, yeah. Keep your shirt on; I was on my way over there now. I had some weeding to do here first."

Kevin stood and walked over to the lawn mower, grabbed it and disappeared around the hedge where Tom could no longer see him. Kevin felt tired and desperate for sleep. Since becoming one of Jack Noonan's regular drug couriers, his extra-curricular activities had blossomed and he was busy almost every night. Kevin did however require a cover occupation to justify his income. He also needed to have a place to conceal his stash. Grudgingly, he made his way over to the fence line and started up the mower.

******

"Have you met Margaret in Unit 110?" Jim enquired, as his wife came through the office door in the Clubhouse.

Di sat down heavily on the spare swivel chair and picked up files distractedly, as she shook her head and rifled through them. "No, why do you ask?"

"I was talking to her yesterday. She has a problem with the afternoon sun coming into her little bed-sitter and she hoped we might provide an awning to help protect her lounge room from the heat and glare. I explained it could be done at her expense, but one look at her expression when I said it made it clear that, for her, it was not an option. I said I'd look into it but didn't really know how we could do it for her, without having everyone else ask for one. What you say you'll do for one, you have to be prepared to do for everyone."

"I see," said Di, still preoccupied with files and showing little interest in Jim's conversation.

"Anyway, as I left her unit, her neighbour Ethan approached me. What a nice man. He says he's known Margaret for some time, as far back as school together. He expressed concern about her and offered to help in any way he could."

Di looked up. Jim had her interest now, and she sat back to give him her full attention.

"Ethan knew her late husband, but not the kids. Apparently, after her husband died, Margaret's children convinced her to sell her home in Sydney and invest the proceeds in their place at Surfers Paradise. They said they would look after her for the rest of her life."

"Oh, what a nice thing to do. I hope our children might be as caring if one or both of us reach the stage where we need help."

"Whoa, hang on, the best, or I should say, the worst part is yet to come. As soon as the money had changed hands, they convinced her to give them Power of Attorney. Ethan said Margaret's husband had always handled the finances, so she was happy to hand the responsibility to them."

"So, what was the problem?"

"The problem was, my dear, that as soon as the Power of Attorney had been signed, the kids cashed in the house, stuck Margaret in a tiny bed-sitter here, and took off with the rest of the money."

Di looked back at Jim, wide eyed. "But surely it was not her intention to have them exercise the Power of Attorney at that time?" she asked.

"Hell, no. Ethan said that the kids totally abused the process and exploited it so quickly and secretively, that Margaret never discovered the betrayal until it was too late. Sounds impossible, I know, but such may be the depth of parental love and trust, eh? Ethan reckons her husband would never have allowed such a thing to happen if he were alive. He says Margaret did nothing but give to those greedy kids of hers and they did nothing but take. Seems they were adopted, and now they've really shown what they're made of. Ethan also says he doesn't have much money, but he'll help Margaret in any way he can – she's lucky to have such a loyal friend. He's a really nice bloke. I almost had tears in my eyes when he told me her story. I just hate it. But it happens, unfortunately."

"Jim, do you know what sort of Power of Attorney it was?"

"No, why?"

"Well, I seem to remember that if your affairs are mismanaged by your Attorney, and I think it applies whether it's through negligence or a deliberate act, then your Attorney can be held liable. Look, I'm a bit hazy on this, Jim, but I remember when I was working at that last nursing home, where there was a lot of talk about one of the residents having been ripped off by some members of her family. She had apparently given two of her children an Enduring Power of Attorney and the mongrels sold all her assets and transferred property titles to their names. It wasn't just her that was affected either, because other family members were also disadvantaged."

"Yeah, I believe you're right about having legal recourse, love; in fact, I *know* you are, because you've really jogged my memory now. I remember a property I had listed for sale a few years ago. It was real shemozzle. It was a similar situation – the eldest son had Power of Attorney for his mother's affairs and he transferred the title of his mother's house into his name. Trouble was, not only was his mother's trust abused, but he had three siblings who also disputed his right to sell the property. Now, I'm trying to think who got involved ... yeah, I remember – it was the Queensland Civil and Administrative Tribunal which stepped in. They put a stop to the listing of the house and I don't know what happened after that, but I'm pretty sure that the holder of the Power of Attorney can be charged with a criminal offence and also face court proceedings to recover assets."

"You know, having a Power of Attorney for each of us is something we should seriously consider, Jim. What if something happened to one or both of us – say a car accident – and we were unable to control our own affairs? The more I think about it, the more I feel we should do something. What's the procedure, do you know?"

"Well, we can use a solicitor who specialises in that field – the Law Society could probably help there, or – and I think this is right – the Public Trustee in Queensland does that sort of stuff as well. I think they may prepare it at no cost, but I've an idea they may take a fee to administer it though, if and when the time comes. We should investigate both options – no, not *should* – we *will* find out – tomorrow!"

"I agree."

As they sat together, they reflected on their own situation with their families. They had their share of family problems on and off. Di's three girls and Jim's two did not get on well. They mostly ignored one another and any family occasions seemed to bring out the nastiness on all sides. Di and Jim had finally agreed to entertain their families separately, and make no attempt to blend them. It was so easy to upset someone, but fortunately, Jim and Di were a solid force and could not be swayed by what happened with their kids. They took strength from one another and survived – just.

"Keep an open mind and be ready to compromise. That's my prescription," said Jim.

"Nothing is that simple," Di argued. "Parents' feelings for their children may be far removed from what those children feel for their parents." Di brought her thoughts back to the present situation. "Look, as far as Margaret's kids are concerned, I really don't understand. Surely, they must have some sense of compassion and love. As far as Margaret's awning is concerned, I can't suggest how we may finance an awning and not attract unwanted attention, but I'll think about it and get back to you, okay?" Di noticed Jim's usual stern expression soften, as he ran his hand through his wavy, greying hair.

Jim looked up from the computer. "Yes, dear, you do that. I know I can rely on you to come up with an innovative plan to come to the rescue," he said with a chuckle.

Knowing how well he could manipulate her, flattery being Jim's favourite weapon, Di was happy to let him think she did not notice. She enjoyed being resourceful and rising to a challenge and she knew he trusted her.

******

"Hey, get a look at this!" giggled Di to Jim, as she looked out the window of the manager's office to see a car pulled up in the middle of the driveway in, front of the community centre. The driver waved at them. In a little yellow Toyota, one of the residents sat behind the steering wheel. The other front seat bore a smart, black poodle dog. He sat rigidly to attention, stared straight ahead, and looked like he wore his seat belt with pride.

"I'd like to introduce you both to my co-pilot," shouted the driver, an elderly, fashionably dressed woman. She smiled at the managers as she said, "His name's Ben and I couldn't possibly go anywhere without him. As you can see, he's my eyes and ears on that side of the car, so I only have to worry about my side of the road. Any accidents I have now will be the fault of some impatient young men who shouldn't be allowed on the road in the first place. What do you think?"

"Well, yes, sounds like a great idea," answered Di, almost at a loss for words. "Where are you off to now?" Di noticed a little queue of vehicles building up behind the Toyota and was about to suggest that both she and her co-pilot move on, when the driver shouted.

"My name's Jessie. I'm in number 27. I met your lovely husband the other day when he rescued Ben from that awful gardener. I'll come and see you this arvo." She directed her words to Di and waved herself off, oblivious to the line of cars behind her.

"What a character. Can you imagine Ben giving directions from his seat?" Jim laughed, and extended his arm as if he were a dog directing traffic. "I get the feeling Ben might be the brains of that relationship – certainly he's the serious one! Talking to Jessie the other day, she told me he sleeps on his side of the bed, and it's he who decides whether they will have chops or chicken for tea. Apparently, that's all Ben likes – chops or chicken. I wonder how he tells her."

******

Jim looked up from the keyboard of his desktop computer. He had been absorbed, if that was the word for it, in processing the end of month paperwork for the resort. He peered out the office window and watched the summer rain begin to fall on Keeala Resort, as it had done, on and off, for the past few days. It was good for the gardens and lawns, but hard for the staff to get anything else done outside. Many residents tended to stay inside their homes in bad weather, but some stalwarts went to the Clubhouse for activities like snooker or cards. Loose-knit alliances like the writer's group, and others with less serious social imperatives would meet in one of the rooms set aside for just that purpose. Several volunteer groups, such as the Palliative Care Support Service, used the centre for their meetings. Today, the sewing room was busy and an art class was in session. There was no shortage of movement, and noise and the cleaning and preparation for events added to the general hubbub.

Jim had returned his gaze to the pile of paperwork, but his attention wandered. He mused about how he saw the same faces at certain activities and how he had come to be able to address those regulars by name. The hard part was remembering the names, out of the hundreds of residents at the resort, of those who kept a relatively low profile. Even though Jim and Di had been at the resort for several months, they knew very little about some residents. A few chose to remain very private and were rarely seen outside their villas; some because they were not physically active, others were simply not interested in the social interaction of the community. It was always a challenge for the managers to put a name to those faces, but it was something Jim and Di accepted as part of their education in each new posting.

Jim looked up from his paperwork when he heard the sounds of several men coming through the front door. They shook umbrellas and stamped the rainwater from their shoes. He recognised Hank, Basil, and Richard, as he watched them make their way to the pool tables in the back room of the centre. He was aware they were regulars and was glad to see the rain had not deterred them. He turned back to a pile of papers beside his computer and tried to come to grips with the employee payroll. A couple of minutes later, he heard a disturbance. It sounded as if it was coming from the poolroom.

Jim heard shouting, then a few ominous noises that he could only guess at. He left his office and strode in the direction of the sounds. Through the doorway, he saw what looked like seven or eight men gathered at the pool tables, one of them with a cue, raised like a weapon over the head of another man. The other, a small, balding man, cowered under the potential assault but seemed to have a big mouth. He shouted and made a great deal of noise, quite out of proportion to his size, Jim thought.

Jim charged in to the room. He sidestepped instinctively as a cue ball bounced past his leg. The small man had thrown the ball. Whether he had meant it to hit the tall man, Jim could not say, because the ball had hit the floor and seemed more like a warning shot rather than a serious defence of his person. It did, however, because the taller man to react with definite threatening steps towards the ball-thrower. Everyone started to talk or shout at once. They gesticulated as the affray escalated. Fingers pointed, arms waved, and what Jim could only assume were threats, were lost in an unintelligible hubbub of animosity. A group of on-lookers had appeared at the doorway, behind Jim. They jostled for position to get a better view of the disturbance as they peered in. Jim had his hands raised in a gesture of peace.

"Can someone tell me what's going on here?" he shouted.

There was no let-up in the noise. Desperate to control the situation, Jim reached to the wall and turned off the lights in the room. As if he had waved a magic wand, the noise stopped. After a few seconds, Jim switched the lights on and pointed to the tall man with the cue, which he gripped at his side.

"Now, what the hell's going on?" he asked the tall man.

"It's just a misunderstanding, Jim, nothing serious. There's no need for you to concern yourself. I'm sure we can work it out without interference – if you'll excuse us!"

There was muttering in the background but it subsided quickly and silence descended on the room. Jim observed that the tall man, whom he recognised as Richard White, spoke and conducted himself with the assurance of someone with many years of authority and was obviously not going to share the problem with the resort manager. The tension in the room was palpable. Jim looked around. Everyone looked at him and he knew he was not welcome.

"If you can work it out, sure, I'll leave you to it." He turned, left the room and strode purposefully towards his office. He slammed the door behind him.

The incident reinforced Jim's awareness of the fine line he and his wife trod as managers. The residents were property owners in their own right and were entitled to the independence of thought and action that came with that form of ownership. On the other hand, the form of communal living to which each resident was bound meant that Jim and Di also had to administer the complex in the interests of the greater good.

"God, I hate this part of the job," Jim said to the computer screen.

******

"I've got to get to the bottom of that pool room incident," said Jim, as he toyed with the Caesar salad Di had made for lunch. "There's got to be a lot more going on than a spat over a game of pool. Somehow, I have to find out the underlying problem, without treading on any toes. It was made quite clear to me this morning that my interference, and that's the word Richard White used, is not wanted. I can't let it fester, though. The atmosphere in the place is not right. Remember the Annual General Meeting of the Resident's Association, not long after we got here? We agreed then that the aftermath of the election was as if the place had split into two armed camps. I know I should've looked into it more, at the time, but we were both so busy finding our feet, I put it on the back burner."

"Look, love, don't beat yourself up about it. They're grown men and women – they're not children. They, if ever there was a group of people it applied to, should have the maturity to sort this out, if not amicably, then at least sensibly. There must be someone you can speak to in confidence – someone without a foot in either camp," said Di.

"Yeah, you're right, but who?" Jim continued to toy with his salad for a couple of minutes, while Di busied herself at the sink.

"Ah, I know who I could see," he said. "I remember Tom, our gardener Tom, that is, telling me some time ago that there was someone I could turn to if I needed the inside information on what's going on here. Now, what the hell was his name?" Jim tapped his fingers on the table in frustration. "Ah, yes, I remember. Harold, from Unit – er, Unit 39, I believe."

Lunch over, Jim returned to the office. He dialled Harold's number. "It's the manager, Jim Watersen, Harold. I wonder if I'd be able to come up and see you for a few minutes? ... Great, I'll be there shortly." Jim took his raincoat off the hook and made his way up to Unit 39.

"Thanks for making time for me," said Jim, as he removed his shoes and raincoat at the door and entered the snug little unit. With soft, draped curtains and a great collection of ornaments and old wares, it was easy to see that both Harold and his partner, Robert, had been avid antique collectors. Harold, Robert, and Jim sat down and sipped tea from delicate china cups.

"How are you settling in then?" said Robert, in an attempt to start the conversation. This was good, because Jim was not sure how to approach the topic, now that he was there.

"I'm glad you asked that, because I'm at a bit of a loss as to how to find my way around some of the locals – if you get what I mean."

"Certainly," said Robert, who nodded sagely. "Who in particular are you interested in?"

Jim told them his version of the events in the poolroom. They listened with interest and exchanged the odd glance, and a tiny smirk creased the faces of both Robert and Harold. When he finished his story, Jim looked from one to the other of these seventy-something, gay men, who had seen a lot of life and retained a keen interest in everything that went on in their world.

"You're obviously not aware of the politics in this community as yet, and we couldn't expect you to know who the driving forces are. The last managers had an uphill battle to get a handle on things because they didn't keep their eyes peeled concerning some important issues. And they missed some very good opportunities to have a greater understanding of what was really going on around here," Harold commented.

"And that was?" Jim asked naively.

"Settle in first, my friend – plenty of time for scandal and gossip once you get to know us all! In the matter of White versus Miller, I know you have had to intervene at least once in a disagreement between them, but what you may not realise is that they are long standing enemies – were enemies long before they both came to live here. You're probably not aware that one of the grandchildren died by drowning and White's wife blames Tony Miller's younger son for that. You see, there's a complicated story there and one best left for a time when your good wife may be available to hear it too. I'm sure it will be of interest to her – your wife being a nurse and Carmen Miller having a terminal illness and all." Harold looked at Jim quizzically and saw that the manager did not know about Carmen Miller's problem.

"We have a little musical evening here once a month, coming up next week," said Robert. "Perhaps you and Mrs. Watersen would join us and plan to stay on for a chat afterward. We could catch up a bit, if that suits you. I think you may find it to your advantage and an offer that the previous managers unfortunately declined."

Jim stood and shook hands with both men. "Di, and I, would like very much to join you. What day next week?"

"Thursday, Jim. We like to start around half past seven. We provide the coffee and tea but everyone brings a plate."

Jim bade his farewell and walked back to his office deep in thought.

******

"What do you think of our new manager?" Robert asked his partner, as Jim left their unit.

"I like him; seems to be up-front and fairly uncomplicated, and not afraid to get straight to the point." Harold bent to collect the cups and walked towards the kitchen. "Mind you, he has a pretty big job ahead of him – they both do. Let's hope his wife is made of stronger stuff than the last one."

"Yes, I agree," Robert said. "The situation bears a close watch. It would be a shame to see this pair go the way the last ones did. Let's hope we can support them where they need it."

For quite some time after they arrived in the resort, Robert and Harold had come in for a fair amount of criticism from their fellow residents. They withstood the snide remarks and innuendo with a quiet dignity and eventually established a reputation as sensible and reliable members of the community. Human nature being what it is, there remained a few critics, but generally, they enjoyed the respect of most of the residents.

******

"You may think this is my being a little psychic, darling, but I have strange feelings about this place," said Di, as she joined Jim on their veranda at the end of another busy day. "And, maybe it's true, but even you must admit there are undercurrents and suspicious characters everywhere. They're around every corner. I've met a new, strange character every day since we came here."

Jim laughed, "I think you may be right, love. This is the most interesting lot of people I've ever seen in one group anywhere, certainly out of all the resorts we've managed. Such a diverse lot of characters, aren't they? They all know something about someone else. The factions have started to emerge for me, and I find I constantly scratch my head and wonder what to expect next. I don't have to look for trouble – it finds me, every day. Oh, by the way, don't forget we're having coffee with Harold and Robert tomorrow night after their musical soiree."

"I can hardly wait," Di said and, with just a hint of sarcasm. "Oh dear, what to wear?"

"I liked Harold when I met him. He seemed direct, honest – not afraid to be blunt if necessary. I'd like him on my team. He told me that the last managers didn't take advantage of his offer of insight, if that's what you'd like to call it. I won't make that mistake. Now, don't you make any smart remarks about Robert when you meet him, please," warned Jim.

"Of course, I would not..."

"No, I mean, you'll see he's a gentleman, and obviously the one responsible for the softer touches about their little house. Don't underestimate him, though. I think we should just listen and observe when we go up there. I think we may have a lot to gain."

"I know what you mean. I'm not insensitive to such situations, you know."

"Of course, of course, my dear." Jim patted her hand. "Now, tell me about your day."

Chapter Four

"Nice to meet you," Jim repeated, as he was introduced to another couple at the music appreciation group. Harold offered him a glass of red wine and lifted his eyebrows in question. Jim swirled the glass just below his nostrils, inhaled, sipped the wine and held it in his mouth for the obligatory few seconds and said, "Yes, thank you Harold, very nice indeed; deep colour, an earthy nose, great depth on the back of the palate. Is it Victorian?"

"You're pretty damned good, Jim!" effused Harold. "I can see you're a man who knows a thing or two about wine. We'll have to compare notes more often, eh?"

Jim took a seat on the end of an already crowded lounge and perched the wine glass on his crossed knee. *I look a right gay fellow*, he thought, and he suppressed a grin at his private joke.

The room was humming. Jim heard chatter from around the room and was amazed at how many people could fit into what was, by most standards, a small lounge/dining area. Glasses clinked and laughter interspersed with the odd loud exclamation.

Robert stood and tapped a fork on an empty wine glass. He smiled, and said, "It is nice to see everyone here tonight! It is not often we have such a big turnout."

Harold cleared his throat as he tapped a silver cake fork against his wine glass. "Let the music begin. We'll start tonight with Symphony No. 6 in E Minor, by Vaughan Williams." He moved to the sound system and turned on the CD. The room filled with music. The talk stopped and Harold turned out the overhead lights, leaving only two soft lamps glowing. There was an ambience of peace and comfort, overlaid with the tiniest touch of excitement. Jim closed his eyes and began to soak up the atmosphere. Di surreptitiously let her eyes wander around from face to face, from shoe to shoe. She waited – she did not know for what.

******

She found out the next morning. Diane walked to Unit No.15 to check on Lydia Dern. She liked to reassure herself each morning that Lydia was okay, and that she had passed the night safely. Lydia looked forward to their daily chats. Finding all was well with Lydia, Diane continued along the path past the three-bedroom units.

Miriam Turner approached. "Morning, Diane," she said, as she reached out her hand to stay the manager. "Could you please indulge me and check on Jessie Thornton in No. 27?"

"Certainly," responded the manager. "Are you worried about her for some reason?"

Miriam hesitated. "Not normally, but I haven't seen her today. She usually walks Ben past my place each morning about eight. You know, I wave, and Ben can't wait to get out to the grass. Sometimes we chat, but not always. This morning, I saw Ben at the window; he paced up and down as though he hadn't been out. Well I wondered if Jessie was alright, and then I saw you come along and thought perhaps we should take a look."

"Sure."

Di selected her master key from the small bunch in her pocket. Together they walked up to No. 27. Di knocked, waited, and knocked again. No response came, so she opened the door. Ben barked and ran at her, then raced around the room as he jumped from one chair to another and barked excitedly.

Miriam stayed at the door and Ben ran to her. His tail wagged as she bent and patted him.

Di called out to Jessie.

No response.

Miriam said, "She rarely leaves Ben behind – only if she absolutely must. I think I'll take him for a walk while you look." She turned and took Ben's lead from the hook beside the front door. Ben followed her for a couple of steps, but turned, and bounded down the tiny hall to the door of Jessie's bedroom. He barked and squeezed through the partly open door.

******

"She's been dead for some time I'm afraid, Miriam. I've checked and she's quite cold and there's nothing anyone can do for her now. I'm sorry. Perhaps she had a heart attack or something, but whatever it was, she is very peaceful. By the way she is snuggled down in bed, it looks to me as though she has died in her sleep. I can't think of any better way to go, can you?"

"No, of course, you're right. It's just so unexpected. I can't believe it, I really can't." Miriam sighed deeply, and with a look of sad resignation, flopped down on a chair in the corner of the bedroom. She looked at Jessie as Diane laid the body out straight in the bed.

Di aligned Jessie's limbs and spread her hair out on the pillow in a fan. Di had performed this ritual many times.

They both sat quietly for a couple of minutes and then the manager asked Miriam, "Do you know if Jessie was religious?"

"No, she wasn't. As a matter of fact, she was anti-religion. We talked once about the service I go to each Sunday. Jessie believed in God, but not in any religion. She was brought up a Catholic, but I gather she rejected that long ago," answered Miriam with another deep sigh, as she shook her head.

"Well, I'm going to say a little prayer for her now to speed her on her way. I don't think she would object if we have a chat with God and let him know she's coming, do you?"

Ben sat quietly curled up on the end of the old woman's bed.

Miriam shook her head again. "No, I think she would like that."

Both women bent their heads and began to pray to themselves quietly. After a few minutes, the manager stood and reached out to assist Miriam. They headed for the door but turned to face one another in the lounge.

"It would be appropriate if no one was told about this until I've been able to inform the relatives," Di explained. "I'll check the files and see who her next of kin are."

"Oh, you won't find any. She had no one. Don't worry; I won't say a thing to anyone. I assure you though, everyone will know soon enough. People just figure things out, as you've probably guessed if you've worked in this job before. There are no secrets, well, not for long, anyway."

"Well, I'll ring the doctor now to have him confirm the death and issue the Death Certificate. I'll take a look at Jessie's file in the office. Are you okay to go home now?"

"Yes. Thank you. I'll be fine, just a little more excitement for one morning than I would prefer."

As Miriam turned to go, Di reached out for her and said, "Thank you for your concern. I certainly wouldn't have checked if you hadn't alerted me."

The other woman nodded and walked down the path to her unit.

The manager pulled Jessie's unit door closed and strode off to initiate a process well known to her. *All part of the job,* she thought.

******

As Di walked purposefully in the direction of the Community Centre, she became aware of the young gardener at her side, keeping pace with her.

"What's your problem, Kevin?" Di said, as she kept up her pace, not looking at the awkward, untidy young man.

"Nothing. Not a thing. Quiet day isn't it?" He danced along beside her, then hopped on one foot, then the other, and finally walked backwards and skipped on the spot.

Di glanced quickly at Kevin. "Shouldn't be quiet for you. You have a ton of jobs to get through if I'm correct. Unless of course, you've finished everything and you're looking for some more work?"

"Huh. That must be a joke, I suppose," Kevin laughed. "No, I saw you come out of that bloody mongrel dog's unit – 27 – thought maybe there was a problem. The animal hasn't been out for his walkie this morning. You know, I missed him and all."

"Yes, well everything is fine. Thank you for your concern. You'd better run off now and start to push around a lawn mower or something, don't you think?" Di looked after him as he cut away from the path without another word.

"Bitch!" Kevin mumbled as he retreated out of earshot.

Di looked around at the trees and the birds and thought this a good day to die. Jessie must have been at least eighty, could still walk and participate in activities, enjoy herself, drive her car, sort of. She really did seem full of life. So she quit while she was ahead. *Well done, Jessie.*

Di recalled a conversation with Jessie a few days previously. Jessie had commented about how well she had felt. She had thought it would probably be a good idea to sort through her collection of medications, many of which she had not used for a long time. Di had a rush of concern and could not help but remember how close she had come to almost losing her career because she had not been vigilant in the case of out of date drugs. *But that was years ago and God help me, I hope she didn't sample any last night. I expect she'll be a post mortem, dying suddenly like that. We'll know soon enough,* Di thought as she walked through the door of the centre and straight to the office.

"Hear you have a problem in 27," whispered Tony Miller, as Di edged past the group gathered in the foyer.

"Good morning, Tony," said Di, as she smiled and kept walking.

"Got a problem with Jessie Thornton, love?" asked Jim.

"What!" She looked at her husband incredulously. "What!"

Chapter Five

The doctor arrived a couple of hours later, and it was afternoon before Jessie's body was taken away for a post mortem. Ben had become distressed when he could not go with Jessie, and Jim was the one who had to pick up Ben and bring him down to their residence.

Di made him a bed on the end of the lounge and looked sadly at the little pet as he whimpered and scratched at the door, desperate to return home. It broke her heart to see the tiny, proud little figure reduced to such a pitiful sight.

******

"I wanted to find out about arrangements. Why haven't Ron and Gwen taken Ben home?" Miriam asked Di. Miriam sat opposite the manager, in her office, the morning after Jessie's death.

"Who are Ron and Gwen, Miriam?" Di looked up from her increasing file on Jessie.

"The cleaners. They cleaned and shopped for Jessie, ever since she fell and fractured her hip a couple of years ago. They looked after her when she came out of hospital – mind you, they were paid well – very well from all accounts. I don't think it was all from the goodness of their hearts, either. At the time, she did need a lot of help, not so much lately, but they were always around to support her and when she named them in her Will, they acted like family."

Di leaned towards Miriam to make sure she had heard correctly. She raised her eyebrows and asked, "She named them in her Will? How do you know this?"

"She told me – and her solicitor. He knows what Jessie's wishes were. He was a close friend as well. She really had a lot of friends, more than I do, but a bit short on family, unfortunately."

"Maybe fortunately," Di smiled "If you met my family, you'd know what I mean."

"So why then, have Ron and Gwen not come to collect Ben?" asked Miriam. "That was part of the deal. She left them what she had on the understanding that they would look after Ben for the rest of his life, once she was gone."

"Well, perhaps they don't know yet, despite the whole resort knowing before me, it seems. I've only just begun to go through Jessie's file and so far haven't contacted any friends or family. I see here the name of the solicitor I was about to contact, when you came in. I'm sure he can shed some light on her affairs."

"Indeed, but if you want to see the Clarkes, that's what they're called, they're up there now, packing up."

"They're what!" exclaimed Di, as sprang to her feet. She knocked her chair over in the process.

"I saw them on the way down here. They were loading boxes into their car. I presumed you knew and I waved to them. They're quite agreeable people." Miriam looked askance as Di marched out from behind the desk towards the door.

"I bet they are!" was all Di said, as she took off in the direction of Unit 27.

"Excuse me!" Di said loudly, as she came through the open front door of Jessie's unit. She almost collided with Ron, as he struggled under the weight of a loaded box.

They both said together, "Who are you?"

"I'm the manager."

"I'm Ron Clarke, old and dear friend of poor Jessie. She died you know."

"Yes, I know. What are you doing here? I left this door locked. How dare you enter Mrs. Thornton premises without consulting the managers?"

Di was perplexed. How did the cleaners know Jessie had died? Di certainly had not contacted them, and they had come so well prepared with packing cartons. Di took a breath and stood back. Ron put his box down on the nearest chair and his wife came out of the kitchen to join them.

"I think there's a misunderstanding here," Ron said. "You see, we're the closest thing Jessie had to family and it was her dearest wish that we clean out her unit after she died. We've always looked after her and loved her. We're truly sorry to see she is gone. We'll miss her sorely."

"But not her things, I see," answered Di, as she looked around at the unit, full of packing boxes and disarray.

"Life has to go on, as you well know," said Ron. "The unit will have to be sold, and before that, cleaned and got ready for sale."

"It will – but all in good time. I'm led to believe you were to be responsible for Ben after Jessie died. He is one very distressed dog and would like to be with faces he knows right now."

"No, that's not possible!" Ron said. "We live in a small flat and I'm afraid no animals are allowed. Someone else will have to look after Ben. I'm sure you can sort that out. Isn't that part of your role here?"

"No, it most definitely is *not*, but what *is* part of my role here is the protection of the homes and ensuring the security of the residents, and that includes making sure there is no unauthorised entry to their home, in their absence. That said, I would like you to remove the boxes and other stuff that belongs to the estate of Mrs. Jessie Thornton, from your car, immediately. This unit will be locked, with no entry permitted until after her solicitor has dealt with the estate and all proper legal affairs attended too. There's to be a post mortem and investigation into her death. Until that time, no one will enter her home or touch a single item of her property."

The manager had drawn herself up to her full height and now looked down on the two cleaners.

Ron and Gwen looked back, aghast.

"Post mortem! What on earth for?" asked Gwen, her face red with embarrassment.

"Do you know how she died?" questioned the area manager.

"For God's sake. She was an old woman. She couldn't live forever," Ron said.

"Fortunately for you," answered Di.

"What do you mean by that?" was the immediate response from Ron.

"By what?" Di walked around the room. She picked things up and put them back where she thought they might have been previously.

"What you just said," Ron stammered.

"I think you'd better start to empty that car, right now." Di walked into the bedroom and checked to see what the pair had removed.

Di Watersen was not a person to be angered easily. She had seen enough in her life to realise a calm approach to an emotional situation would usually achieve a happier outcome, but such mercenary behaviour, as displayed by the Clarkes, was something she had trouble accepting. She would not tolerate it, and would make sure they knew it.

It took about ten minutes for the Clarkes to empty their car, accompanied by door slamming and mumbling as a background chorus to their labours.

Di checked their car as they got in to drive away.

They did not look back as they moved off.

As Di locked the front door, she heard a car pull up behind her. She turned.

The Clarkes had returned. Ron got out and ran around to the door of the unit.

"Just so you know," he yelled, "we're aware of everything that belongs to Jessie, and we know what her wishes were. We'll check that everything's in order when it's settled." Ron stood his ground.

"I'm sure you will check, Mr Clarke, and maybe, while you're being so particular about details, you'll even remember Jessie's wish, and *your promise*, that you would look after Ben."

"How do you know about ... ." Ron knew as soon as he had opened his mouth that he had made a mistake, but he could not stop the words.

"You might be surprised what I know about, Mr Clarke. Good day."

Di turned and walked away. She looked down as she walked slowly, barely noticing the day. Trees swayed in the breeze and cast a weaving, lacy shadow onto the paved roadway. A lawn mower roared and rattled in the background, and residents chatted to neighbours as they hung out their washing. The motorway traffic hummed incessantly in the distance. Di heard none of it.

Life just goes on; as though it doesn't matter that one of us has left forever, like a hole that closes over – another insignificant life lost to ever diminishing memories. Life may be a struggle or it may be easy, but it all ends, just the same. And so it is for everyone. Di thought, as she turned off the driveway onto a path, and absentmindedly kicked little stones on to the grass.

After years of seeing people and friends off, so to speak, Di recognised the usual melancholy that descended on her

45

whenever she participated in someone's death. She went back to check on Ben.

******

For the rest of the morning, Di attempted to make contact with people who would need to know about Jessie's death. There was the Palliative Care Group, of which Jessie was Treasurer.

"She'll be sadly missed," said Frances, the president. "It was a cause dear to her heart, and Jessie was one of the founding members. There had been a few problems lately, such as Jessie being a little forgetful, sometimes confused, but that's sometimes part of the aging process, as you well know. I must say though, we had considered asking her to step down from the position of treasurer – but no one knew how to do it. After such a dedicated history, how do you tell someone they're no longer up to the job? I'm glad now that we waited, and didn't have to put her through all that. Actually, it had gotten to the stage where my husband had to check all the books and figures after she finished. She had no idea that she made so many mistakes. Thank God, now she never will. She was reliable, honest and often gave money to people short of cash at the time of a relative's death, you know." Frances enjoyed the opportunity of talking about one of her favourite people. "Yes, if Jessie thought a family member was not able to meet the bills of one of our clients, she often offered to pay. She must have a lot of grateful friends out there."

"Do you think people remember that sort of generosity?" asked Di.

Frances said thoughtfully, before she said, "We wouldn't survive without the contributions and the time of volunteers who support us. Of course, no one can expect reward or recognition for such work, but I believe it does come back to us in some way. What do you think?" She looked at Di and could see an answer was not forthcoming.

They both smiled and nodded.

******

"I can't believe it!" said Jim, as Di met with her husband in the kitchen for lunch. "That bloody gardener has just wasted a whole morning, arguing with no less than three of the residents about their front gardens. He thinks he knows everything, and so do they. However, that's not the issue. He takes his orders from me, and he knows it. Then, he starts taking 'requests' from this one, and that one, and nothing gets done properly. Then the complaints start rolling in from all the others. It's as if he was their personal gardener and had nothing else to do. I suspect he takes 'money for favours' as well, that's why he's never where he's supposed to be."

"We all have our problems. You should have been me this morning!" Di told Jim about the situation with the Clarkes and how they refused to take over Ben's care and how they planned to strip Jessie's estate at the earliest moment. She finally ran out of breath.

"Nothing surprises me anymore, love. People can be very disappointing sometimes. You know, you shouldn't get so personally involved. You said you wouldn't, remember?"

"Yes, I know that but this whole situation gets more and more complicated. Someone should stand up for Jessie's rights, protect her interests, and so on. I'd like no less for myself, or for you, for that matter."

"Thanks a lot, darling. I know I can rely on you to look after my affairs when I die."

Jim continued to make himself a sandwich at the kitchen bench. He began to wonder how many other things were going on around the place that he should know about. How deep did he want to dig?

Chapter Six

"I think I may have the solution to the problem of Margaret Robilliard's awning," said Di, as she swept into the manager's office. It was two mornings after the removal of Jessie Thornton's body to the morgue.

"Really?" Mild disinterest was evident in Jim's voice. "Perhaps you can come up with a solution to the problem I have with Kevin, the gardener. I could also use some help with Miller and White again. They've both been in this morning to complain about plants and trees dying in their backyards."

"Maybe the gardener is responsible for all your ills. Sack him and see what happens," Di suggested.

"I'd like to, but if only it were that simple. I've been up to see the plants in question and they are indeed dying. You know White and Miller live either side of Jessie's unit. They each said Kevin, the gardener, said he thought Jessie was the one who had an axe to grind. Apparently, she often complained about the fact that the Millers and the Whites were both awful neighbours and made her position intolerable, with them always at war." Jim sat back in his chair. He stretched his legs and watched as his wife made herself comfortable on the other seat.

"I'll come back to that; first let me tell you what I think we should do about Margaret's awning." Di crossed her arms and said, "Repair."

"Repair?"

"Of course. We do it all the time, accidental damage. Let's say Margaret has a broken window. We have to repair it and the awning will go up at the same time to prevent any chance that it will happen again. Problem solved." Di looked smug.

"But she doesn't have a broken window, does she?" Jim looked mystified, as he usually did when he could not keep up with his wife's thought processes.

"Just think about it. Margaret is on the end of the row and very exposed to balls from the park next door. She could, at any time, have glass all over her lounge room floor. You know what they say 'an ounce of prevention' and all that. Are you with me now?"

"I think I may be and that in itself is a problem; I really don't want to think about it right now. So do what you will and make everybody happy and tell me nothing, okay?" Jim looked resigned.

"Sure!" Di answered.

"Now, getting back to our problem at hand, Miller versus White," said Jim. "Could they have poisoned each other's plants? Not likely. Could Jessie have poisoned both of their plants before she died? Not likely. Could the gardener have poisoned the plants in the hope Jessie would receive the blame, and thus revenge himself on Jessie for her dog Ben's attack on him? God knows." Jim felt frustrated. "I know what I'll do. I'll get Kevin to remove the damaged plants and plant new ones and say no more about it. I'm sure both Miller and White would like nothing better than to draw us into their dispute and waste our valuable time. Kevin can do it tomorrow."

"I actually do have other problems anyway," said Di, becoming more serious for a moment."

"Really, I thought you'd solved Margaret's window dilemma."

"Seriously now. Yesterday, when I called Jessie's doctor to write a death certificate, he wouldn't!" Di began.

"Wouldn't what?" Jim looked up.

"Write the death certificate. He hasn't seen her since her hip replacement over eighteen months ago. He thought she was seeing another GP. If so, we don't know who it was. I would have found out by now if she was still alive. We were planning to go through all her old medications and hopefully chuck some of them out," Di said thoughtfully.

"Well, I certainly hope she didn't chuck any of them down her throat first."

"My thought exactly. It was the first thing I thought of when I began to wonder about her unexpected demise, but she was so buoyant, so involved with life. If she couldn't sleep, maybe she took the wrong drug or maybe too large a dose, but I find it hard to imagine, unless of course she took a sleeping pill and then forgot and took more. That happens you know. People can get confused after they've taken sleeping tablets or tranquillisers. She may have woken up, and in a confused state, re-dosed herself. Oh, yes! This is possible you know. I think she may have been in the early stages of dementia, based on what Frances says about her deteriorating mental faculties in the job of treasurer with the Palliative Care Group."

"So who did write the death certificate before they took her away? I saw the van leave. What happens in cases like this?" Jim looked interested now.

"If they can't find a doctor who has seen her recently, she will be a post mortem – a coroner's case. We'll find out the cause of death then and we can bury her. I have a meeting with her solicitor this afternoon. Do you have time to join us?" Di looked questioningly at her husband.

******

"Peter Burrows, Mrs. Thornton's solicitor, how do you do?" A tall, lean, middle-aged man came through the door and shook hands with Jim and Di in the manager's office. Burrows didn't wait for an invitation, but sank into a chair and, after the usual preliminaries were dispensed with, he said, "It was not commonly known, but Mrs. Thornton did have a brother. They were estranged, for years I believe, but he was the original beneficiary of her Will."

"But no longer a beneficiary?" Di asked, as she leaned towards the solicitor.

"Ah, no. Needless to say, I can give you no more information concerning Mrs. Thornton's Will, but I thought it appropriate to let you know that she does have a brother. You may want to contact him."

"Do you have an address?" Jim asked.

"I do, I do, but I have no idea if it is current. Mrs. Thornton left no instructions for me to contact him. I believe their disaffection may have lasted until her death, but it is possible he may still believe he is a current beneficiary."

"I see," Di said. 'So this is when the Clarkes must have filled the slot as major recipients of the old lady's money. We've been told that a husband and wife, Ron and Gwen Clarke, are now the major beneficiaries and that they made an agreement with Jessie to look after her dog, when she died."

"If they have told you that, then I cannot confirm or deny it, but, in the best interests of the dog, I can say I will see he is cared for until the Will is read. Where is he now?" Peter asked.

"At our residence. He's grieving and presently in our care. He deserves better than a kennel or that pair of grave robbers to look after him." Di said, and proceeded to explain to the solicitor about the Clarke's attempt to take possession prematurely of what they reckoned was soon to be theirs anyway.

"You wouldn't credit some people would you?" Peter shook his head. "I won't take up any more of your time," he said, as he stood. "We'll await the outcome of the post mortem and then we'll get the go-ahead to settle Jessie's affairs. She was a lovely lady. She was getting old and a bit forgetful, and it was time she stopped driving. I warned her of that, of course, but she said she knew when she would be ready. Anyway, God bless her. I'll be talking to you in the next week." The solicitor shook hands again and made his way out to his car.

Thoughtfully, Jim and Di looked at one another.

"A brother – that's interesting. Another job for me I guess," said Di, as she too made her way out of the centre and up the path to check on Lydia Dern. "Families never fail to surprise," she sighed.

A few days later, the coroner brought back an inconclusive finding of the cause of Jessie Thornton's death.

******

"Detective Frank Pekalski." The detective reached out to shake hands with the managers. They were vaguely familiar with the name. Pekalski had headed the investigation into the death of a protestor killed during his involvement in the development of the first stage of the resort. Pekalski explained to Jim and Di that he was now heading the investigation into Mrs. Thornton's death.

"I seem to be very attracted to this place," he smiled. "There was a large amount of barbiturates found in her system, but whether it was enough to kill her, it's hard to say."

The investigating detective sat opposite Jim in his office and explained he would need access to Jessie's unit.

"There'll be a police investigation into the death before she can be buried. We need to satisfy ourselves as to how Jessie died. Probably natural causes, maybe misadventure, suicide, or even murder. Unlikely, but nothing can be ruled out as yet."

******

"I always knew there was something odd about that woman," said Tony Miller to his mates around the pool table that afternoon. "She was a troublemaker. I'm sure she poisoned our plants. You know we had to have new ones planted the other day." He spoke to anyone who would listen. His friends' responded with nods and grunts.

Jim observed the men from a distance. They were all well aware of, and supportive of the ongoing dispute between Tony Miller and Richard White. For some, it had been an ongoing saga, something interesting to gossip about. For others, it had been a cause in which to be involved. They could be part of a war no one could win, but which provided ongoing entertainment. Jim thought it gave vent to pent-up talents and energies no longer used in the boardroom or workplace. He wondered if most men always needed to be combative or competitive; was it part of their basic nature?

******

"I thought it would be a simple affair – clean up, and sell the property and move on," Ron complained to his wife, after yet another interview with the detective. Both had ceased to work at their domestic cleaning jobs in the expectation they would soon have a life of leisure. While at least $350,000 was tied up in the property, there was something like another $500,000 or so in cash, sitting in the bank, waiting for them to enjoy.

"$850,000 may not be considered a fortune by some around here, but it would certainly be enough to keep us happy," agreed Gwen.

The fact that Jessie did not have a funeral straight away and that her unit remained sealed, sparked quite a bit of speculation in the resort over the next few weeks. Then the questions started. A police investigation initiated, and just about everyone had a theory or an opinion about how Jessie may have died.

The Will was read and, not surprisingly, the bulk of Jessie's estate went to the Clarkes. There were small bequests going to her favourite charities and enough set aside for her funeral and legal expenses, but the estate remained frozen until the conclusion of the police investigation. The sale of the unit remained frozen, and the Clarkes became increasingly frustrated at being unable to access their inheritance.

Interestingly, as Gwen Clarke made a particular point to Di after the reading of the Will, there was a sum of $20,000 bequeathed to Peter Burrows' son, for his 'education'. "How's that?" Gwen had said, "And he charges his exorbitant fee, being the executor and, in this case, an indirect beneficiary as well."

Gwen made these canny observations before she and Ron left the Clubhouse following the reading of the Will.

******

"It's the stress of the job," Kevin said to his 'connection', as he bent to pick up the money he dropped after their exchange. Kevin's thin hands shook, and his usual pasty complexion was blotchy and sweaty. His stringy hair was uncombed and his clothes dirty.

"You don't look too good to me, mate," said the bloke from the ute, as he leaned against the passenger side door. They rarely ever used names and shared the minimum of conversation. "You should lay off the stuff yourself or you won't live long enough to enjoy all this dough you're pulling in."

"Ah, shut up. What would you know? I got problems you haven't dreamed of."

"Okay, mate, it's just friendly advice; we're both in the same business, you know. It's just I don't partake – made that decision long ago and now I might live to enjoy what I got for the risks I'm taking."

"Yeah, yeah, fair enough. I got a nervous disposition and a boss breathing down me neck, not to mention a doddery old fool of a partner to work with. This bunch of geriatrics don't improve me life either." Kevin began to move away; he could not afford to let anyone see him in this condition.

"So, next week?"

"No, mate, there's troubles down the line. I'll let you know when. You'll be contacted in the usual way."

The man nodded slowly, and went around the front of the vehicle to the driver's door. He hesitated before he got in, stared at Kevin, and said, "Your troubles better not last too long, mate. You're not the only guy I can do business with, you know." He slid into the cabin, slammed the door, and squealed the tyres as he took off.

Kevin stared after him and he wondered what else could go wrong. He owed too many people now, and simply could not afford any disruption to his cash flow. He made his way back to the lawn mower he had left near the swimming pool.

******

Di had not been able to contact Jessie's brother, Stan Connelly, but she felt it was not really her job to search for him if he did not want to be found. She put Jessie's file in the bottom drawer of the filing cabinet to review later, perhaps.

When Jim answered the phone in his office, it had been ringing for some time. He reached over his desk and grabbed the receiver.

"Yes, hello, Keeala Resort. This is Jim Watersen."

"My name is Rena Connelly," was the softly accented response. I have a sister-in-law living there. I've rung her and there is no answer. I am a bit worried in case she may not be well. She is usually home; she is very old, you see. I wondered if you could check on her for me please."

"Certainly. What's her name?"

Jim reached for a pen to write it down.

"Mrs. Jessica Thornton," the speaker's accent more noticeable now.

"Oh." Jim sat down behind his desk. "Who did you say you were again?"

"My husband is Stanley Connelly and he is, well actually he was Mrs. Thornton's younger brother. He died nearly a month ago." A sniff suggested emotional distress at the mention of Mr. Connelly's death.

"Mrs. Connelly, I'm very sorry to have to tell you this on the phone, but it's my sad duty to tell you that Mrs. Thornton has died also."

There was silence on the other end of the line. "Mrs. Connelly? Are you there?"

"Yes, I am here. Can you please tell me what happened to my dear sister-in-law?"

"Last week, at the request of a concerned friend, my wife checked on Jessie and found her dead in her bed. It appears she died peacefully, in her sleep, but as yet the police are not sure of the cause of death."

"The police! What have they got to do with it?" The woman seemed very anxious suddenly.

"In this case, Jessie had not been in contact with her doctor for some time. He was not able to satisfy himself as to the exact cause of her death. He could not write out a death certificate."

"But surely anyone could see she was an old lady and she probably had a heart attack or something," Mrs. Connelly suggested.

"Yes, but that was not borne out in this case, unfortunately."

"What do you mean?"

"I wonder, Mrs. Connelly, if perhaps you would like to come and see me or my wife. We could talk better, face to face, rather than over the phone. There may be some areas you could shed light on also."

"I will come, I will come this afternoon. What time?"

"It would be good for me about three, and I'll try to see my wife is free also. She's more aware of the finer details than I. So we'll see you then, if that time is suitable."

"Yes, and oh, you will need to tell me about when the reading of the Will is also. Thank you." The woman hung up before Jim was able to say that the reading was over already.

Not to worry, we'll sort it all out this arvo. First, we have no relatives at all, and now, suddenly they're coming out of the woodwork. Jim grinned to himself at his own wit.

Chapter Seven

Jim joined his wife for lunch, as was his habit, about 1pm. They seated themselves at the kitchen table. Although the sun's rays streamed in through the window, there seemed to be a chill in the air.

Di picked at her food and ate in silence, sparking fears in Jim that he had offended her in some way. He studied her face and could see that Di was deep in thought. Suddenly, she looked up and asked, "Well, what happened after the music session the other night? Did Harold get a chance to tell you about the Whites and the Millers? Did you get the whole story?"

"Oh, ah, yeah, I think so, yes. Why do you ask?" Jim answered, looking at Di as she pushed a slice of tomato around the plate with a fork. *Oh, shit*, thought Jim, *I know what's coming. I forgot to tell you about it. Bugger!*

"You may not have noticed, Jim, but I had to give most of my attention to Harold's sister, who had arrived unexpectedly. I was supposed to be privy to Harold's exposé of the White/Miller saga, remember, and I am a joint manager, supposedly. Seems you're treating me like the proverbial mushroom. Can you repeat that story to me now?"

Jim realised Di was not making a request – it was a direct order. He usually treated Di's requests for action more as 'suggestions', something to be acted upon, or discarded, depending on his judgment, but a direct order had no wriggle room. It had to be obeyed.

"Sure," he said. He sat back on his chair, and tried to appear relaxed, as he started to recount the gist of the story. "As I remember the story, Richard and Beryl White lived in the same country town as Carmen and Tony Miller. The fact that they both ended up living here, in the same resort, is a pure coincidence. Apparently, they were both on the local council and were at odds over a land development of Richard's. Tony did everything he could to obstruct the passage of the application and it dragged on for several years. It was finally passed, but not before there was irreparable damage to the relationship. In the meantime, White's daughter, I think, married Miller's son because she was pregnant, and that alone caused a massive argument. I believe Harold said that they were not together more than a year and they divorced. There was a custody battle and a dispute over property. It still isn't settled. There was a tragedy also; a child died – drowned. I don't know the details about that."

Jim drew in a big breath – *so far, so good* – and continued, "When they came to live here, neither couple realised that the other pair was going to call it home, with only Jessie's unit separating them, and by the time everything was settled, neither couple would move out. So, they simply carried on the feud, to the great discomfort of the other residents. Eventually, other people joined in, and they took sides. Both families have pretty forceful characters. Depending on your point of view, they have attracted either a healthy or an unhealthy following. All this has made for a divided camp. Harold says the competition between the couples overshadows many events. Sometimes, it seems farcical, but it's almost dangerous. None of the parties involved will back off, and the previous managers came in for lots of criticism about how they handled the situation."

"Do you think that's why the last managers left?"

Jim could see the concentration on Di's face. He thought he detected a softening in her voice – but he had been wrong before.

"Well," he said, "I'm not sure. Neither is Harold. Robert suggested that money was involved in their demise. He said Allen and Georgeina, the area managers, had something to do with all that. He says they're a shady pair and we'll find out ourselves soon enough what they're up to." Jim looked at the clock then started to shovel food into his mouth. "Sorry, love, I've got work to do and I'll have to continue this story later. By the way, we have a special visitor this arvo."

Jim chewed his salad and wiped his mouth as he stood and pushed the chair back to the table.

"Really, who?"

"Jessie's sister-in-law. At three, in our office." He threw the last few words over his shoulder as he took off for the front door. He wanted out of there.

"So who's going to wash up? And who's Jessie's sister-in-law, anyway?" Di said to the empty doorway. Di stood with her hands on her hips and shook her head slowly. She wondered how Jim always managed to escape the mundane duties and give the overwhelming impression that he was running the show every time.

Di turned back to the table and began to clear away the dishes. Her mind was on a notation in the diary. There was a wedding reception booked in the main reception room in two weeks' time. It was the wedding of Narelle White. One could safely assume that the coming event would be an opportunity for White and Miller to sharpen their axes again. She had an awful vision of blood on white tulle.

******

"Please come in, take a seat." Di looked her guest up and down. "My husband tells me you are – *were*, sorry – Jessie's sister-in-law. I'm so sorry for your loss. We didn't have your name on any of our records or we would've contacted you when she died. As a matter of fact, we could've used some insight into Jessie's background at the time."

The woman who had appeared in the office doorway fifteen minutes before the appointment time, smiled and she held out her hand for Di to shake. She was small, petite, attractive, and about fifty years old. She was nicely dressed, if a little old fashioned, and she spoke with a soft, Asian accent.

"My name is Rena Connelly." She dabbed at her eyes with a lacy handkerchief. "I can't believe my dear sister-in-law is dead. She was so kind to me when I came to this country to marry Stanley. I stayed with her, here in her unit, until Stanley and I married. She helped me to understand many things, and taught me what I needed to know to make a good wife for Stanley." Rena burst into tears. "And now, they are both gone. They have left me to find my way alone. I have no family in this country and no wish to return home. If only you could understand how difficult life is, where I come from. You have no idea. Things you take for granted here, is impossibility in my country. We have little money and no opportunity like here. I have worked hard to support myself and my husband since he was unable to work." Rena gave a loud sob.

Di jumped in at this point. "What was wrong with Stanley, that he couldn't work, Rena?"

"He had a very injured back problem in the beginning, but after that he had a very high blood pressure problem. We had so many plans to enjoy ourselves, but Stanley was always sick. He stayed at home, and then he was told he had a kidney problem – and from that he died – with high blood pressure."

"I'm very sorry; none of us know what's ahead, do we?" Di made soothing sounds and patted Rena's hand.

Rena sniffed, and dabbed at her nose and eyes. "Can you tell me please when the Will may be read? Stanley told me we would be the only living relatives of his dear sister, and she may leave some money to help us in our old age." She gave a wan smile to Di, then once again dabbed at her leaking nose.

"The Will was read the day before yesterday, here in the conference room in the presence of the major beneficiaries. I wasn't there, but I'm reliably told that the bulk of Jessie's estate went to the couple who have been looking after her since she fractured her hip some time ago. I'm afraid she divided her money between a few charities, her solicitor's son and the Clarkes, Ron and Gwen." Di reached for Rena's hand to comfort her, but Rena pulled away and stood, her face a mask of suppressed rage.

"No! This is absolutely not possible. He was her brother; he promised me we would have that money." Rena stamped her foot.

"I agree it's hard to understand, but it was Jessie's prerogative to leave her money wherever she saw fit. Obviously, she wished to reward her carers in some way, and she also hoped they would look after her dog, Ben," Di tried to explain.

"Stupid dog! Always biting and running around making a big mess. He should have died." Rena paced around the room. "I believe they tricked her, these carer people – made her leave our money to them. Jessie was by way of being very mixed up the last couple of years. They have taken advantage of her. They have forced her to sign this Will and probably she did not even know what she signed." Rena gestured with her palms facing upward in despair.

"There was a solicitor present, Mrs. Connelly. He drew up the Will. It is a legal document, and it was his responsibility to satisfy himself that Jessie was of sound mind at the time she signed it. I have no reason to think she was otherwise. I also had several discussions with Jessie and, aside from a little forgetfulness, I found her to have her mental faculties intact." Di stood and faced Rena again.

"Oh, you! How would you know anything about an old woman? She was always taking the wrong pills and having car accidents. You know nothing about my sister-in-law."

Rena was standing close to Di, looking up at her, saliva gathering in the corners of her mouth. She was obviously very distressed.

Di did not know how to defuse the situation, or whether she wanted to listen to any more of the woman's tirade.

"I wish to go to the home of Mrs. Thornton. Please give me the spare key, and I will see for myself what needs to be done about her things." Rena put her hand out for the key.

Di shook her head. "I'm sorry, but I can't do that. There is a police investigation in progress and no one is allowed to enter the unit. If you wish to discuss this, I'll give you the name of the police detective to see. I'm sure he'll be interested to talk to you as well. He'll need all the information he can get, to allow him to close this case quickly."

"Why would he wish to talk to me? I know nothing about how my sister-in-law died." Rena took on a defensive air as she turned, dry eyed, to pick up her handbag. She made for the door.

"Can I have a contact number for you please?" asked Di, as Rena turned her back.

Rena spoke as she hurriedly walked away, "I may be moving soon. I will ring you in a couple of days."

Di called after her, "But what about the funeral? Don't you want to know about the funeral?"

The woman ignored her and strode out of the building towards her car.

Di shrugged and dialled the detective's direct number.

"Detective Frank Pekalski speaking."

Di introduced herself, and then launched into a description of the past few minutes she had spent with the elusive Mrs. Connelly. "So I thought you may like to know that there are a few relatives around after all," she concluded.

"I appreciate your interest, Mrs. Watersen. The Connellys had come up on our radar, and I was hoping to see the person in question sometime today. I have an address here and I'll give her a buzz pretty soon. By the way, I'll be down there tomorrow to go over the unit again. That okay?"

The request sparked Di's interest, and she fished for information. "Is there something special you're looking for, Detective?"

"Yes, I'm always looking for something special, Mrs. Watersen. I don't always find it, but I usually recognise it when I do," the detective laughed.

Di could see she would gain no more information from that source today. "Well, to answer your question, then, yes, I'll be around tomorrow. I'm not too hard to find – call out if you need me. The keys are here in the office."

They both hung up.

Jim walked in a few seconds later. He saw Di sitting there, deep in thought. "Penny for your thoughts," he said brightly.

She looked up and stared at her husband. They were good together; in tune – most of the time. They gave one another enough space to express themselves and operate independently, and yet they seemed to be able to judge one another's moods and respond on a deeper level – a sympathetic and intuitive level.

"I'm really sorry about the White/Miller thing, darling. I done ya wrong. I's a naughty little fella sometimes," said Jim, with a chuckle. Before Di could answer, he put his hand on her shoulder and bent his mouth to her ear. He kissed the lobe with exaggerated kissing noises, and then blew his warm breath in her ear.

Di gave an involuntary shudder. "You – you ... "

Jim spun Di's chair to face him. "You what?" he asked before she could continue. He raised his eyes and held his hands palm upward.

"You smooth bastard." Di's face softened with a smile and her eyes sparkled. "You do this to me every time. I don't know why I keep falling for it."

"Ah, it's 'cause ya love me, baby!"

Jim broke up the ensuing laughter by looking at his watch and saying, "It's three minutes past three. She's late."

"No, darl, she's been and gone."

"What?"

"Yep, and she's *not happy, Jan.*"

"What happened?"

Di gave Jim a rundown of the conversation she had with Rena, but her tone alerted Jim to her disquiet about the encounter.

"What's up?" Jim asked when she finished. He looked at his wife closely.

"I've been thinking about Jessie's death. There are some things that stand out, won't fit in the puzzle, so to speak."

"Like what?"

"Well. There are the people. An odd bunch. Think about Gwen and Ron, and now there's Rena and Stanley. I can't help but wonder about the solicitor, he was a bit odd too, you know. None of them seems to fit in with a nice person like Jessie. I also wonder what her husband was like. I suspect nothing like that lot."

"Don't resurrect him too, please. Did you meet with the sister-in-law?"

"I did."

Di told Jim her story about Rena, and then related her conversation with Pekalski.

"It seems to me you may be just creating a problem for yourself," said Jim. "Let the police handle it. We have enough to do around here – and make sure those Clarkes organise the funeral. They're getting all the money and they aren't even taking the dog. The least they can do is see the old girl off properly."

"I'll give them a ring now. The funeral can go ahead, I believe. I'll tell them we'll keep Ben, not that I think they'll care. I have a thought in the back of my head that keeps coming up, though. It's about Jessie's medication. I had arranged to go through all the bottles and packets with her, but she died the day before we were due to do it. If she died of barbiturate poisoning, how did it get into her system? I can't help but wonder if she may have died as a result of an accidental overdose." Di was staring out the window, again lost in thought.

"I'm sure you're not the only one who's asking that question," said Jim. "Forget it for now. I've a list here of things you need to follow up. I could use some help with this wedding reception coming up as well. Could you meet with the caterers, and Beryl and Narelle White? They should be here this afternoon, about four-thirty."

"Sure," Di replied, absentmindedly.

She's off in her own world, thought Jim. He threw his hat on the hook and sat down to shuffle through the papers he had taken from the file earlier.

Di slipped out of the office and went off to make some coffee.

******

There was a knock on the door. "Ah, just the people I want to see. Take a seat," Jim said.

The gardeners entered and sat at Jim's desk. Kevin looked uncomfortable. Tom looked like a man with something on his mind.

Jim got straight to the point, and asked, "What was the problem this morning. What's going on between you two? Have you had these problems before? Have you always found it so hard to work together?" Jim pointed to Tom. "You first please, Tom."

"Jim, I can't work with this lazy arsehole anymore. Either he goes, or I go. That's about the size of it."

Jim looked at Kevin. "Got anything to say to that?"

The younger man looked at Tom and then back at Jim. "You can both get stuffed. I quit." He stood, knocking the chair backwards as he turned on the spot to leave.

"Now just a minute!" Jim raised his voice. "I'd like to hear what you have to say, Kevin. You don't have to go racing off like that."

"You aren't interested in anything I got to say. You'll only listen to that silly old bugger, and he lies like a pig in mud."

Jim leaned over the desk, and still speaking loudly, said, "So, you don't want to discuss the problem? You're just going to fly out of here and see yourself put out of a job, because you're too stubborn to sit down and talk about it?"

"Fuck off!" Kevin walked out and slammed the door behind him.

Jim and Tom both sank back into their seats and breathed out loudly.

Jim sighed again, and then asked Tom, "Can you tell me what this is all about?"

Tom pulled himself up. "Yeah, well, he's never been easy to work with. A loner, wants to work his own way, can't take direction. He came here to make things easier for me. Used to do all the work meself. Got a bit much over time, so you put him on. He's a good gardener, has a real feel for plants and knows a lot about colour and design, but can't work with me. Doubt he can work with anyone; and he has to be in the mood. If he comes to work after a night out on the sauce, he's useless the next day. He holes up somewhere and sleeps it off. The residents find him in some secluded, common-area courtyard, then come looking for me to have a whinge about him. Today I spied him hanging around Unit 27. I think he may have been in there, like, broke in an' all. Can't say for sure, but I got a feeling he knows more than he's saying."

"So Tom, are you telling me that he may have had something to do with the death of Mrs. Thornton?"

"Oh no, prob'ley not, it's just he's such a sneaky bugger. He coulda been in there snooping 'round in the old lady's stuff. Prob'ley harmless – who knows." Tom shrugged and now seemed less inclined to criticise Kevin when he thought about it, than previously.

"So, the upshot of today's incident is that you caught Kevin in the back courtyard of Mrs. Thornton's unit, and he said he was doing the garden, but you say it didn't need doing and then you had a brawl." Jim laid it out.

"Yeah, that's 'bout it. An' good riddance, I say." Tom pursed his lips, in conclusion.

"Tom, I know you're a hard worker and I'll try and get someone to help you as soon as possible, okay?" Jim nodded as he looked at him.

"Sure. Thanks boss." Tom turned and left.

Jim sat and sat, not knowing what to think. He spaced out, as Di would have said, staring ahead at nothing.

Later, when he told her about the afternoon interlude, she said, "Your brain just needed a rest, that's all. Mine does it all the time. Goes on autopilot, takes a walk on the quiet side, and chills out. You know what I mean?" she explained.

"I'm afraid I do. Now I'm a very worried man." Jim slumped in his chair.

Chapter Eight

J essie's funeral day arrived. Jim and Di stood at the rear of the assembled mourners.

"There seems to be quite a turnout, must be more than twenty of her friends from the resort, and that lot over there." Jim pointed to a small group; mostly women. "I wonder who they are?"

"They're from the Palliative Support and Lion's Club. She was a really socially engaged lady."

Di looked at the gathering, as they all slowly moved into the chapel. She shook her head and tut-tutted to herself. *Another thing you probably wouldn't have agreed to, Jessie,* Di thought – *the clergy being involved in your affairs in death, when they took no part in them in life. But that's the Clarke's decision, and it only proves how little they really knew or cared about your personal preferences.*

As they walked to their car after the ceremony, Di said to Jim, "Did you notice the subdued atmosphere? It was unusually sombre, wasn't it? It's not that funerals are laughing affairs, by any means, but these days, there generally seems to be an acceptance that the ceremony can be more a – well, I was going to say, 'joyous' – but that's probably not quite the right word – perhaps a 'rejoicing' celebration of the person's transition from this life to whatever lies beyond. I guess the problem for Jessie's friends may be that there is still no closure. Everyone's aware that the cause of Jessie's death is still open to conjecture until the police investigation reaches a conclusion. I think it's fair to say that everyone knows she died from an overdose of barbiturates. Most people probably assume it was an accident, 'cause I'm sure no one wants to imagine that Jessie would deliberately do such a thing to herself. Even harder to accept – but I have heard the gossip – is the possibility that someone else administered a lethal dose of drugs to Jessie."

"Yeah, I'm sure you're right about the solemnity today," said Jim, "but I'll tell you what – I want lots of laughing and singing and joking when you spread my ashes. I want a happy trip!"

"Who said you're going first, mate?" Di chuckled, but a more serious look spread over her face as she said, "Maybe I'd rather go first. I can't envisage life without you."

Jim clicked the car's remote entry key and heard the answering chirp. He looked at Di, and said, "Hey, I'm not going anywhere."

As Jim opened the car door, he became aware of a couple approaching him, almost at a run.

Gwen and Ron Clarke arrived, out of breath, just as Jim slammed his door shut behind him.

"Have you heard anything about the police investigation?" Gwen managed to ask, between her laboured gulps for air. She looked worried.

"Nothing this week," said Jim, shaking his head. He was not interested in any conversations with the Clarkes, who had abandoned Ben to the managers without concern for their responsibility, indeed their solemn promise to Jess, about the dog's care. Jim was disgusted by their lack of compassion for Jessie, and their mercenary interest in what they stood to gain from her death. As far as Jim was concerned, if Jessie had been given an overdose of pills, the Clarkes would be his prime suspects. Jim hit the starter button and took off.

The managers drove home from the funeral in silence, each deep in thought. It was time to move on, but impossible to do so yet. The overcast day only increased their sober mood. As Jim and Di drove into the garage next to their house, it started to rain.

Di remembered she had a meeting with the Whites about the wedding, and they would be waiting for her in the community centre. She grabbed an umbrella from the boot of the car and headed off in the rain.

"Hello, everyone." Di waved to the women gathered around the table in the conference room. "Sorry to be late – funeral finished on time, but it was a slow drive back."

"Did all go well?" asked Beryl White, Narelle's Mum.

Di smiled. "Yes, it did thanks, but let's talk of a much happier occasion now. Are you looking forward to Saturday, Narelle? Oh, of course you are, silly me. I only have to look at you to see that." Everyone turned towards Narelle. She blushed. She was a pretty girl; did not say much. Her mother seemed to have all the answers, even when they were directed towards Narelle.

"Can we talk about the table arrangement now?" said Beryl, sounding very businesslike. It took longer than Di thought it should, and she thought that Beryl could have had a meeting for one, since Beryl's opinion was the only one that seemed to matter, and was the final word in every discussion. They finally agreed on tables, flowers and decoration, speeches, dancing and music. Di eventually had to beg off, saying she had to see a resident who was unwell. She figured Beryl did not need her there anyway, and there was a cold bottle of wine waiting in the fridge at home, which did not need to get any older.

Di walked out with a sigh of relief. She waved to Harold and Robert who were taking their King Charles spaniel for its afternoon walk. They both looked fit and happy; so did the dog.

******

Saturday was a great day for the wedding. Brilliant sunshine spilled from a cloudless sky. The gentlest of breezes tempered the air, giving the atmosphere a cooler edge. It was mid-November, so the oppressive humidity that usually descended on Christmas Day, and lasted for two or three months, was still weeks away. Richard and Beryl White had booked the Clubhouse reception room for their daughter's wedding. She was being married in an old church only a few streets away and the reception was to commence at 4:00pm.

The room looked lovely. Di wandered around in the mid-afternoon glow, touching a flower here, pushing in a chair there, adjusting flowers in tall vases, and rearranging the bows in some of the white ribbons tied around the chairs. There was a beautiful enlarged photo of the happy couple, taken on their engagement, mounted behind the seats of the bride and groom. They expected about one hundred and fifty guests. The caterers had arrived at two-thirty to begin setting up food and checking last-minute arrangements.

Di retired to the manager's residence, her work done. She put her feet up on the banana-lounge on the veranda and opened her hard-to-get-engrossed-in novel, not for the first time, at page twenty-six. Two minutes later, she dozed quietly.

She woke with a start. The telephone in the hallway was ringing and Di looked around to see if Jim was nearby. She could not see him, so she hurried over and grabbed the phone.

"Get over here to the office quickly, please." Jim slammed the phone down.

Less than a minute later, Di ran to the office door.

Jim was in the office, the phone to his ear. He waved her in, and put his hand over the mouthpiece as he said, "The shit's hit the fan! Take a look." Jim pointed to the reception room as he spoke into the phone. He was speaking to the police.

"Oh, my God!" said Di. Her hand flew to her mouth. She could see a great commotion down the far end of the room and guests had gathered there, some shouting, some pushing. Chairs lay tipped on their sides and backs. Food, drink, crockery and cutlery, obscured the parquetry floor. Di saw someone lying flat on his back amongst the mess. She rushed to see if she could help.

Tony Miller lay unmoving. Several men knelt next to him. One put his hand on Tony's head, and called his name. He did not respond.

Di moved in next to him quickly, and after a brief assessment, she could see he was unconscious, but breathing. Blood oozed from a head wound, and a laceration on the palm of his right hand looked like it would need stitches.

Di looked up as Jim approached with a blanket in his hand.

He spoke to her, over the heads of those gathered in a crowd around Tony's prone body. "The ambulance and police are on their way," he said, rolling his eyes at Di.

"Can everyone stand back, please?" Jim said, as he jostled a couple of onlookers aside. He handed his wife the blanket.

Di turned Tony on his side and checked his airway again. She spread the blanket over him and became aware of someone crying. She looked up and saw the bride, surrounded by bridesmaids, sobbing loudly.

"What's going on?" she asked, as Jim knelt beside her..

"A big brawl," Jim replied. "Tony Miller decided that the community centre was not going to be out of bounds to him, just because the Whites had booked the place for their wedding. He and his cronies came in during the reception and started to play pool. At first they all ignored him, and then he started to heckle the family during the speeches. I was in the office. When I came out to see what the hell was going on, Richard had gone down to take the pool cue off Tony and there was a struggle. I saw Richard hit Tony over the head with the cue. Tony punched Richard, and then a few of the others got into the act. Next thing, Tony just fell to the floor like a stone. I had to help drag some of the others apart. I've never seen such a bloody punch up."

Jim stood, and pushed his way to the front of the room. He grabbed the microphone. "Can I have your attention please?" He waited a moment, tried again, but louder. "Can I have everyone's attention here, please? Can you please move up to this end of the room and clear a passage to the doorway. The ambulance will be here soon – and the police."

An outcry followed the last statement and the crying soared to further heights. Jim walked back to the group gathered around Richard White. He looked distressed and very pale.

"He came looking for a fight and he bloody well got one," said Richard. "I can't believe that idiot couldn't even stay away from my daughter's wedding. He couldn't let us even have that in peace. The bastard got what he deserved." Richard was still strung-out tightly, both fists clenched.

Beryl was at his side. "He'll pay for this, the mongrel. He's gone too far this time. We really should never have decided to have the reception here in the first place," she said. She made her way, pushing through the crowd, back to her daughter's side. She put her arm around Narelle's shoulder and rocked the sobbing girl. The new bridegroom stood with his own parents, trying to comfort them.

The ambulance arrived. The police came in, not far behind.

There was not much to retrieve of the promised happy occasion after the ambos took Tony away, and Carmen left in tears to meet her husband at the hospital. The police arrested

Richard. Beryl followed him out of the building. She stormed along the driveway to get her car, muttering loudly as she went. She followed Richard to the police station. If Richard had been able to see the look on his wife's face, he would probably have asked to be put in a cell for his own protection.

The bride and groom were huddled together on a small lounge, stunned into silence. The caterers stood around the edge of the crowd, throwing their hands in the air and shrugging their shoulders.

"Would everyone like to take a seat please?" Jim addressed the guests. "Since we'll be unable to continue with the celebration as planned, may I suggest that everyone has a meal. We can't let this good food go to waste and I'm sure you all must be hungry. I'll leave you to disperse in your own time. I can't say how sorry I am that this should have happened here today. Of course, we'll have to get to the bottom of it, and hopefully Tony will recover soon. Please relax now, enjoy your dinner and have a safe drive home."

The two managers escaped to the office to take stock. They sat down looking at one another. "What else can happen in this place? It must be jinxed," said Jim.

A couple of hours later, the caterers finally packed away the last of their equipment into their van. Jim turned the lights out and said to Di, as they walked up the path to the manager's residence, "Please don't forget to call the cleaners on Monday. I doubt they'll get the carpet clean again and the walls were all splashed with red wine. If things always go like this here, I can easily see why the last managers left when they did. I feel like walking out myself tonight."

"Nothing like a bit of excitement, I always say," answered Di, but not looking a bit as if she meant it. They heard the phone ring when they got to the house. It continued to ring all evening. It seemed every resident wanted a personal description of the afternoon's events directly from the manager. Di eventually left the phone off the hook. "If there's an emergency, they'll have to ring the bloody buzzer. I'm not answering that phone again tonight. God, why can't these people respect our privacy?"

******

"You still awake?"

"Yeah," Jim sighed. "What time is it?"

"A little past four."

They both turned over and tried to sleep.

******

Both Allen and Georgeina turned up at the Resort on Monday, Allen a little before 10am, and Georgeina a few minutes after. They asked to see the managers in the office straight away.

They took their seats and Allen started. "I want answers and I want them now. Since the two of you arrived, there's been nothing but trouble. I thought I could trust you to sort things out here, but all you've managed so far is to make things worse." He stared at the managers. Georgeina sat there and nodded her head in agreement.

The manager's mouths fell open in astonishment.

Allen charged on. "What I'd like to know first is, where were you when all this trouble started and who called the police? What the bloody hell do you think we pay you pair

82

for? Can't you bloody well keep order here? It's not rocket science, you know!"

Jim stood up and pushed his chair back. He walked around the room looking like he was trying to digest what he had just heard. All eyes were on him, waiting.

"Is this an inquisition?" He leaned over Allen and drew close to his face. "I don't like your attitude, not one bit. If you've come here today with a belligerent attitude, a closed mind, ready to cast blame on my wife and myself, without even attempting to find out what's happened, you can sit there while we pack our bags now. You can take over immediately. This minute!" Jim stood up and looked from one to the other, waiting for a response.

Allen pursed his lips, took a deep, audible breath, and then put up his palms in a gesture of peace.

"Sit down. Of course I want to know what happened. I'm responsible for everything that happens in these Queensland resorts. The buck stops with me. Sit down, for God's sake."

Georgeina piped up, "Maybe we all need a cup of coffee. I certainly could use one."

Di got up to go to the kitchen.

"I'll come with you," Georgeina said.

"Don't think I can make coffee any better than I can run a resort, I suppose" said Di quietly, as she followed a few steps behind Georgeina and into the kitchen.

The tension hung in the room when the women walked out. Jim decided he would not make the situation any easier for Allen, and he would have plenty to say.

"I don't take kindly to being treated like a naughty child," Jim said, "and I don't expect my wife or myself to be spoken to without respect. I can go over your head just as easily as you can go over mine, but I suspect you have more to lose than I. Fortunately, I'm able to work in any number of other positions. I suspect you don't have that luxury." The swords were drawn.

"Why do you suspect I have more to lose than you? What are you suggesting, and what makes you think I came here to argue? You're overreacting – get a hold on yourself. We both have a lot to lose if this scandal gets out of control."

Allen crossed his arms. Jim mirrored his unyielding body language. Neither spoke, just stared at one another across the desk.

Di and Georgeina finally arrived with a tray. It rattled as Di put it down on the desk between them and handed out cups. They all sipped in the loaded silence.

Allen finally broke the awkwardness. "So, start from the beginning."

"The death or the punch up?" asked Jim.

"The death. I heard it was murder."

"In that case you know more than the police," Jim said, with a hard edge to his voice. "There's an ongoing investigation. Mrs. Thornton's death could have been an accident, suicide, or murder. When the police tell me, I'll tell you. Next?"

"What has a wedding got to do with it, anyway?" asked Georgeina.

"Not a thing," said Jim. "I really don't know where you get your information from, but I can assure you these incidents are not connected. The wedding reception was booked long before we took over, and it all went to plan until Tony Miller turned up at the centre and decided to play pool with his mates. He knew the centre was out of bounds to him on that afternoon, but he decided to be bloody-minded and gate crash the function. First, he marched in past the wedding guests and started playing pool, thus disrupting the event, and then he and his mates started heckling the speechmakers. I don't think any father would be able to ignore that on their daughter's wedding day. I'm surprised there wasn't more damage and more violence."

"And it's only thanks to Jim that the incident was curtailed as quickly as it was," put in Di.

"And thanks to Di for so swiftly coming to the aid of the injured man," acknowledged Jim.

"So, pat yourselves on the back, why don't you," said Allen, "but remind yourselves that that's what you're here for. How much damage is there in the reception room?"

Jim stood. "Let's take a look."

The four of them walked out of the office and strode purposefully to the big central room. Two men were cleaning the carpet.

"How's it going, boys?" asked Jim, as they entered.

"I think it's all coming out, mate," said the tallest man. "Looks like we've got rid of the worst of it. I'm sure you'll be happy with it when we've finished." He went back to work with a steam cleaner.

"It's all covered by insurance, including breakages," added Jim.

Just then, two residents walked in the front door and waved to Jim and Di.

"I'm sorry, we're closed for cleaning this morning," Di said quickly, and she walked towards the men to divert them.

"That's okay; we just wanted to tell you both what a great job you did. This type of thing has been on the boil for a long time, and most of the residents who were at the reception say it was only thanks to your cool headed handling of the situation that it wasn't a lot worse. We all appreciate you very much. That's all we wanted to say." They waved, turned, and walked back down the path.

"Oh, how timely, how very convenient," commented Georgeina, with ill-disguised sarcasm.

They all looked at her.

"I think we might be finished here, don't you?" said Jim, as he ushered the area managers towards the front door. "So, you can see everything is in hand, and when we have an outcome in regard to the death of Mrs. Thornton, you'll be the first to know. I suggest you tell whoever is your source of information here that they should get their facts straight, before they create trouble where there isn't any."

"You haven't said why the gardener was sacked," Allen cut in, as Jim edged them closer to the door.

"Oh, so he's the one giving you your information, is he? He wasn't sacked. He quit, and, if he hadn't, I certainly would have given him his marching orders. He was lazy, and a troublemaker to boot. I intend to replace him. Anything else?" Jim bristled.

Neither Georgeina nor Allen answered. They walked off towards their vehicles together, glancing at one another when they reached the car doors.

"There's more to those two than just being business associates, I reckon," said Di, as another vehicle pulled into the visitor parking area.

Chapter Nine

Detective Pekalski waved to the managers and strode down the path to the door. "Hello. It's nice to see you both looking so well on this beautiful day," he said, with a broad smile.

"Sure," Jim answered.

He ushered Pekalski towards the office. Jim looked slyly at Di and gave an almost imperceptible shrug. He could see another day slipping by and no work done. The management would be asking him next what he did all day.

"Nice to see you again, Detective," said Jim.

"Can I offer you a cup of coffee?" asked Di, as she gestured Pekalski to take a seat.

"A cup of tea would be great, and please, call me Frank."

"Certainly," said Di. She couldn't help smiling every time she saw this man. *He's so attractive,* she thought, *but it's more than that. He has a way of making light of everything, and such an irreverent way of speaking, nothing is too serious for him.*

"Hear you had some fun here this weekend," said Frank. "You guys can't seem to keep this lot under control. What have you done this time?" he asked, grinning.

"Well, when we're not knocking-off old ladies, we're assaulting the members of the wedding party and arguing with the management, for starters," said Jim.

"Yes, I heard you had the assault team here. This place is a hot bed of insurrection. What next?"

"I think we might pack up and move on," answered Di. "We've just about had it for excitement. We thought this was going to be a quiet posting. We thought we could take it easy – sort of semi-retire. You know what I mean?"

"Unfortunately, I do. I still look for excitement in my job though, but even dead bodies generally fail to get my blood pumping anymore. By the way, great cup of tea, Mrs. Watersen. But now to business," Frank nodded to the pair. He continued, "The forensic team has been over Mrs. Thornton's unit with a fine tooth comb. We'll need to do some fingerprinting, to eliminate some people such as yourselves. I wanted to ask you, Mrs. Watersen, about those medications you planned to go through with the old lady."

"Call me Di, please."

"And Jim."

"Fine. Now, please refresh my memory about what you said to the deceased lady when she came to you about the tablets."

"It was a few days before she died. I met her outside her unit, and in the course of our conversation, she mentioned she would like to get rid of a lot of old medications, but wasn't sure which ones to keep. I said I'd take a look then, which I did, but only briefly. When I saw how many there were, I said I'd be back in a few days to go through them properly with her. One thing I did notice was that she had medications that are rarely prescribed now, especially to elderly people." Di looked at Frank.

"Such as?"

"There was Seconal and Nembutal. These barbiturates have largely been replaced by benzodiazepines, which are safer and less addictive."

"Really?" Frank raised his eyebrows.

Di nodded. "Yes, I can't imagine how old they must have been, but most of them did have her name on them. Taken with alcohol, they could knock an old lady flat."

"What sort of bottle were they in, can you remember?"

"They were in small, brown bottles, not used anymore – very old. There were plenty of other medications too. I also noticed some with what I now know to be her brother's name, Stanley Connelly. I asked Jessie about that at the time, and she just passed it off. I think she said, 'Don't worry about those,' or something like that. She had quite a collection."

"So far, we've been unable to locate any tablet containers at all in her unit. I mean empty containers," said the detective. "When we examined her unit for the source of the barbiturates found in her body, there were none. If she administered the drugs herself, there would be a container of some kind left behind. The fact that there are no sleeping pill containers left, and certainly nothing like the ones you mentioned, means that someone has removed them. Someone wanted her to look as though she died in her sleep – with nothing to suggest any misadventure. Had she seen her GP in the last three months, he probably would have signed her death certificate with a diagnosis of heart failure. It seems she didn't have a robust heart, and of course, she was getting on in years. But she didn't fill her body with pills and swill them down with alcohol, and then remove all sign of the pills and their containers, either."

Frank took a breath. "Let's walk up to the unit now, if you don't mind. I want you to take me through a few steps of the day you found the body. We won't need you, Jim. I'll catch you later, thanks for your time." He waved as he and Di walked out the office door.

That could be a good thing, Jim thought, as he tried to decide what job he had to tackle first, *but he sort of makes a bloke feel superfluous, somehow. Oh well.* He looked at his desktop and the paperwork waiting for him. He started to shuffle paper.

The resort salesperson, Matthew Weatherlee, knocked on the office door. "Can I come in?" he asked, with a smile.

Another slimy character, was the first thought that came to Jim's mind.

"Be my guest," Jim said, and pointed to a chair. He sighed deeply, and with dripping sarcasm, finished with, "I didn't have much to do today anyway."

******

Allen Sinclaire answered his mobile phone at the first ring; he recognised the caller's number instantly. It was Georgeina.

"Yes, sweetie," he breathed, his voice completely different from what everyone else normally heard – just as he had a different persona when he was around her.

Georgeina said, "I'm worried. Do you think anyone suspects anything? I don't trust that pair at all." She spoke breathlessly into the remote microphone as she drove toward their usual meeting place.

"Nah! I'm not worried," he said. "How could they know anything? You're overreacting and you're getting yourself upset for nothing. I'll keep my eye on them. You just worry about where you'd like to eat tonight. I told my old woman I'd be back about midday tomorrow, so we'll have all night together and a big sleep-in tomorrow. How does that sound?"

"Great," she answered. "Can't wait."

Sinclaire smiled as he heard Georgeina sign off. He reflected on his thirty-year marriage. He had no children and a wife who never questioned where he was when he left their house. He started married life as a travelling insurance salesperson and he spent lots of time on the road, sometimes up to two weeks away from home. Now, as joint area manager for the Sleighmen Group, no one, including his wife, seemed to know where he was at any particular time. Even the Adelaide office accepted that he was wherever his mobile phone was.

He thought about how he had made his move on Georgeina, a few weeks after she had taken over his old partner's job. He could not believe his luck when a woman had been assigned to the position. *A real smart chick, too,* he had summed her up.

******

Georgeina clicked her phone off and managed to subdue her guilty conscience. When she had first met Allen, it was obvious to her he had done this before. She could see he had all the moves; perhaps that was what excited her. She had a husband and a son at home and they managed fine when she had to stay away overnight for work, but Georgeina managed even better with the comfort and company of Allen Sinclaire when they were on the road.

As it had turned out, she had been on the lookout for a bit of excitement in her otherwise dull life, and she knew he had been broken up with his previous girlfriend for a year. The pair had fallen into a relationship as soon as they had both sized each other up. Georgeina felt they seemed made for one another; they were both willing to break some rules to get what they wanted out of life, and that added an extra spark to her relationship with Allen. She had readily agreed to become involved in the fraud perpetrated by the resort salesperson. She knew that when Allen had discovered what Matthew was up to, he had been able to demand a share of the spoils. Georgeina had always admired resourceful men and she liked the way Allen had used his position to force Matthew to cut a deal. She was also realistic enough to realise that the alliance with Matthew would have to be treated, if not with trust, then at least with respect, because Matthew knew about Allen and Georgeina's liaison. The arrangement with Matthew was '*Going to be like a Mexican standoff,*' as Georgeina had said to Allen when the deal was done.

93

Allen set off for the hotel that was going to be their love nest for the night. As he drove, he could not let go of a nagging thought. *What would happen if the managers ever cottoned on?* He knew his little band of thieves could be in big trouble. Maybe he could offer Jim and Di part of the action? The only problem with that was that the scam would become a five-way split, and that was not an attractive proposition as far as Allen was concerned. It would be far better, Allen had thought, if he could dig up some dirt on Jim and Di. *No one is squeaky clean*, he thought. *Who knows what might turn up?*

The trio were not amateurs anymore, but Allen knew they must proceed with caution. The police were hanging around the resort now, doing two separate investigations; the three of them would need to remain on their toes. Allen also knew they must be careful not to overreact, or appear defensive and draw attention to themselves. He knew he had come on a bit too strong with Jim Watersen at their meeting that morning and he did not need to put him offside unnecessarily. He actually had needed to make a friend out of him. *It may be too late for that now,* he thought, and he banged his fist on the dashboard of his car in frustration. He acknowledged he had let his ego get in the way of his good sense.

******

"Hello, darling. How's it all going?" Georgeina's lovely voice was a delight to her husband, Morris.

"All the better for hearing your voice, my pet," Morris answered. "We always miss you when you stay over. You would have loved the pizza we had for tea. Kainen and I watched a movie, and we're just about to go off to bed."

"So soon? Oh, it's almost eight-thirty, and it is a school night, I suppose. Well, sleep well, and I'll see you tomorrow afternoon when you get home from work."

"Love you. Bye now."

Georgeina felt guilty. Her affair with Allen had gone on now for two years. To begin with, it was wonderful. He had been the perfect lover. He was mature, over fifty, good looking, although greyer and wrinklier every day. He was loving, but not as sincere as her husband was. Georgeina had begun to wonder why she ever started this affair. It would be hard to have any control over Allen. She had seen how little he cared what his wife thought about him. Allens's wife, Eileen, seemed to have her own reasons not to care what her husband did when he was out of sight. Perhaps she liked it that way. He gave her the freedom to do as she pleased when he was out of town, but none of this helped Georgeina to figure out how she could extricate herself from a situation that no longer suited her. She also had a feeling Morris would one day discover what she had been up to. Then she would lose everything of value in her life. She felt helpless and stupid.

******

"Are you coming to bed, sweetie? I'm getting lonely here without you." Allen moved over in the bed and threw the cover back.

"Yes, I'm here." Georgeina smiled, but felt cold inside as she walked to the bed.

******

"So what did Matthew want? I saw him leave when Frank and I came back from Jessie's unit," asked Di, as they got ready for bed that night.

"I wish I knew. A fishing expedition I think. He says he's going to be away for a week and wants me to do the sales while he's away."

"That's not a problem, is it?"

"Normally it wouldn't be, but I'm behind in all my work this last week, and I still haven't replaced the gardener – and there's been a heap of buyers through the new units. If this keeps up, that idiot Sinclaire will have something to complain about. Can you believe the two of them?"

"One thing I can say about those two is that they are a pair. You know, in bed together, literally," answered Di.

"I think they're both married, aren't they?"

"Yes, but not to one another! They don't fool me or anyone else, I'd reckon. Frank asked about them. I couldn't tell him much, but I think Sinclaire is a sleaze; don't know about her. Maybe just stupid. Do you think they'll report us to head office?"

Jim slid down under the sheet. "Hard to say. I really don't know what got into them. They're so defensive about the police being here, I can't help but wonder if they've got something to hide. Hey, maybe that's it!"

"What's it?"

"They probably killed Jessie and mugged Tony Miller and now they're afraid we'll put two and two together so they want us out."

Di laughed and gave Jim a hard nudge in the side, "You're overtired, and that's what I think. Go to sleep."

The early morning sunlight fell in shafts across Jim's pillow and he squeezed his eyes tight to keep it out. Di had forgotten to close the blinds the night before, but it was just as well. They both needed an early start.

"What time is it?" mumbled Jim, from under the sheet.

"Time to get up, my love." She rolled over and put her feet on the floor. "I have so much to do today. Where to start?"

"What do you have to do that's so important today?" Jim's disembodied voice rose from the bed.

"Heaps. You may have forgotten, but unfortunately, I haven't. We have guests to entertain this weekend."

"We have, who?" was Jim's muffled response.

"Your dear daughter, Sheeree, her husband Brian and their two sons, Tom and Jack, that's who!"

"Oh, well I really had forgotten. I suppose it's too late to put them off?"

"It is, and I won't. If this is what life's to be like here, then we just have to get on with it. We haven't had a single guest since we arrived, and our family all probably think we've left the country. You know, like when we wanted to go and live in Tasmania."

"Yeah, I wish we had; beautiful cool weather with none of this humidity. No murders, no punch ups. Oh, God, I have to be in court today. Richard White's hearing is today."

"Say no more then. Get up and face the day." Di left the room.

******

Outside the courtroom, Jim, Richard White, and his solicitor, Lawrence Bradach, huddled in discussion.

"There is his age, and there was provocation. Tony Miller's improving condition will count too. He'll be out of hospital today," stated Bradach.

They waited for the Magistrate to hear the case. They were called in, only to experience an anticlimax. The case was adjourned until Tony Miller could be present, and a date was set for six weeks time. They all went home to lick their wounds.

******

"What I'd like to know is how two mature, seemingly intelligent men, could carry on like such imbeciles," said Jim to Di, as they walked back to the office after lunch. "The more I think about it, the more I feel they've both gotten what they deserve. I was told today that they'll both enjoy airing their dispute to a court. That's what Harold said. He said the both of them will relish the opportunity to air their grievances in public."

"I believe you, but I'm sure that won't happen. When did you see Harold?"

"This morning; I met him as he was taking his dog for a walk. He seems to be a very well informed man. He's known Tony and Richard since they came here, and he says there's so much unresolved stuff between them that they may never work it out – not without a lot of help, motivation, counselling – whatever."

******

"Jim, Frank said he hadn't interviewed Rena Connelly yet. He said he hadn't caught up with her. I can't help but wonder why she's so elusive. One minute she wanted to know all that had gone on, and then the next she disappeared. Her husband died shortly before Jess. That's a bit odd, don't you think? I mean, it's suspicious to me. She thought she would inherit whatever her sister-in-law left behind."

"You may speculate all you like, but there won't be any answers," said Jim. "Let Pekalski do his job and we should do ours." Jim put his head down to the paperwork that continued to mount up on his desk. He had no time to talk.

A car horn beeped and Jim and Di looked through the office window. Matthew Weatherlee waved as he headed slowly out of the resort.

"So now I'm on duty for the next week, selling houses," said Jim. "Shit!"

Chapter Ten

Matthew Weatherlee adjusted the rear view mirror of his white, soft-top Saab convertible as he pulled up in his driveway. A good-looking, strong face smiled back.

"You handsome bugger," he said to his alter ego.

Matthew did not get out. He started to think about his mum. She had said he should stay unmarried, continue to play the field and enjoy his active social life. She thought thirty was still too young for family responsibilities. Matthew had heard his mother's views on marriage often enough to have an understanding of her advice to him. Myra Weatherlee did not have much time for the institution of marriage – she had told Matthew it had not done a thing for her. Her husband had left twenty-six years ago and had remarried, with a whole other family.

"We are the family now, Matthew. Just the two of us," she had said, after her husband had walked out.

Matthew agreed with his mother's sentiments, but for other reasons. He felt he still had plenty of time to develop his career and wanted no impediments in his way. Real estate sales provided him with a living but he got no excitement from it. He wanted to become a reputable, if not totally honest, businessman. He thought about his most recent scam, involving himself and his old school friend, Davo.

"I want a lot more money than selling houses will ever get me," he said to the face in the mirror, "and more than poor old Ma can ever earn."

Matthew thought about how hard his mother had to work to raise him on her own. He remembered his angst when she had told him how guilty she had felt because her cleaner's salary was not sufficient for her to provide a university education for her beloved son. He let out a prolonged sigh, got out of the car and went to the house.

******

"I don't think it's a safe place for a holiday." Myra was in the kitchen, and she shouted so that Matthew could hear her from his bedroom, as he packed.

"I know what you think, Ma," he shouted back, "but I don't agree. I know heaps of friends who've had the best time ever in Bali. It's cheap, and I'm going to bring back some clothes. You still haven't told me what you want."

"Nothing. I don't need a thing, thank you. Look, love, I'm sure it's very easy to get picked up and thrown in jail in that country. It's uncivilised and bombs can explode at any time, no matter where you go. There are terrorists around every corner."

"Yes, well thanks a lot for your informed comments, but I intend to relax and lie around on the beach and surf and check out the night life – nothing else. What size are your joggers, Ma, and what type would you like? Write it down for me please."

Matthew came out from his bedroom with a packed bag he pulled along behind him. He was stuffing papers in his jacket pocket and looking around the room for anything he may have forgotten.

"Love ya, Ma." He kissed Myra on the forehead. "Don't worry; I'll be fine – back in a week. Any calls for me, write them down. The new manager is doing the sales while I'm gone. I'm leaving my car at home. Davo's giving me a lift to the airport. That's him now. Bye."

******

Matthew had not planned this trip before last week. Fortunately, his passport was in order when an old friend, someone he knew from school so many years ago, approached him. He and Davo kept in touch occasionally. At first, Matthew had said no, absolutely, no, to the proposition put to him by Davo. There was no way he planned to spend the rest of his life behind the bars of a Bali jail.

However, things had not gone so well lately for Matthew. He had two investment properties, still owned by the bank, and he knew he could lose them if he did not inject some money in that direction soon.

Before Allen Sinclaire had come on the scene, Matthew had reaped the benefits of a couple of little scams at the Resort, which he had run for the last couple of years. He thought angrily about the intrusion of Allen Sinclaire and his floozy into what had been a nice source of extra income for him alone.

The normal practice when a villa became available for re-sale was that the unit would almost always be refurbished. The exception was unless the departing owner had been in residence for only a very short time, and had left the unit in a state that was pretty much the same as when it was new. Matthew, however, picked his marks and often had those short-term units undergo a major refurbishment, on paper that is. He submitted falsified invoices from his own dummy businesses. The costs of new carpets, internal painting, and so on, were billed to the vendors. More often than not, the re-sales were on behalf of an estate and handled solely by solicitors. Matthew had one particular solicitor to whom he directed enquiries when clients asked for a recommendation. Matthew had realised that in those cases, executors had little interest in coming to the units and were never aware of the state of repair. Matthew would give the units a cursory going over, and sometimes carry out a minor touch-up. Rarely was there any major work needed on the short-term units, so Matthew pocketed the money that the estate paid for a major refurbishment, less a percentage for the solicitor. Matthew needed the solicitor to have some incentive not to question the refurbishment costs.

Matthew's other little earner was to import furniture from Thailand for the display units. Matthew printed his own dummy invoices and added on a hefty mark-up. He then submitted the accounts to head office and the payments flowed to his dummy business – *Not a king's ransom, but a nice sideline, all the same,* he had often thought. These had been small, but regular earners for the young man, but now, following the discovery of his illegal activity by Sinclaire and Georgeina, there was almost nothing left for him after the area managers took their cut. Matthew was not happy, and, to add insult to injury, Sinclaire had stolen his ideas and started the same schemes in some of the other resorts he oversaw. Matthew had wracked his brains trying to think of a way to get rid of Allen Sinclaire, without implicating himself. He also needed to replace his lost income. Now, here was an opportunity to get out of the red with the bank, and maybe even buy another investment property. He decided it was worth taking the chance. All he had to do was carry some drugs back into Australia from Bali. He had never been searched before, when he had left the country. He looked like what he was – a businessman.

******

Brian stretched his legs out under the dining room table as his wife, Sheeree, helped Di clear the dishes from the table. They disappeared into the kitchen. Brian always enjoyed his mother-in-law's meals and had not had one for some time. Br but wished he had not. His eyes met Di's over the top of Brian's head. His mouth fell open, but no sound came out.

"Of course," said Di. "We'd love Tom and Jack to have a little holiday with us." Di was nodding.

Jim widened his eyes and mouthed, 'No!' as he vigorously shook his head from side to side.

"What do you think about that, boys?" Di said, as Sheeree re-entered the room.

"I have to bring me bike," said six-year-old Tom, "and Jack's not sleeping with me. He wets the bed." Tom put his crossed arms on the table and lowered his chin on to his wrists. He looked around and dared anyone to challenge him.

"Jack does occasionally wet the bed, don't you my darling," his mother whispered to him, just loud enough for the rest of the table to hear, "but not very often now. He's four soon, and after his birthday no more wet beds, hey?"

Jack nodded and looked embarrassed.

"Where're you going? What're your plans," asked Jim, as he sat at the table. He knew he had been out-manoeuvred, and he still felt negative about the idea.

"We have an opportunity to get Brian's brother to do the bread run for us while he's home on holidays. He's quite capable of holding down the fort for us for about five days. Since he offered, we felt like taking him up on it. It's hard to get someone you can trust and, as I'm sure you can imagine, we don't want to come home and find our business gone down the gurgler," Sheeree explained.

Brian and Sheeree had a bread run and they both worked very hard to maintain it. The hours were unsociable and they were sometimes out in inclement weather making deliveries to shops and supermarkets. They usually worked well together, but sometimes the pressures would build up and they both needed 'timeout'.

"What are the chances of looking after the boys while we take off for a few days?" asked Brian, when Di came back into the room.

Jim was standing slightly behind Brian, about to place a cup of tea on the table in front of him. He heard the question.

"No, of course not," agreed Jim, resigned to the inevitable now. "Why don't you take our boat and go fishing. The camping gear's there too," he offered.

"Exactly what we were thinking," said his daughter, as she clapped her hands. "Oh thank you, thank you Daddy, we're in great need of a break. You can be such a nice old fella when you want to be." She leaned over and kissed her dad on the head.

Jim grinned, suddenly he felt magnanimous and happy with himself. "When do you want to go?" he asked.

"How about the day after tomorrow? Too soon?" asked Sheeree.

"No, not at all," said Jim, looking at Di again as she grinned at him.

"Well, Brian's brother is on leave from the Army for another two weeks, but we'd like to strike while the iron is hot, if you know what we mean," replied Sheeree.

"I do, I do. Pack up then, and I'll make sure the camping gear and boat are ready for you by Friday morning. Okay?" Jim wondered how he was going to find time to do all this. He shrugged and thought *Just sleep less, I guess.*

After Sheeree and family had left that night, and Di and Jim were on their way to bed, Di said, "That was very kind of you to offer all that to the kids tonight, dear. I think they'll really appreciate the time out and the boys will give us something to do as well." Just a hint of sarcasm coloured Di's last statement.

"It's my absolute pleasure to help out whenever I can," answered Jim sincerely, while he felt proud of himself. "The kids will be no trouble. They can spend their time with you. They'd like that."

"Oh, thank you," said Di.

Friday dawned bright and shiny and the Simpson family were on the doorstep at 7am. After that, they crashed, dragged, packed and tied ropes. An hour and a half later, Brian's car sat a few centimetres lower, and the boat held enough gear to take the couple around Australia. The boys were watching TV when their parents left. Jack curled up on the lounge and sucked his thumb, eyes wide as he watched a program his mother would not have allowed. Tom selected it for just that reason; he knew his grandparents would not know the difference. Non-stop, inter-galactic battles and violence were the best way for a kid to have a good time; that, and riding bikes on the endless paths in the 'old people's place'.

"Darling, I need you to sit in on the interviews with the gardeners when they turn up this morning, please. I think you're a better judge of character than I am, and I don't want to make another mistake and make a bad choice. Old Tom has had enough problems managing alone these past weeks, without being stuck with another lemon."

Jim and Di returned to the lounge after waving the parents off.

"Certainly, I'd love to, my dear husband, but no can do. Have you forgotten already that we have two little boys here who need to be looked after," Di circled the two small bodies now stretched out on the lounge room floor.

"Well surely that doesn't mean you have to sit here and stare at them all day. They'd be fine while we did the interviews in the office. They can keep the phone on hand and ring if they need anything." Jim had the idea that to leave kids in front of the TV was a great way to look after them. The fact that they needed exercise and activities, as well as supervision, had escaped his notice.

"I trust your judgement, Jim. You'll be fine with the interviews. You should move – your first appointment is at nine."

Di turned her attention back to the kids. "Would you boys like to do some cooking with me?" she suggested.

"Yes, please," they cried enthusiastically.

Chapter Eleven

Rena Connelly was staying with a friend, a boyfriend, Daniel Milou. He had come to Australia from Rena's home country and taken up employment in the health care industry. He had planned to work in pathology, but had been unable to raise the funds he would need for his tuition. Rena worked in the same aged care institution as Daniel.

She was good at her job but had not expected to have to work after she and Stanley married. When Rena had arrived in Australia she had been both disappointed and surprised to find Stanley Connelly did not live up to her expectations. When she had corresponded with Stanley, she had gained the impression he was a man of some means and would be a partner who enjoyed travelling and socialising. Friends had warned her not to take his description of his circumstances at face value, but the lure of the good life in Australia had clouded her judgment. Stan had proved to be none of the things he had described. A year after their wedding, Stan somehow managed to become an invalid pensioner and Rena could see that his pension would not keep them; she had no choice but to get a job. She had been qualified as an Enrolled Nurse in her own country but she had to do some refresher courses to enrol in Queensland. Having done that, she worked in a hospital at first, and then obtained a position in aged care. She discovered this was her forte, but it was certainly not her pleasure; only the easy life she had expected would make her happy.

Rena had been Stan's wife for eleven years. Stan's health had deteriorated over the past ten years, and Rena had looked after him as he became ever more dependent. He was not a well man, and it was only after confiding in Daniel that she began to see this as a positive thing. *Stan could die; sooner, rather than later*, she had thought. At least now, she was an Australian citizen. She had a job and a boyfriend. There were elements of happiness in her life, but she would not be truly happy until Stan died and she reaped the rewards of the inheritance she expected to flow though to her from Stan's elderly sister. Now, she was waiting for Stan to die. He was just not ready to oblige.

******

Rena had a certain amount of access to drugs, but Stan had his own supply. He was careful about what he took and he depended on Rena to check everything. His eyesight was poor, and after a few drinks in the evening, he could make a mistake. Rena could see all this.

Rena was a little older than Daniel, but they had hit it off straight away and now they worked the same shifts, five days a week. Rena had the added responsibility of looking after her husband, but as time went on, she cared less and less about Stan and spent more and more time with Daniel. Daniel had a three-flight walk-up in West End, and they usually went back there after the end of an evening shift at 11pm. Rena expected Stan would be asleep at their home, long since.

One evening, two months previously, they had made their way to Daniel's home and settled on the mattress he had on the floor of his bedroom. Daniel handed Rena the tablets he had secreted in his uniform pocket.

"Thanks, I'll need more though."

She reached in her pocket for her own stolen stash and added them to the little plastic bag in her purse. Between them, they collected enough sedatives to keep Stan in a drowsy or drunken state much of the time. Several older patients of the pair would not sleep well that night, now that mild analgesics replaced their prescribed medications.

"Stan never complains. He also never goes to see his sister Jessie anymore," Rena said to Daniel. "His overall health has deteriorated and he's lost a lot of weight. He also has no interest in food and sleeps much. Of course, he takes no exercise."

Rena leaned close to Daniel, and stared into his eyes to emphasise the seriousness of her next statement. "I do not give him his heart and blood pressure medications anymore. When he complains of any symptoms, I just sedate him. We will be so happy." She leaned back and gave her lover a tight grin of satisfaction.

Rena and Daniel had a plan – assist Stan into the next life, so they could pool their resources and live happily ever after. So far, it was going to plan.

That same evening, Rena went home to find Stan dead in his bed.

The doctor had written Stan's death certificate the next day. Rena discussed how difficult it had been for her to care for Stan, and she said she would miss him terribly. The doctor advised her about a reasonably priced cremation service and Rena contacted them as soon as she arrived home. A few days later, Rena disposed of Stan's ashes. Rena's next chore was to inform Stan's sister, Jessie, about her brother's unexpected death. Rena felt sure Jessie would be happy to compensate her for the cost of Stan's cremation; what she had not expected was that Jessie would refuse any money, and be so angry that Rena had not informed her about Stan's death prior to the cremation. Rena had underestimated Jessie's depth of feeling for her brother, and harsh words were exchanged when Rena last visited Jessie.

******

Rena parked her car outside the building where she and Daniel worked. It was almost two in the afternoon, and she was running late because she had spent the last hour or so with Jessie's solicitor, Peter Burrows. Burrows had drawn up Jessie's first Will and had been aware that the changes she had made, only months before her death, would affect both Stan and Rena. Now that he had been made aware that Stan was dead, he assured Rena she did not have any chance of contesting her ex-sister-in-law's Will. She was no longer related and the present Will was sound. Burrows had his own reasons for not wanting the Will to be scrutinised by anyone else. His son's 'education' had benefited greatly from the terms of the document.

Detective Pekalski and his team were on the lookout for Rena. He wanted to question her, and now realised he would have to speak to her at work, since she had not been at her own home for over a week. It was almost two months after Stan's death that the detective finally caught up with Rena.

"Good afternoon, Mrs. Connelly."

Rena was locking her car. She swung around, wide-eyed, and saw the ID flashed in front of her face.

"Who are you?" she asked guardedly, as she fumbled her keys.

Pekalski introduced himself, and said, "I need a few minutes of your time – to talk about Jessie Thornton. Or, you could come to my office tomorrow morning and have a more private discussion."

In her best, softly spoken, accented English, she agreed to see him the next day and went to work.

Rena did not go to the police station to see Pekalski the next morning, and she did not go to work that afternoon. She had the idea that if she could avoid a confrontation long enough, he might give up and go away. Of course, she soon found that investigating police officers were not like that, and Pekalski eventually caught up with her again three days later, outside Daniel's flat in West End.

"You're a hard lady to find when you don't want to be," was the first thing the detective said to Rena's back, as she put her key in the front door. She stepped inside the open door and turned with her hand on the back of the door, ready to close it in his face. His big foot lunged into the doorway and he pushed the door open.

"We need to talk," he said.

Rena started to sob, as she backed into the room and sat on a lounge chair.

"My husband is recently dead and I cannot talk about his sister, it upsets me too much," she blubbered.

"What was the cause of your husband's death, may I ask," said Detective Pekalski softly, but forcefully. He remained standing. His sheer bulk was enough to intimidate most people, but he realised he was dealing with a woman who was not going to be easily flustered.

"He had heart failure. His doctor had treated him for many years for that and other conditions as well. I'm missing him very much. How could I be of any help to you in your questions about his sister? I was told by the manager of her resort that she had died and I have not seen her for a long time." Rena made her way to a chair nearby.

"How long since you had seen Jessie Thornton?"

"Maybe a year – or more."

"Why so long?" he continued to question.

"I had to work and look after my husband. He was unable to do anything for himself at the end."

"Why wasn't he in a hospital?" The police officer walked around the room.

"There was nothing they could do for him. He wanted to stay home with me. I loved him very much and I wish he was with me now." Rena dabbed at her nose again, but Pekalski ignored the affectation.

"Who looked after your husband when you were at work?"

"He was alone. There was nothing I, or anyone else could do for him. I cared for him, washed and fed him, and made sure he was comfortable before I left for work. I had to earn a living. Why do you want to know about my Stanley?" Rena was tiring of the questions and wanted the police out before Daniel came home and they started to ask him questions also.

"Why aren't you living at home? Who lives here with you?" Detective Pekalski already knew the answers to these questions, but wanted to hear Rena's response.

"I'm staying here with a friend. I was too sad to live in that house alone, and I will have to move out soon anyway. I can't afford to pay the rent on what I alone earn." She looked so sad.

The detective played the game and handed her another tissue from the box.

The woman sniffed and accepted the tissue; she tapped her nose and looked miserable. She continued with her sob story. "My friend has been kind enough to allow me to share his hospitality until I find a place of my own. He is very kind."

Pekalski pointed to the mattress on the floor of the only other room in the flat. "He must be. I see he even shares his only bed with you. A true friend, indeed," said Pekalski, with sarcasm dripping from each word.

Rena knew this man would not be deceived or misled. She decided there and then that there was nothing to gain by trying to convince him of her sincerity. The gloves were off; she just had not realised it thus far.

"If that is all, Detective, I have my own life to attend to now. I hope you find the information you are looking for." Rena stood and made her way to the door. She opened it and looked pointedly at the police officer.

He walked to the door, turned, and looked at her eyes, still moist with tears. "I'm very sorry for your loss, Mrs. Connelly. I don't think there is any reason we need to bother you again. Please contact us with your new address when you have one."

They had the measure of each other now. They both knew they would be seeing each other again.

Chapter Twelve

Matthew had spent almost a week in Bali, supposedly relaxing. What had seemed a good idea back in Australia now looked to be a very stupid idea, but the thought of the payoff kept him going. He had done his 'pick up' in a busy market place. As pre-arranged, he had simply picked up an inconspicuous shopping bag that had a sarong stuffed in the top, then returned to his hotel room. Here he transferred the drugs, white powder, into two empty talcum powder containers and placed them at the bottom of his wash bag. Now he could be on his way home; he had only to pass through customs undetected but he was terrified and knew how much he had to lose if caught. After having slept fitfully the previous night, he arrived at the airport on the last leg of his nerve-wracking excursion. Matthew tried to lose himself in the crowd at Denpasar Airport. He sweated, and his hands shook. He also noticed he was hyperventilating as he sat and waited for his flight call.

He got up and started toward to the men's room to try to calm himself. As he left his seat, he noticed someone else move in the same direction. He gave a small sideways glance and saw it was a young European man. They both headed for the toilets. Once inside, the other man made a direct line for Matthew and edged him toward the end stall. He nudged him inside. Matthew made no attempt to resist him. The other man stood on the toilet seat so that only one pair of feet showed on the floor. His deft movements were very quick and he whispered into Matthew's ear.

"You've been followed. Give me the drugs quickly and get on that plane. You've been set up. You're lucky Davo was able to contact us in time."

Matthew rummaged through his backpack and found the talc containers. He handed them over and said, "Who are you?"

"A friend. When you get home, Davo will explain. Think yourself very lucky. Now piss off and don't look back."

Matthew did exactly as the man instructed. His legs shook so much he could barely walk. A few minutes later, his boarding call came over the PA system. Matthew boarded without incident. He took out an anti-histamine tablet and allowed the sedative side effects to sooth his nerves. He eventually dozed off.

Matthew cleared customs at Brisbane, and headed for the car where Davo waited for him. He was both relieved to be home, but still confused about what had happened to him.

"Must have gone well?" his friend said, as Matthew slipped into the front passenger seat.

"Depends on what you call well." Matthew had started to get angry, now that he felt the security of home soil. "I didn't carry the stuff."

"What the fuck do you mean?" Davo asked, staring at Matthew.

"I was cornered in Denpasar airport and told to hand over the stuff."

"What? Who was it?" Davo shouted in Matthew's face.

"Dunno. Some Aussie guy – said I'd been spotted, and I had to hand the stuff over or I'd be picked up by the cops. He said you'd explain when I got back home. I did what he said, no questions. There's no way I wanted to spend the next twenty years in a Bali jail, or worse," Matthew said.

"You mean he actually used my name? I can't believe this! You've been had, mate! Did you get searched?" Davo stared at him incredulously.

"No, and I'm not sorry I offloaded that stuff either. I think I would have had a heart attack on the plane before we touched down in Australia. I never want to go through that again. Not ever." Matthew shook his head.

"Well, I have a feeling a few people here at home won't be as relieved as you, mate. I'm the one that has to come up with the answers about where the stuff is now. It's been paid for, you know?" Davo began to get fidgety as he considered where they stood now. "I sure as shit hope they believe me. I can't tell you how bad this looks for me, mate."

"Sorry, but that's the end of it as far as I'm concerned. Count me out from now on. You stick your own neck on the bloody chopping block. No amount of money's worth going to prison for. Drive me home, please. I've got to get to work tomorrow."

Ever since his scare in Bali, Matthew's head had been filled with images of the inside of Bali's jails. The long flight home had given him too much time to think, and he had kept remembering television news reports he had seen, about Australians languishing in those terrible conditions. He had always believed the only fate worse than incarceration in those places would be death itself, but now he was not so sure. The incident in Bali had for the first time, concentrated his mind on his own vulnerability.

Matthew shuddered, and said, "Let your mob do their worst, I got nothing to lose anyway."

"You reckon, do you?" was the second last thing Davo said to his now 'ex-'friend, when he let him out in front of his house. "Piss off!" was the last.

******

Monday found Matthew back at the retirement resort, determined to be the best real estate salesperson in the country. No more scams. He planned to tell Allen Sinclaire where he could go as well.

He did not hear from Davo in the weeks that followed, and he had no idea what happened to him. He lived in fear that Davo's friends might come after him as well, but he heard nothing and tried to forget about the incident.

As it happened, Allen Sinclaire was the first person through the sales office door on that Monday morning and Matthew was ready for him.

"I want to talk to you, Sinclaire," Matthew said, as the area manager walked in.

"So talk."

"It's about the refurbishment of the last three units," Matthew started.

"Keep your voice down kid, do you want to tell the whole resort what you've been up to," Sinclaire hissed.

"What *I've* been up to?"

"Well, it was your idea. You've enjoyed the spoils, haven't you? I hear you also just took a little holiday. Profitable, was it?"

Matthew stood up and said, "What do you mean by that?"

"There aren't any secrets in the circles I move in, kid. I know all about you. And I've got influence. You're only here today because I want you here. So forget what you were going to say and get started on the refurbishment of those units. I can approve the budget right now and be on about my own genuinely important business."

Matthew sat down again. His thoughts tumbled over one another, as he tried to come to grips with what he had just heard.

"I'll be back in a few days, kid, have it sorted by then. I got more on my plate than watching you squirm around about every little uncomfortable situation."

Sinclaire walked out and over to the manager's office. He spotted Jim, just as he emerged from the building.

"Hello, Jim." He waved in a companionable salute. "Can I have a word?"

"Sure. What can I do for you?"

"Heard any more about the police investigation – the old lady who died?" Sinclaire put his hand on the wall of the community centre, as he attempted to lean in a casual stance.

"The unit has been released for sale, but the investigation is ongoing as far as I know. There's still no culprit but Detective Pekalski seems happy enough with progress. Why don't you give him a call?" suggested Jim.

"No thanks, I'll take your word for it." Sinclaire could have sworn he saw a glow in the manager's eye when Jim suggested he would like to see Allen in a conversation with the detective. "I'll get the kid to see if the unit needs to be tidied up. Can't let our standards fall, can we. The new owners can bear the cost – they're getting it free anyway, aren't they? Can't help but wonder why the cops haven't taken a keener interest in that pair who inherited it. Looks suspicious to me, but I'm no cop." Sinclaire laughed and they parted ways.

You may well laugh, thought Jim, as he continued down the path to catch up with the new gardener. On his way, he thought he might stop and see Harold for a moment. *Got to keep my ear to the ground,* he thought. He knocked on Harold's door.

Robert answered. "Morning, Mr. Manager," said Robert, with a sunny smile. "Haven't seen you for **a** while. I hear you've been busy sacking gardeners and refereeing punch ups at wedding receptions, just to name a couple of your manager's duties." He stood back to allow Jim to enter and waved him to a chair in the lounge.

Harold walked into the room. "Well, good morning, my friend," he said. "Nice to see you. Hear you've had your nose to the grindstone."

"Seems to me there's not much you two don't know," Jim responded with a smile. "Actually that's why I'm here. I wondered what you might be able to tell me about a couple of our employees, that is Matthew Weatherlee, the salesman, and also the famous area manager duo, Allen Sinclaire and Georgeina Bunning." Harold and Robert both nodded,

Jim rubbed his hands in anticipation of some tasty gossip. Actually, he was making light of a subject he thought may well turn out be very serious.

"Glad you asked," said Harold, "it's one of my favourite subjects. To put it simply, as I have said to you about them all before, I believe they are crooks and are up to more than a couple of very shady deals."

"Hmmm ... go on."

"When Robert and I came here, we were amongst the first to move in to our section. We had plenty of opportunity to watch as the other new units sold, and sometimes resold. As you can see, properly looked after, they are in good condition." He waved his hand around their unit. "Some of the older residents died, or otherwise moved on, not long after they arrived, and the family or the estate had to sell the units, of course. One day, Robert walked the dog and stopped to see a re-sale unit on the way. He told me on his return, that nothing had been done except for a bit of a cleanup. The advertising said 'completely refurbished', and the estate would have been charged for it. I know that, because a daughter of one of the deceased old men told me what she had paid for work on her father's unit. The solicitor involved was Peter Burrows, and the salesman always directed the clients to him. I've seen other cases which I suspect may have followed the same pattern."

"But how can you be sure that this is an ongoing thing?" asked Jim. "I mean, the unit you mentioned that Robert saw – couldn't that have been just an isolated case?"

"No, Robert and I believe they always pick their mark. We've looked at a few of the resales over time. Sometimes a unit can look almost 'as new', especially if the owner has only occupied it for a short time. Maybe they've died, or gone to a nursing home, or gone to live with family, whatever. If they haven't lived in the unit for very long, say if it was new, or if a genuine refurbishment had been done prior to that short term resident's occupancy, then it's difficult to tell if it's newly painted or had new carpet laid. Look, call it a gut feeling or whatever, Jim, but there are little tell tale signs – scuff marks on the walls, indentations on the carpet where furniture has been – even the lack of the smell of fresh paint or newly laid carpet."

"I'm not making light of what you say, Harold, but isn't it a bit circumstantial?"

"Well, maybe, but that unit over there," Harold said, as he pointed to a unit diagonally opposite their own, "that was advertised as 'refurbished', yet we saw no sign of any tradespeople there, and we don't miss much, I tell you."

"So, what's your take on the whole thing," Jim asked.

"I suspect they divide the profits between the salesman, the area managers, and the solicitor. I also think that's not the full extent of their activities. I suspect this job here is a cover for something more lucrative. The last managers may have stumbled on to whatever it was, and were somehow encouraged to leave. Keep your head down and act dumb, that's my advice to you." Harold took a breath and settled back into his chair.

"Much of this is what I had already suspected, Harold. As you say, I believe they've gone further than simply the refurbishment rip-off, but that's enough for me to go along with. Thank you for your help. As yet, I don't know what I will do with any of the information, but it doesn't hurt to be aware. My friend, Detective Pekalski, might be the person to give me some advice next, even if it's off the record." Jim took his leave and went off thoughtfully.

As he approached the Clubhouse, on the way to his office, Jim saw the new gardener sweeping leaves from the deck around the pool.

"Lachlan, how you going?"

Jim opened the gate and shook hands with his new employee.

"I see you've found your way around already. Straight into it, hey? That's what I like to see. Please use your initiative as much as you like. Come and sit down and tell me what Tom has already told you about the job."

They walked over to the dappled shade of a native frangipani tree and sat on a garden bench. Jim welcomed the opportunity to talk to someone keen and intelligent, and was open to any new ideas Lachlan had to offer.

******

The emergency buzzer sounded at 10.27pm. Jim had gone to bed early, after a busy day had sapped his energy. His body was about to enter the deep sleep phase.

"Ah, crap!" Jim shook the sleep from his head and searched for a pair of shorts. "No, don't get up. I'll go. You shouldn't have to have your sleep disturbed," he said to Di, as he slipped out of his pyjamas and into his clothes.

Di only half heard the facetious remark and could muster no more than a grunt in reply. She buried her head in her pillow.

Jim shoved his feet into a pair of slip-on canvas shoes and went somewhat unsteadily down the stairs. He flipped the 'cancel' switch on the alarm box, and grabbed his master key and a torch from the hall table on the way out. *Unit 15 ... well it's been a while I guess,"* Jim thought, as his body came to life on the way to Lydia Dern's unit. He walked purposefully, but no more than that. He knew he was taking a chance, but he could see Lydia was becoming like the boy who cried wolf. Since his arrival at Keeala Resort, there had been four false alarm call-outs to her unit, all late at night, and the unnecessary disturbance to Jim's life was testing his patience.

He arrived at Unit 15, knocked on the front door and waited a few seconds – no answer. He found the door was locked, so he used his key and went in.

Lydia was sitting in her recliner. She turned to look at Jim and pointed to an area of smouldering carpet. She said nothing.

Jim went to the laundry and returned with a small dish of water, which he splashed over the affected area.

"What happened, Mrs. Dern?" Jim walked over to face the woman.

She looked up at him and shrugged. "I got up to go to bed and noticed the carpet was smelly. When I took a closer look, I saw a cigarette butt and thought I'd better ring for the manager. I don't deal with these sorts of problems."

Jim sat down on the lounge, took in a deep breath, held it for a couple of seconds, and exhaled, as he silently counted to ten. *God help me with this woman.*

"Would you like a cup of tea, Lydia? Are you upset?"

"No, of course not, I trust you to take care of these little situations. Mind you, I wish it hadn't happened just as I was going to bed. I suppose you might be going to bed soon yourself." She moved as if to stand.

"Please, just sit for a minute, Lydia. It's time we talked about the problem of your smoking. I'm afraid that one day I may be too late, and you could be burnt to death in your chair; not only that, but there are the other residents to consider as well. Look, I'd like you to talk to someone I'll invite to discuss this problem with you."

Lydia was already shaking her head. She said, "But it's such a minor thing and you have dealt with it so efficiently. I don't see how that can be anyone else's problem. You can take yourself off too bed now, as I will."

"No, Lydia, I won't go yet. We do need to discuss this – now. Anything like a fire, as in this case, is not just your problem, Lydia – especially when it happens as often as it does in your situation. You have neighbours in close proximity, and you cannot put their lives or property at risk."

Jim tried to keep his voice calm, but authoritative, and at the same time, he tried not to offend the woman.

"This has never happened to me before. I only smoke occasionally. You are really being very harsh, young man." Lydia looked close to tears.

It had been many a year since anyone had addressed Jim as 'young man'. His tone softened a little as he said, "I suspect you may have forgotten about the other incidents, Lydia, but they did occur, and that's why I want you to see a counsellor. I don't want you to take offence at what I'm saying, but this is a very, very serious issue, and I can no longer stand idle when there are things that can be done to prevent a major catastrophe."

"Major catastrophe! Now I've heard everything." Lydia shook her head and started to cry. "I know I sometimes forget things, but this is absurd. I won't allow you to treat me this way." Lydia stood and shuffled toward her bedroom. She dabbed her eyes then turned to Jim and said, "My husband would never allow anyone to speak to me in this way. I shall tell him what you said – and I will ring my daughter in the morning. You can let yourself out."

Jim moved to assist Lydia to her room but she pushed his hand away. He turned and surreptitiously removed the lighter lying next to her cigarettes. He watched her disappear into her bedroom and close the door. He could hear her as she sniffed and mumbled to herself.

Jim let himself out and locked the door. As he made his way back to his own bed, he thought about the smoking incidents, which were worrying enough, but he also knew that Lydia's memory loss was causing other problems as well.

Neighbours had told him she often did not eat properly, and so far had refused all offers of help. Jim knew Lydia had neither a husband, nor daughter – in fact, no relatives at all. Jim was well aware that for some, aging was a cruel and undignified journey, but that he could no longer delay in recommending Lydia for ongoing care in a special facility. How sad; and now she would have to deal with a counsellor, another stranger, and someone who would doubtless commence the process that would see Lydia enter into formal care.

Jim started to jog, but pulled up suddenly when he almost ran into someone on the path.

"Whoops, almost ran into you, sir," said the other man.

They both laughed and Jim said, "You're out late. Doing laps?"

"As a matter of fact I am, sort of. I always jog at night – it's cool and I usually have the place to myself. I don't expect to run into the manager at this time. Working overtime are you? My name's Martin Judd, by the way," and he put out his hand to shake with Jim.

"Nice to meet you, Martin. I have just visited a resident with a little problem. It's the nature of the job, you know."

"Of course, of course," replied Martin. They both started to walk briskly again alongside one another.

Jim recalled that Martin had been an Olympic athlete, competing for Australia in 1956.

"Any closer to a solution of the old lady's death?" asked Martin.

"Not really. But I'm sure you know as much as I do. It's quite a mystery, not the sort of thing that you expect to happen in your own backyard, so to speak," Jim continued lightly.

Martin said, "I know there is speculation about the Clarkes and I agree it's warranted, but my money is still on the sister-in-law."

"Really, why?" Jim knew the residents would all have their opinions but he had no idea they had it down to a few suspects.

"Well, it stands to reason. She expected to inherit the old woman's money. She was living here with Jessie when she married the old boy, Stan. Of course, they all fell out and the Connelly's did nothing to help old Jess when she needed them. Then the Clarkes stepped in. We know now that Jessie changed her Will in favour of them. Not that they deserved it, because they haven't fulfilled the spirit of the old girl's wishes. However, I'm sure Ben is much better off with you and your wife than he would ever have been with the Clarkes. Be that as it may, the Clarkes had good reason to see the old girl dead. So did Mrs. Connelly. And then, of course, the previous gardener had an axe to grind with Jessie and her dog. Ben went for him on several occasions and he even had stitches after one bout. There was a big dispute about it at the time. Kevin, the gardener, wanted the dog put down, but it was finally agreed that he was just protecting his own property, and Kevin had been loitering about without permission." Martin took a breath.

"You seem to know a great deal about all this," said Jim.

"In fact, it sounds to me like you've got enough material for a book," he laughed.

"Well, that's not all. She did keep cash in her house. Several people knew that. Maybe she caught someone stealing, and he or she decided to shut her up. I should also mention her neighbours on either side, the Whites and the Millers. They were in a long dispute, which you well know. They have both received poison-pen letters and they both had trees poisoned. Who could have done that, I ask you?"

"You may well ask," Jim said, and laughed again. "You may very well ask. If only I had the answer, but I suspect you are much closer to the answer than I am. You've given me a lot to think about. Perhaps we can talk more about it next time I meet you on the path, late at night?"

Martin grinned and they parted, each to his own bed and his own thoughts. Martin's thoughts again drifted to one thing that he had not mentioned, and he was not sure why. The night Jessie died, he had been out jogging as usual; he saw someone leaving Jessie's unit after 10.00pm and he thought he knew who it was. He wondered if Detective Pekalski knew about this late night visitor.

Chapter Thirteen

"I thought you'd already got rid of those medicine bottles," Ron said to his wife Gwen. "I told you to," he said scathingly. "You're a fool, woman. How could we explain having those things here? Get rid of them today – right now. Understand me?"

"If we both did what you think we should do, we wouldn't have a cent to our name. Shut up and let me decide how I'm going to do this." Gwen Clarke knew she had always been the brains of the outfit. After all, she had often thought, wasn't it she who decided to befriend the old woman in the first place? Wasn't it Gwen, who first offered to sleep overnight in Jessie's spare bedroom when she came home from hospital? She had offered the woman a lifeline and made it possible for Jessie to come home and have physiotherapy there.

Gwen recalled how she had first visited Jessie in hospital after she had broken her leg. She intended to find out about cleaning her unit for her, as they did weekly. She discovered Jessie in tears because the brother and sister-in-law, who should have visited and supported her, were nowhere to be seen.

"Not a word. Not a card or a flower. They have completely and very conveniently forgotten me," Jessie had cried. "Just when I need them to help me, they desert me. Bugger both of them. That's what I say. Sorry to swear like that Mrs. Clarke, but I'm so upset. The least Stan and Rena could do is pay me a visit."

Gwen saw herself as a compassionate soul. She had put her arm around Jessie's shoulders and patted her. "There, there, my dear, don't worry, you still have Ron and me. We can help in any way you like. What say I take your nighties home and bring them back nice and clean? And if you need anything, we can get it for you. What do you say?"

"You're very kind," Jessie had said. "Of course, I'll pay you for your time; it would mean a great deal to me. Thank you, Mrs. Clarke."

"It's my pleasure love, and please call me Gwen – I don't stand on ceremony. We can talk about money at a later date – just to cover our expenses, you know."

"Of course, and perhaps you can help me with another problem I'm having?" Jessie had begun to feel a little more positive than she had all day.

"What problem is that, love?" Gwen had smiled; the soul of kindness.

"I was told today that I must have someone live with me at home when I'm discharged, if not, I'll have to go to a rehabilitation hospital and then maybe a nursing home, or even worse, straight to a nursing home. What if they never let me out? I can't bear the thought of living out my days in a place like that." Jessie had been distraught at the possibility.

"Well, I may be able to help you there too." Gwen had thought fast. "Let me have a word to Ron and I'll come back to you tomorrow with an answer. I can't see why I can't live in for as long as you need me. Ron could manage by himself, he's big and strong. It won't do him no harm to make his own bed for a while."

"Oh, you're a lifesaver, dear Gwen. What can I say? I'll sleep soundly tonight knowing you're going to have a solution to my problem. I'll be waiting to see you tomorrow. Thank you so much." Jessie had reached out to hold Gwen's hand and even kissed it. She was so grateful. That was how their relationship had begun.

Next day, Gwen had gone into the hospital with a bunch of roses, Jessie's favourite flowers.

"How sweet. You're so thoughtful. Come and sit down here, dear." Jessie had pointed to the chair next to her bed.

"Now tell me, what have you and your husband decided?" Jessie had waited eagerly for Gwen's response.

"Well, I thought I'd see what you thought of the idea that Ron and I both come to stay with you for a while. He wasn't real pleased about the prospect of cooking for himself, so I said, why don't we both help Jessie? He was okay about that and said he thought he'd like to take Ben for a walk, as you normally do. I sort of thought you might need a helping hand when you're getting about on your feet again." Gwen had looked pleased with herself.

Jessie had hesitated and then said quietly. "It's been so long since a man lived at my house. But of course it's an excellent idea. There are plenty of ways Ron could help out; maybe he could even build that ramp I need before I'm discharged?" Jessie had smiled as she said it. "It really is an excellent idea. I wish I had thought of this to begin with and perhaps I would have spared myself a lot of worry. And, as I said yesterday, I will certainly make it worth your while."

"We don't want you to stretch your finances," Gwen had said, but Jessie had interrupted her.

"No, no, I insist. I have some money put aside and what good is it if I can't use it at a time like this? You and your husband have come to my aid and the least I can do is pay my own way and not leave the two of you out of pocket. I know you have a living to earn. Now, it's settled." Jessie leaned back on her pillow.

"Well, Ron will still go and attend to some of his regular clients; you know he can't let anyone down, but that won't interfere with his helping you. And I'll be with you all the time. You can rely on me." Gwen had looked very satisfied with herself. "Now let's discuss what has to be done first. Would you like me to do any shopping for you today, is there anything you need?"

Jessie smiled. "I feel so lucky to have found such agreeable people and at a time when I most need them. It seems the first thing will be a ramp at my front and back doors – to accommodate my walking frame, you know. Do you think Ron would be up to constructing that?"

"Don't see why not, he's a jack-of-all-trades. Sometimes I say, master of none, but don't really mean it. I can't help but like the old sod. Excuse my French."

The relationship evolved and all three benefited from the arrangement. It was not until more than a year later that Jessie talked to the couple about changing her Will. Ron and Gwen were delighted at the prospect of an inheritance to begin with, but waiting became harder as time went on.

"I've begun to feel like this old girl will live forever. The thought of having to wait maybe ten or more years seems impossible," Ron complained to his wife. "The possibility that Jess may meet with an accident is becoming more likely every day. She could have a fall; but that's uncertain and then she could recover and end up in a nursing home, completely out of our control."

They had both begun to think of Jessie's money and property as their own. But, should she even become aware of their thoughts of treachery, she would disinherit them. They both gave much thought as to the best way to see their friend Jessie meet her maker, and sooner, rather than later.

******

Gwen took a drive down to her local supermarket. The rubbish bins at the rear of the building presented her with the best possible disposal place for the bag of small brown medication bottles. She thought smugly, *Problem solved.*

She had really grown to like Jessie over the years. Their relationship had been easy and Jessie had been quite undemanding. Gwen wondered if her own expectations would have been much greater, had their positions been reversed. Gwen shook herself. There was no room for sentimentality in her world. It made a person weak. It gave a person unrealistic expectations and it was a waste of time and energy. Gwen knew that, in the end, she could only rely on herself and that to invest in other people would always end in heartache. Life had taught Gwen that nothing came easily and whatever she had could be snatched away in the blink of an eye. The fact that Jessie had been generous to her and Ron, without a second thought, had really unsettled her. Gwen had always said she would not leave anything behind for anyone else. She would spend every penny she had and certainly none of her thankless children would get a cent – even if she did know where they were now.

This last thought brought an unexpected tear to Gwen's eyes. She could not afford to think about her children. Long gone, they had made their own lives and not given a thought for the woman who had given them that life. *Stop,* she said to herself. *Enough.* She made her way back to their little flat where Ron sat with his feet up, watching TV.

******

The previous day, the Clarkes had met with Matthew Weatherlee to discuss the sale of Jessie's unit. "I can assure you that refurbishment of the unit before it's offered for sale will guarantee you a better and quicker sale," Matthew had said.

They had agreed with him at the time, but while they drove home Ron commented, "I personally don't trust that sales kid as far as I can throw him. He may have the gift of the gab, but I'll keep a close eye on how he spends our money. If it helps to sell the unit, fine. He had better not plan to rip us off. I'll be watching him for sure."

Gwen nodded. "Those pill bottles, I got rid of them – a waste bin," she said as they drove into their driveway.

"Well, they had better not lead anyone back to us. That's all I can say," said Ron.

"Don't worry, they won't," she returned.

******

At a small shopping centre, two resourceful young boys rummaged through the waste-bins in the lane at the rear of the shops, which had closed for the day. As was their regular habit, the boys looked for anything of value they could sell and they quickly scattered the rubbish onto the footpath. Damian stood on guard while Tim, the oldest boy, was the first to see the little bottles as they clattered to the ground. He stooped and picked up one and pulled a face as he attempted to open the lid. Nothing, it was empty. He shook the others and peered inside them; several contained some tablets. He shoved them into his back pockets then threw more garbage to the path and examined it as it fell. Not much luck, so they moved on to the next bin down the lane.

******

"Why were the police here today? I thought now that Stan was buried there'd be no more problems." Daniel stood in the kitchen in his work clothes; he looked tired and worried.

"There are no problems. It had nothing to do with Stan. They asked questions about Stan's sister, Jessie. Remember she also died recently?" Rena continued to prepare the vegetables for their dinner. She turned back to the cutting board.

"But you said she died of a heart attack." Daniel said, as he took a soft drink from the fridge.

"That's what I thought, but she hadn't seen a doctor in a long time and no one knew what caused her death. So, there's a police inquiry." Rena continued to move about the kitchen.

"Well, why did they want to see you? Do they think you had something to do with her death? When will we know about the Will?" Daniel's face brightened at the thought of money.

Rena turned to face her lover. She sighed deeply, her shoulders dropped as she bent her head and quietly mumbled. "There'll be no inheritance for me. Stan's sister has willed her money to the people who looked after her when she broke her leg, more than a year ago."

"No. Oh, no! So now we have nothing again." Daniel sank down on to a chair, his head on his chest. Nothing had been as easy as he thought it would have been since he arrived in Australia. He had struggled to find a place where he could afford to live, and although work was easy to find in the aged care industry, it was not what he had hoped for. Daniel worked five or six days a week, depending on what casual work was available and was too tired at the end of the day to do any study. He wanted to start a course to become a laboratory assistant but he needed to have enough money to buy a computer and pay the tuition fees. His English language skills also required some improvement. He saved as much as he could but there was little left after all his expenses. Daniel was impatient to be a success and make money. He had not left his home in the Philippines to live like a servant until he was an old man, and die in poverty like his father.

"Are you sure about this?" Daniel spoke to Rena's back.

She turned, "Yes, I've also been in contact with Jessie's solicitor to ask him some questions. He was no help and he was really quite rude." Rena sat down with her elbows on the table; she looked at her lover and he lifted his eyes to her. "I was very disappointed with Stan, my husband. He deceived me when I married him and now we're both here with a living to make and no one to help us."

"Maybe you could marry a rich old man this time. Together we could make sure he really did have money and, after a year or two, he also could join Stan." Daniel raised his eyebrows and leaned questioningly toward Rena.

"Perhaps, but rich old men are hard to find, especially one that may be looking for a wife – that's the problem." Rena shook her head in resignation.

The two sat there for some time. They thought over what they could do next, imagined possibilities and discarded them. They had no moral constraints and were not hampered by any particular compulsion to stay within the law. They both knew they were not prepared to risk being caught, so whatever their next venture was, it would have to be foolproof.

Chapter Fourteen

Di was on grandson-sitting duties again. The boys were back again for the day, and were about to get into the pool with Di when she heard the office phone ring.

"Damn," she said.

"It's okay, Mrs. Watersen, I'll keep an eye on the boys if you want to get that call." Lachlan, the new gardener, was cleaning the pavers surrounding the pool. Jim and Di had been impressed with Lachlan's demeanour and Di had no hesitation in leaving the boys in his care for a few minutes.

"Who're you?" Jack was walking toward the pool ladder when he stopped abruptly. He stared at a clump of golden cane palms, some of the many that gave shade and privacy to the pool and outdoor spa.

Lachlan heard Jack's voice and looked up. Jack appeared to be speaking to the golden canes. Lachlan walked over to see what was going on.

"Making friends with the trees, Jack?" Lachlan said with a laugh.

As Jack turned toward him, Lachlan saw a youngish man, crouched close to the ground behind the golden cane foliage.

"Who're you? What are you hiding in there for?" The gardener was at first suspicious and then on guard. He took a step back to allow the stranger to come out and stand.

"I was just checking the mulch you're using on these plants in here. You must be the gardener. I'm a bit of a tree man myself, you know, a greenie. I just can't pass an opportunity to take a closer look." The stranger emerged from the garden, brushed himself down and took a few steps around Lachlan. Just then, Di returned and walked over to the little gathering of Jack, Tom, Lachlan and the other fellow, who was doing the talking.

"Mrs. Watersen, I just found this bloke crouched down in the bushes here; I think he's hiding or something. He looks like he's ... " Lachlan was interrupted by the stranger.

"Look, I'm just waiting for a friend and decided to check out these plants, I'm sorry if I scared you. I'll buzz off now and see if I can find him."

He made a move to go around the group, only to feel Di's hand on his arm as she restrained him. "Now hang on a bit, tell me first who you are, what you're doing here, and who it is you're waiting for."

"My name's Dave, I'm waiting to see my mate, Matthew, and I was just enjoying the garden. Will that do, missus?" The man tried to stare Di down and again made to move away, but Di was not fobbed off easily.

"Matthew Weatherlee? Is he who you're waiting for?" Di let go of his arm and stepped back. "If you wait there I'll get him for you right now, I just passed him on the path."

Dave went to interrupt, but Lachlan put his hand up and signalled stop. Out of the corner of his eye, he had spotted Matthew walking toward his sales office.

"Matthew. Mr. Weatherlee," he shouted, then again, "Mr. Weatherlee!"

Matthew turned and walked toward the pool. Di had heard the shouting and turned around to join Matthew on the path.

"Hi, Matthew, what's up?" Davo walked toward the pool gate to meet him; he made to shake his friend's hand.

Matthew was nonplussed. *What the hell are you doing here?,* he wanted to say, but he kept his mouth shut. He had no idea what was going on but went with the flow and shook Davo's outstretched hand.

"I was waiting over here to see you, mate. The gardener thought I was some kind of intruder or something. No harm done; just a little misunderstanding, eh?"

Matthew nodded, and tried to figure what Davo was doing at the Resort and why he was lurking about the pool. He looked back at Di and the kids, then to Lachlan; they stood together and stared at the two men.

"It's okay," Matthew said. "I know this bloke. He's an old friend – don't worry." Matthew waved and pointed Davo ahead of him toward his office. The others watched the retreat in silence.

When they were out of sight, Di turned to Lachlan and said, "So, please tell me again what happened here just now."

"I noticed Jack talking – excuse my apparent flippancy – to a golden cane. I went over and saw someone hidden in the bushes. When the guy came out, he said he was checking out the mulch. He didn't convince me, but then you came back. He was definitely hiding, from what I don't know, but he was lying about checking out the plants – even Jack could tell you that." They all looked at Jack.

"Can we go for a swim please, Gran?" Jack and Tom both walked toward the edge of the pool. Di bent down to pick up flotation jackets and she put one on each of the boys.

"Thanks for your help, Lachie," she said, as she turned to the gardener. "We'll talk again later at the office, maybe after lunch when these fellows are asleep and Jim can join us."

"Sure," said Lachlan. He went back to pulling weeds from the gaps in the paving.

******

Matthew and Davo stood in the sales office and faced one another.

"What's going on, mate? Where did you get to after you picked me up from the airport? I thought you must have done a runner or something." Matthew sat down behind his desk and waited for Davo's explanation.

"Yeah, well what do you think? It was my arse they were after. They know you picked up the stuff and left Denpasar with it. So they came looking for me. What could I tell them? Oh, it was snatched at the airport. Yeah, sure, pig's arse! So now, they'll want to get their hands on me. Nothing I say will convince them that the stuff didn't even arrive in the country. You should talk to them, maybe they'll believe you."

"Shit no, Davo! I've got enough problems and I've got a mum to think of. Imagine what would happen to us if they turn up at my place." Matthew's expression was adamant.

"Well, you're going to have to help me get away. They think you passed the stuff to me; they don't buy my story – that is – your story."

"What do you want?" Matthew asked.

"Hide me out until I can get away." Davo was thoughtful for a moment "I have a few contacts in W.A. They won't find me there. I can come back in a year or so, if I want to. I've thought about making a new start, this is my best chance. What do you say?"

"Okay, you can lie low in one of these empty units until I organise a flight. That's the quickest way to get rid of you. I'll buy a ticket and get you a disguise as soon as possible. But you'll have to be as good as invisible here. I'll get you some food and some clothes..."

"And money" interrupted Davo.

"Yeah, well, once I've paid for the ticket you'll have just about cleaned me out. This whole venture has been the worst and stupidest thing I've ever done. You're a bloody trouble magnet, not a mate at all."

"Well, what about the fact that I haven't turned you in, I could have. And this has wrecked my plans too, you know. Now I'm on the run – can't contact my family."

"I didn't think you had any family," said Matthew.

"Course I have, just don't talk about them like you. Mind you, they don't talk about me much anymore." Davo grinned and then his face quickly crumpled. He looked as though he was about to cry. He walked over to the window and looked out while he sniffed and recovered his composure. He turned back to Matthew and said, "I'm real sorry this has turned out such a shit of a mess, and I'm sorry I got you involved. I do appreciate your helping me now, but honest, I got nowhere else to turn." Davo looked at his old school friend and wondered how things had ever become so complicated.

"It's okay, mate. We all make mistakes and I've probably made just as many as you. The fact is, I've got the best mum in the world and, if it weren't for her, I'd be in jail right now. So let's get on now and you tell me where in W.A. you want to go." Matthew sat behind his desk and picked up a pen and the telephone. He pointed his thumb over his shoulder to direct Davo to the toilet.

When Davo emerged, Matthew said, "You're on a flight to Perth, tomorrow at 4.30pm. I'll drive you to the airport. I have some I.D. you can use. I've used it myself a few times. You can post it back to me when you're finished with it. That's all I ask. I can probably scrape together 500 bucks, so there won't be any luxury accommodation when you get there."

"Gee, thanks Matt. I can't tell you how much this means to me. I'll pay you back some day, I promise." Davo looked relieved.

"Sure, no problems. I'll go out and get you some food and that disguise from home. I've used it all before and it should suit you just fine. I must impress upon you to keep quiet while you're here. The residents here have nothing better to do than watch out for what their neighbours are doing. They hear and see everything. Don't even flush the toilet when I'm not here. I'll bring you back a book, but no light, no torch. When I go home this evening, I'll lock up and there can't be a sound from this place after I leave. Comprende?"

"Aye aye, sir," Davo saluted and looked much happier. For the first time in weeks, he had some hope for his future.

******

The evening closed in and Davo sat in Matthew's office chair. He swivelled from side to side and drummed on the desk. Now he could make some plans, but who to ring first? He had contacts in Perth but no phone numbers. Email, yes – an old girlfriend. He began to think about Darralyn. He had been in touch with her last Christmas, almost a year ago. He wondered what she might be up to and whether she would welcome a visit from him.

He thought about the good times he and Darralyn had shared when they first left school. In those days, they were inseparable – until he started playing around with her best friend. That was really dumb, stupid, he knew, because in the end he lost them both. They had reconciled since then, and she had come east last year. They did revive some of the past feeling, but, as usual, he had neglected to follow it up.

Only one way to find out if I'll be welcome, he thought. He opened Matthew's laptop and typed in her email address. He gave little thought to the glow of the screen. Davo sent off his email and then sat on the two-seater couch under the window. He looked around at the prints on the walls and ate the cold hamburgers his friend had supplied for his dinner. It was becoming dark as Davo once again sat in front of the computer. He opened the email inbox and there it was; the answer he had hoped for, 'Looking forward to seeing you tomorrow night. Will be at the airport before 8.00pm. D.' *Yes! That's my girl.* Davo had a grin from ear to ear. He knew now that there was a chance he could restart his life, maybe even with Darralyn, and hopefully, reform.

He got up and walked to the hallway leading to the toilet door. Suddenly, he froze; he heard a noise at the front door. A key was turned and someone was fumbling for the light switch.

Davo knew if it were Matthew, he would definitely have called out first. He slipped into the hallway and flattened himself against the wall. He heard someone walk over to Matthew's desk and pick up the phone. He identified the voice of Allen Sinclaire.

"Let me speak to Norman Noonan, please," Allen said, and then waited. Finally, the other party answered and Allen said, "He's gone, or gone to ground. Anyway, I don't want to spend any more time on him. He'll eventually turn up, his type always does, and then I'll get him. I've begun to think he may have been telling the truth and didn't collect anything anyway. We need to check at the other end again, and, if my suspicions are correct, your son should be able to come up with some answers. He may have decided to branch out on his own."

After a pause, Sinclaire continued, "Yeah, yeah, maybe, but I've got my own ideas. He's been learning the business from the ground up, or the inside out, as you well know."

Another period of silence followed, then, "Okay." Sinclaire hung up and walked to the door, turned off the light, slammed the door behind him and was gone.

Davo breathed out and stepped over to the window to watch his boss walk to his car and drive off. He thought about the conversation he had just overheard. Pieces in a puzzle started to fall into place. Norman Noonan was a local Brisbane politician. His son, Aaron, went to school with Matthew and Davo. The boys had been to Bali with a group of surfers on several occasions, so now, Davo could see the pieces beginning to fit. *Could Aaron have been involved in Matthew's foiled attempt to leave Denpasar with the drugs?* he wondered.

Norman Noonan was not above making some extra money and he had plenty of contacts. Aaron had probably suggested Davo to Allen in the first place. On more than one occasion at school, Davo and Aaron had been involved in distributing drugs. That was how Davo first become involved with the drug-running scene. Davo had no idea Aaron was still involved in the business but he was not surprised either. Davo knew Aaron regularly surfed in Indonesian waters and travelled wherever the best breaks beckoned. *Of course, he could be a carrier,* thought Davo. He would not be afraid to move drugs himself or set up his own business – just like Daddy.

Davo sat down on the couch and thought about what he might be able to do with this new information. At least the heat was off him for the time being. *Maybe I'll just keep it to myself for now, not share with Matthew. You never know when that sort of information might come in handy.* He needed an ace up his sleeve for a change. Davo curled up on the couch and drifted off to sleep. He had a smile on his lips when he woke; his dreams were full of money, beaches, and girls.

******

Matthew arrived early the next morning. "How're things going?" he asked his friend when he handed him a toasted cheese sandwich his mother had prepared for her son's lunch. Matthew was surprised at how good Davo looked compared with when he had seen him the previous evening.

"Great. Got it all sorted. Darralyn will pick me up from the airport tonight and I can hang out at her place until I get a job. She was cool, maybe not so surprising since no one can resist the famous David Winton charm."

"Well, no wonder you feel good, at least now I don't need to worry about you. Once you piss off to Perth I'll expect you to keep your head down and stay there." Matthew moved around his desk.

"Sure, sure. I've got a feeling things will work out just fine. I got a few ideas about how I can make some dough, and with Darralyn at my side, who knows?" Davo's barely suppressed excitement threatened to break out. He paced around, touching things, dancing on the balls of his feet.

Matthew focused on his friend. "Well, just don't tell me your plans and I don't want to hear from you again until you're fifty, okay? You can keep out of sight today, I've got heaps to do and people wander in here all day. Keep to the bedroom."

Davo spoke quietly, "You had a visitor last night."

"What?" Matthew looked up.

"Allen Sinclaire. Came in here and made a phone call – had his woman out in the car."

"He didn't see you?" Matthew asked anxiously.

"No, mate. I was lucky to see him first and I stayed out of sight."

"Who did he ring?"

"Dunno, couldn't hear. Left after a few minutes, the mongrel."

Matthew was thoughtful. "I can't help but wonder what he needed to come here for."

"Well, the conversation he had, he could hardly have in front of his missus, could he?"

Davo suddenly realised he had trapped himself.

"I thought you didn't hear the conversation." Matthew was quick to notice Davo's slip.

"No, well I didn't, but you don't have to be a genius to figure out he must have made a funny-business call if he couldn't use his mobile in front of her."

"Suppose so." Matthew sat down then shook himself. "I got work to do. Get out of here now." He pointed to the empty bedroom and Davo obliged.

******

Jim knocked on the door as he entered. "Busy, Matthew? Can I have a minute of your time?"

Matthew pointed to the chair opposite the desk and looked at the manager. "Always have time for you, Jim."

Jim could not help thinking that Matthew was always respectful. "It's about some guy showed up here yesterday, hiding out in the garden near the pool. What do you know about it?"

"Yeah. My friend Davo. Mad as a cut snake. He was looking for me. I sent him on his way. Nothing to worry about, honest." Matthew put his hands up, "He's an old school friend, just wanted to borrow some money. I loaned it to him and he took off. Like a bad penny, always turns up at the wrong time. He won't be back. No worries."

"Well, I hope you're right," said Jim. "I don't want any undesirables hanging around here. As you know security is my responsibility and I take it seriously."

"Sure. I understand completely. I promise you won't see him again." He stood in the hope of giving the manager the hint.

"By the way, how was your holiday?" said Jim, as he turned to leave.

"Good, good. Just got heaps of work to catch up on now. I saw the notes you left me, thanks for that – I really appreciate it. I'll follow up those leads." Matthew walked to the door with the manager.

As he walked back to his own office, Jim had the impression he had been given a polite brush off. He sat and stared at his computer. He did not know what to make of the salesman; he just could not figure him out.

Jim was still sitting, staring, when Allen walked into the office without knocking. He sat down heavily on the other chair. "You look busy, Jim, no wonder you can't keep on top of the work around here." Allen leaned toward Jim.

Jim roused himself and looked back at Allen. "Is there something I can do for you, Mr. Sinclaire?" Jim did not care if the area manager sensed his animosity.

"I heard you had dealings with a young bloke hanging around yesterday. Someone looking for the salesman," Allen prompted.

"Is there something you want to tell me about him?" Jim threw the question back.

"I'm asking you, Jim. What happened?"

"I really don't know, Allen. Di said there was a young bloke hanging around the pool, waiting to see Matthew – which he did. End of story."

"I see, okay. Well, that's about all I wanted to know."

Allen could see now he had made an enemy out of the new manager and he would not get any co-operation. He wished he had handled him differently from the start. Enemies he already had enough of.

"I'll be off now, Jim. I have to go up north for a week. Try to keep a lid on disputes and keep the cops outside the gates 'til we get back." Unable to help himself, he made no attempt to hide his sarcasm as he stood, gave a perfunctory wave and walked out the door.

Jim looked at the receding figure. "Anything for you, Allen," he said with equal sarcasm, but at least it was barely audible.

Chapter Fifteen

Jim stared out the office window and his thoughts focused on how inappropriate Allen Sinclaire was an area manager. In an industry filled with senior citizens and an environment focusing on a relaxed and happy retirement, Allen Sinclaire would be the worst choice. He was rude, arrogant; he completely lacked any compassion, or even interest, in anyone but himself and maybe his floozy. He never asked about the welfare of the residents or the amenities that were there for their benefit. He simply did not care.

Jim thought there had to be some other reason that man held the position he did; Sinclaire must have another agenda. *Well, of course he does, you idiot. You just haven't figured it out yet. But you will.* Jim turned to his diary and put Allen Sinclaire out of his mind. *One thing's for sure, I've got to get some work done.*

******

The area manager drove out of the resort and back to the motel where he and Georgeina had spent last night. She was arranging her hair when he came through the door without a knock. He threw his keys onto the bed.

"That's a real bad habit you have of never knocking before you come charging in on someone," said Georgeina, looking up.

"Well, if you weren't doing anything you shouldn't, you'd have nothing to worry about, would you?" Allen was in a particularly unpleasant mood this morning.

"What's wrong with you? Worried about going all the way to Cairns by yourself or something?"

"On the contrary, I'm looking forward to a bit of peace and quiet. This place gives me the shits. And you're beginning to get on my nerves as well." Allen slumped in the armchair.

Georgeina put her comb down and walked over to her lover. "Well, I don't know how you'd expect me to react after finding those drugs in your laptop case. Shit, Allen, I still can't believe it. I don't want to be a part of anything like that, and I don't know why you do either. You don't earn a bad living; you get plenty of freedom and travel and you've got either me or your wife on tap. What does it take to make you content?"

"Money. I don't intend to retire on the pension. In ten years from now, I'm going to be long gone from here and I'll never work again. You can play house with hubby and the kid but I want more and I'll get it, wait and see." Allen stood and started to pace around the room.

"You're taking risks though. How will you feel if you end up spending your retirement rotting away in jail?" Georgeina continued to pack clothes into her bag. She intended to go home for at least a week. She also planned not to come back to work with Allen. She had had enough and now, finding drugs in his possession was scary, though it gave her some ammunition to use in her favour. She had thought about nothing else all morning. She had been given a glimpse of how ruthless he could be when he dealt with anyone he did not like, and she did not want to join that ever-expanding group of people. *Get out now – before it's too late*, she told herself.

"You know you can't tell hubby about what you found in my case. The one you had no right snooping in, in the first place." Allen was still quite angry that Georgeina had found his secret stash. Not that he indulged himself, but they were his best currency and could buy more favours than any money.

"Of course I know that, you idiot. There's a lot at stake here." She picked up her bag and walked toward the door.

Allen collected his things and they walked out to their respective cars.

"When will you be back?" he asked, as Georgeina opened her car door.

"Probably next week," she lied. "Got stuff to sort out at home and I'm due several weeks off now, anyway."

Allen walked over to her door and leaned in. Something in the air told them there was a sense of finality about this parting. "It's been good, hasn't it, girl?"

"Yeah. It has. We just need a bit of a rest, that's all. Talk to you in about a week," she said as she turned her ignition on and drowned out his response. She took off out the gate and back toward Brisbane.

Allen got into his car and wondered which would be his best route north. He had loose ends to tie up here but he was no longer in the mood. What he needed was a bit of open road and fresh air. He turned on his CD then upped the volume. He wished he had a car with the top down, like the one owned by that little shit, Matthew. He cleared his mind and put his foot down. *Bugger 'em all,* he thought.

Georgeina too was experiencing a great sense of freedom as she drove down the motorway. She thought about Allen and seriously wondered why she was ever attracted to him. She could see now he was a very dangerous man. Maybe that sense of danger was what stimulated her interest in the first place. She had been tired of her mundane life, of Morris and his quiet, accepting demeanour. He was so content, even trusted her to go off for days at a time to work. He could have objected, or insisted that she accept a job in a company that ensured she came home every night. She knew how much he loved her and their son. He managed to look after the house and their son and put in long days at work himself.

Georgeina decided to call at a shopping mall on her way home. She knew this was to be her homecoming. She wanted to cook for the man she loved, the man who had loved her through all her transgressions. Suddenly she felt tears in her eyes; they rolled down her face and almost blinded her. She pulled over to the side of the road and began to sob – big heart wrenching sobs that took her breath away. She dabbed at her wet face until she quietened and allowed her emotions to subside slowly. She sat in the driver's seat, staring through the windscreen; Georgeina began to think about all the mistakes she had made. She had a sense of drawing back and looking at herself as she had been. Now, she seemed like a different person. Who could have been the person who blithely walked out of Morris's house and into the arms of another man, on a weekly basis? How could she have deceived him like this? He would never have done that to her and he probably would not even believe she could do it either. Morris had a beautiful face, with keen, smiling eyes. His hair was thin, but he did not need any to be handsome. He was tall and lean, and walked with big strides, eating up the path before him. He was patient, kind, and generous. *Oh God,* thought Georgeina, *Allen had none of her husband's attributes, how could I ever have betrayed Morris?* Guilt washed over her and she began to tremble and shake.

She sat there for over half an hour, overwhelmed by the shame of her own behaviour. She wondered whether she should not go home, perhaps keep driving; go away and start her life over where she could be the sort of person she did not have to be ashamed of. She sat slumped in the driver's seat, closed her eyes, and dozed off. A sudden noise woke her with a start as someone tapped on her window.

"You okay there?" An old man with a dog looked in the window, he stepped back as she wound her window down.

"Oh, yes, thank you. I must have been a bit tired; just as well I pulled over, hey?"

"Sure is. Are you okay now?"

"I am. Thank you for your concern." Georgeina waved and the man nodded and walked on. Georgeina opened the car door and put her feet on the gravel. She walked along the roadside, head bowed, thinking how badly she had treated the two people who truly loved her. She resolved to make amends to her husband and her son.

Georgeina returned to the car and drove directly to the supermarket. Later, with the back seat full of groceries, she wondered if perhaps she should have checked at home first before she duplicated stuff they already had. *Who cares?* She thought, as she turned into the afternoon traffic toward home. There were a hundred recipes going through her mind. But what were their favourites?

******

Morris looked up from his computer and saw two police officers outside his office. One knocked. The other stood back.

Morris pushed his chair back and walked to the door. He opened it and said, "How may I help you?" As he asked the question, a shiver went up his spine.

"Mr. Bunning? Morris Bunning?"

Morris nodded.

"I'm Senior Constable John Stokes and this is Constable Andy Potter. Your wife is Georgeina Bunning?"

Morris nodded again and stared at the two police officers. He thought they seemed to take up all the space and all the air in the room.

"I'm afraid I have some bad news for you, sir. Your wife has been involved in a motor vehicle accident on the Motorway at Springwood."

"Oh, my God. Is she alright?" Morris asked quietly but visibly cringing at the thought of what the answer could be.

"No, sir, I'm afraid she died at the scene." In unison, the two police officers moved forward as Morris fell toward them. They supported him to his chair. The younger constable turned to a woman seated at a desk opposite Morris's office and said, "Can you get us some water, please?"

She was out of her chair immediately and in a moment returned with a paper cup filled with water.

"Thank you," Morris said, as the woman handed the cup to him. John Stokes supported Morris as he bent forward on the seat, breathing heavily.

"Try to slow you breathing down, sir, small breaths – slowly – in – and out. Sit back and have a sip of water."

Morris did exactly as he was told. He stared ahead, then looked up at the two men, and asked, "What happened? Are you sure it was my wife? I wasn't expecting her home until tomorrow."

The senior of the two police officers removed a wallet from his pocket and handed it to Morris. He looked at the photo on the driver's licence then offered it back.

"No, you keep it, sir. I'm afraid we're going to have to ask you to come and identify your wife at the morgue. We'll take you there and then bring you back later. Do you have some family we can contact? Any children?"

"Oh, Kainen. Oh, no." Morris shook his head from side to side. He began to sob. "No – no – no," he repeated, as he rocked forward and back.

Andy Potter sat next to Morris and put his arm around his shoulders. They sat like that for a few minutes and then Morris stood up. He sucked in a deep breath, held it for a couple of seconds, and let out long sigh.

The men walked slowly out of the building and down to the police car.

The next day, Allen heard about the tragedy when he contacted his head office. He sat in his motel room and held the mobile phone. He knew he felt sad, unbelieving even at first, but then stood up and walked toward the door and his car, he said aloud to himself "At least dead people don't talk. That's one good thing about it."

Chapter Sixteen

The early evening darkness cast its gloom as the police car cruised quietly alongside the kerb. A tip-off had alerted them to some suspicious activity behind some commercial premises.

The young, female probationary constable looked left and right then back at the sergeant at the wheel. She pointed up ahead. "What's that?" she said.

They both peered ahead at a small boy, as he disappeared around the corner at the end of the street.

"Look, Serge!" she yelled.

Another young boy ran off in the same direction. The sergeant drifted a little closer and parked the car quietly. They both got out and edged along the shop walls to the corner. An alley full of wheelie bins and industrial garbage bins opened up before them; a group of boys and two men huddled at the end. The cops drew their extendable batons and walked forward. One of the kids spotted them and screamed;

everyone looked up from the corner and started to run around in a panic.

"Stop – all of you!" the sergeant shouted.

A few of the boys tried to scamper over the back wall. One made it, but it was too steep for the others. They turned like caged animals, one ran at the cops, and ducked between them. The female officer made a grab for him and yanked him by his collar. The other two boys stood frozen to the spot.

"Stop, all of you, right where you are." The sergeant pointed to the two men. "You two, what're you doing? Come over here."

The men were about twenty and dressed roughly, with caps pulled low over their faces. They both stepped up with their hands hidden.

"What's behind your backs?"

They both produced hands full of small brown bottles. They appeared to have pills in them.

"These kids here found 'em. We were just takin' a look to see what they were."

"Come with us." The sergeant motioned the men towards him. The probationary constable walked around behind the group as the sergeant ushered them toward the police vehicle. They pushed and shoved each other while they waited in a huddle for the paddy wagon to arrive. The female officer went back and collected all the bottles off the ground.

The police contacted the parents, while the boys enjoyed the drama, sitting in the station waiting room. The older men received a caution; neither had a fixed address. They were known to the local cops as homeless opportunists.

A couple of days passed before Det. Frank Pekalski got wind of the 'pick up'. He was able to track down and interview the men and the two boys who had attempted to sell the drugs to them. They told him where they found the little bottles and were adamant they had not stolen them. Pekalski read the worn labels and saw they were marked either Stanley Connelly or Jessie Thornton. This was the best lead he had had for months. Now a few pieces fell into place. The ongoing investigation into the death of Mrs. Thornton had reached a standstill. Even Frank Pekalski had run out of ideas.

But this is good, he thought. If the medication matched up with the concoction found in Jessie's blood stream at the time of her post mortem then that was one more link he needed. He had no expectation of fingerprints being viable but the bottles proved his theory. The laboratory was his next step.

******

Pekalski asked Di again, who had access to the resident's units.

"We do. We have a master key which gives us access inside the units in emergency situations," said Di. "The gardeners have access, but only to the backyards, by a key to the side gates. Our old gardener accused the gardener who was sacked recently, of maybe accessing Jessie's unit through the backyard entrance, which was often left open because the courtyard common area was supposedly secure. Well, I don't know if I agree with that theory, but I suppose it is possible," acknowledged Di.

"What about cleaners?" Pekalski pulled his seat a little closer to the desk in the manager's office.

"Well, some may have a key, but that would be a personal arrangement between a resident and a private contractor. I suspect you will find many a resident will only allow cleaners access when the resident is present – they often don't trust anyone with a key. I believe the cleaners who operate for the major service provider organisations are actually not allowed to be in a client's house, unless the designated client is on the premises for the duration of the work."

"What about Mrs. Thornton? Do you know who might have had a key to her unit?" Pekalski continued his questioning.

"I really don't know. The Clarkes may have had a key since they lived there with her previously. She was a trusting soul though, and I suspect she may have gone out leaving doors unlocked. I'm sure most residents lock up. That's the problem for us if we need to gain access to someone who has an emergency. That's why we have our master key. Notwithstanding the fact that we're a gated community, you can be sure most places will be locked up tighter than Fort Knox. Older people are concerned about their vulnerability, especially at night. Anyway, the morning I found Jessie, her unit was locked and Miriam and I had to let ourselves in with the master key."

"That's right," Pekalski nodded, as he glanced at his notes.

"So, are you any closer to finding out what happened to Jessie?" Di wondered.

"We do have another lead, but nothing conclusive. I need to go back and question a few people again. I've got to come up with the goods pretty soon or this case will end up on the shelf." The detective stood up to leave, then turned, "Oh yes, do you have an address for the gardener who left, please. The last time I questioned him he was here, and our records are incorrect – or he gave us a false address."

"Sure," answered Di. She sat down in front of her computer and tapped on the keyboard. The detective moved to the back of the desk and smiled down at her.

"Yes, that is different. I'd better check this out." He was off, waving as he strode through the door. Di looked after him with a grin from ear to ear.

"He's so nice," she said softly.

******

The drugs found in Jessie Thornton's body after she died did match those found in the containers confiscated from the kids. The boys had told Pekalski where they found them. He immediately thought about the proximity to the unit where Gwen and Ron lived. It was time for the Clarkes to come up with a few more answers.

"What?" answered Ron, when the detective questioned him about whether he had ever seen the bottles in the evidence bag Pekalski held up for him to look at.

"I said, have you ever seen these bottles before?"

Ron looked suddenly at his wife who was busy trying to make herself small in the background.

"Perhaps your wife knows?" and he held the brown bottles up so Gwen could get a better look.

"No, I've never seen anything like them before." She did not move.

166

"Well, I am surprised!" said Frank Pekalski "I thought you may have recognised them from Jessie Thornton's place, since you used to live with her and look after her. Surely you must have seen these bottles if you gave her medication."

"I never gave her that kind of medication. She took whatever sleeping pills she wanted and usually only took them in the middle of the night if she couldn't sleep." Gwen stood rigid.

"What gives you the idea these are sleeping pills?" Pekalski moved toward Gwen and she took a step back. "You must have great long vision. It puts mine to shame."

"Well, I just assumed they were sleeping pills since we all know that she died from an overdose." Gwen tried to regain lost ground. "I may have seen those bottles in her room, or maybe I was thinking about some I had once."

"I doubt you ever had any packed like this. These are very old. Nowadays they are prescribed in a box, not little brown bottles." He handed Gwen the bag.

She took it and could make out Jessie's name on the labels. Gwen sat down on the lounge chair. "They're not familiar to me. No, I don't recognise them at all." She handed the bag back to Frank and looked at her husband with what looked like a pleading expression.

The detective put the bag back in his pocket when Ron said suddenly, "What about fingerprints."

"Yes, we are still checking those. We'll know more about those this afternoon." Frank knew there was nothing to be proved by the fingerprints – too many – all smudged. But the Clarkes didn't know that.

"I suspect Gwen may have given those pills to Jessie, you know." Ron looked thoughtful. "I mean, I think I may have seen them when we were living there. Don't you remember, love? I'm sure you gave those pills to Jessie. Or you may have handled the bottle cleaning her bedside table. I think it's possible her fingerprints could be on that bottle."

"Even after all this time?" Frank wore a very worried frown with his question.

"Who knows? Surely, you blokes know how long a fingerprint lasts. And what does it prove anyway?"

"You tell me." Frank looked closely into Ron's face.

Ron began to bluster and then got angry. "What do you think you're doing, coming round here, and suggesting we had anything to do with a murder? We, of all people, were closer to Jessie than anyone was. We loved that old lady, didn't we, Gwen?" He looked at his wife.

Gwen said nothing; she just sat there and nodded her head.

"Well, let's go over this again." Frank stood up and began to walk around the little room. "You two are the only people who stood to gain anything from Jessie's death, so you had motive. You two were the only ones who had access and opportunity. These little bottles here may be called the murder weapon, and if your fingerprints are found on the murder weapon, there won't be much left to say."

Gwen began to cry. "It wasn't us. Honest. We had nothing to do with Jessie's death."

Ron got up and put a protective arm around his wife's shoulder. "She's telling the truth. We didn't kill Jessie. But we did dispose of the bottles."

"Why?" Frank asked quietly, not wanting to interrupt the flow of the confession.

"When we found out Jessie was dead, we went to her unit to see for ourselves. The young gardener said he heard she was dead and we were cleaning the unit next door at the time. The manager had left and so we slipped in to see for ourselves. When we saw the bottles in the kitchen, we figured she must have taken them herself. Then we thought someone might even blame us. We talked about it and thought it would look better if she seemed to die of natural causes. We thought there would be no investigation if she looked like she just died of a heart attack in her sleep, so we took the bottles. We got rid of them. We had no idea there would be a post mortem on such an old woman. All we did was to get rid of the bottles. We just wanted to get our inheritance without any fuss. That's it."

"How did the gardener know she had died?" asked Frank.

Gwen piped up and said, "He said he was out the back of the unit when the manager arrived – just checking to see if her yard needed mowing. He looked in the window and put two and two together. He also said the manager told him she was dead."

"Bit unlikely, don't you think?" responded Frank.

"What?" asked Gwen.

"That sort of information coming from the manager to the gardener; the unpopular one as well. Not the sort of person you would expect the manager to confide in."

"No, I guess not," Gwen responded, "but that's what he said."

"Well, let's see what we have so far." The detective put his fingers up, ready to count off the points. He pointed his index finger, "You guys are busy cleaning the unit next door to Jessie's – that must be either 26 or 28?"

"Unit 28," answered Gwen.

"Unit 28. Okay. So then you speak to the gardener. When?"

"When we'd finished cleaning 28. As we came out, we saw him leave Jessie's yard. He called us over. A bit of gossip, that's all. He told us what he had just seen and he left. The manager had just left too. We used our key and went straight in."

"Did it ever occur to you that maybe the gardener might be a suspect?" Frank queried.

"No, we never really thought of that. Well, actually we did think of it, but not seriously."

"Why not?" Frank raised his eyebrows.

"Just didn't think she was murdered is all. We thought she'd killed herself. The gardener wouldn't gain anything by killing her. Maybe her dog, but not Jessie."

"I see. Well this is all very interesting. If either of you think of anything else I may want to hear, please don't hesitate to give me a call. You'd be surprised what I think is useful, even if you don't." Frank turned toward the door.

"What about the fingerprints?" Ron asked.

"We'll have to wait and see, won't we. Don't leave town."

Frank smiled and left.

******

"You two had your day in court and I think you were lucky to get off with only a fine." Carmen Miller's voice was fragile. It sometimes failed her completely. She looked at her husband's back as he stared out the bedroom window.

Tony Miller ignored his wife's comment. He parted the curtains a little and observed Ron and Gwen Clarke on the front porch of Unit 27. He watched them water the pot plants and give the tiles a final sweep. The Clarkes now had the unit on the market and Tony wondered what type of person would be his next neighbour. He let the curtains fall back into place and turned to look at Carmen.

She now spent most of her day in bed and continued to lose weight. Day by day, her strength ebbed. Each morning, she sat in a lounge chair while the nurse made her bed, but even the effort of sitting upright for extended periods was becoming increasingly difficult for Carmen to manage. She was no longer able to sit for any length of time in the lounge chair, so, during the day, she watched some television in the bedroom, but mostly slept with her head propped up with pillows. Conversations with Tony became shorter as her stamina waned. During their married life, Carmen and Tony had shared similar interests and Carmen had always been available to give Tony advice and listen to his opinions. They had revelled in the stimulation of wide-ranging conversations, but now, even that pleasure was slipping away. She did not care to talk much, and she slept most of the time during the day. The sound from the television was like white noise to her. Carmen hated the nights. She was often awake, as the awareness of her mortality pulsed through her mind in the darkened hours. She had always said she was not afraid of death itself, but now, she knew she was afraid of the dying. As each bout of anxiety woke her, she turned on the television, muted the sound, and let the movement on the screen distract her enough to help her doze for another few minutes.

Tony moved to the second bedroom so his sleep was not disturbed.

For the last couple of weeks, there was always a volunteer support person on hand, ready to assist if Carmen needed anything. Tony did not realise how lucky he was to have this volunteer service made available to him. It was largely due to the efforts of people like Jessie Thornton, who had helped set up this community service, that such valuable assistance was possible in helping with people who wanted to die at home. Tony tended to take such things for granted, and never fully appreciated the time, effort, and compassion of the volunteers.

"I'll be glad to see the back of those Clarkes," said Tony. "I don't trust them and I reckon they might have done the old girl in. Mind you, it could have been Richard White. I wouldn't put a thing past him."

"Let it go, will you? I am so fed up with hearing about the Whites. I won't be around to see the new neighbours and you'll probably find nobody killed her." Carmen paused for breath before she continued, "Most likely she just died. We're all doing it, or haven't you noticed?" Carmen turned her back to her husband, who was standing beside her bed. She pulled the sheet over her face.

When Tony heard her cry softly, he walked out of the room and decided to let her rest. *She'll feel better when she's had a bit of a sleep*, he thought. Tony sat in front of the TV in the lounge and flicked around to distract his mind from the quiet sobbing he could hear coming from the bedroom. Now, he really felt sorry for himself. It just did not seem right to him that he was going to be left alone.

******

The Clarkes heard nothing from Detective Pekalski the day after his interview, or the next, or the next. A week went by and their apprehension lessened. They started to think that maybe they were off the hook, and they both started to relax and continued to do cleaning jobs in and out of the resort. They were more patient now and knew it was just a matter of time until the unit sold and they would get their money.

"I can't help wonder what the Connelly's thought about us getting the money they expected to inherit," Gwen said as they drove home at the end of another working day.

"Well, old Stan's dead now and Rena's a blow-in opportunist, so I don't feel any guilt about getting the money," answered Ron. "We were the ones to help her when she needed it, after all."

"True, but who did kill Jessie? That's what I want to know and I can see now that if we hadn't touched those bloody pill bottles, maybe the police would have had the fingerprints they needed."

"Yeah." Ron had had enough discussion – too much talk did his head in.

Chapter Seventeen

Frank Pekalski knew that someone had given Jessie a lethal dose of sedatives, probably washed down with alcohol. There had been no evidence of any rough handling on her body, so she must have somehow been coerced into drinking it. He figured the only reason Jessie would have had a drink in the first place was because she was with someone she felt comfortable with. There was no sign of forced entry and not a thing out of place in her unit. Pekalski wondered what he had missed and who had wanted to see her dead. He cast his mind over all his suspects again and was standing in front of his desk at the station when he took a call from an anonymous voice.

"You might want to take a look at what's going on at the Retirement Resort in North Brisbane," said the voice. "I'm not talking about murder, mate – I'm talking about drugs. The managers; they're the ones you should be questioning. They know more than they're saying."

The line went dead. Frank's mind was replaying the message. He wrote it down and then looked at the words again. He sat and thought, *What the hell could this be about?* It looked like he would have another trip out to the Resort.

******

Jim walked over to the manager's residence and up the stairs to the veranda that had become their retreat at the end of each day. "This spot is compensation for all we've had to put up with since we came here," he said to Di, who was already ensconced on her favourite chair in the corner, under the lacy branches of the Poinciana tree.

"What's up?" She looked up at her husband.

"I was just thinking this place must be jinxed. The death of Georgeina Bunning is yet another sad event to add to our ever-growing list of unexpected occurrences since we arrived here. Maybe this place is being haunted by an unsettled spirit – maybe someone who died here."

Jim was pouring himself a drink from the tray Di had placed on the table.

"Well, if you think we're haunted then maybe we are. When you consider all the places we've worked and how little trouble we've had, this is exceptional," Di nodded.

"I'm serious. I just had a call from Pekalski at the office. He wants to come and talk to us again tomorrow. I wish he'd wrap up this investigation and let everyone get on with their lives. This time he said it's nothing to do with the death of Jessie Thornton. What else can he want to talk about?"

Jim slid down into his favourite chair and looked out at the sunset. He began to think seriously about retirement himself. Allen Sinclaire, his immediate superior, was another thorn in his side and he was not going to go away. Jim wondered what Di would think about hanging up her master key forever.

******

Pekalski arrived directly before lunch the next day. As always, he brightened up Di's day with his cheeky smile.

"Take a seat," said Jim, pointing to the spare chair in the office. Jim did not care if he never saw him again.

"Sorry to disturb you guys again. I'm beginning to feel like I live here lately," he said.

"I wish you did," said Jim. "You can have my job. I'm completely over it all."

Di looked at her husband and wondered if the job was really finally getting to him. She had never heard him so belligerent to a guest before.

"So, what is it this time?" he looked directly at Pekalski and gave the impression this interview should be short and sweet.

"I don't know where to start, really. I think I need to ask you if you have had any indications that there is drug dealing here in the Resort."

"Drug dealing!" The managers leaned toward the detective in unison. "God Almighty, what's this really about?" said Jim.

"I've had a tipoff." He told them about the phone call he'd had.

"That's all pretty personal and only the fact that it's so absurd prevents me from laughing my head off," Jim said, as he stood and walked around the office.

"Jim, do you know anyone who may want to implicate you, make life uncomfortable for you?" Frank looked up at Jim and waited. "Anyone?" Frank prompted after a few seconds.

"Jim, what about the gardener?" Di asked. "He didn't like us."

"Neither does Allen Sinclaire," answered Jim.

"Neither do Richard White and Tony Miller," continued Di.

"Those two are mad but I doubt they'd stoop so low as to set us up. They'll always have to deal with some managers. We could have done a lot more than we have, following their behaviour," said Jim, "and I think they know it."

"Tell me about the gardener," said Frank. Jim sat down again.

"He quit. He thought I was about to sack him so he stormed out of here following an altercation between himself and the other gardener, Tom. Tom's been here since the resort opened, and Kevin started about six months ago. Kevin had the qualifications, but was lazy and unreliable. He didn't like being the junior boy and wasn't able to follow instructions. I suspect he was not trustworthy either. More than one resident complained about Kevin being in the wrong place at the wrong time."

"Don't you think he'd be more likely to have an axe to grind with Tom, than you?" Pekalski was taking notes.

"Yes, I would have thought so. But he had a chip on his shoulder and Di said he was rude to her as well."

Di nodded, and, said, "I think he's a mischief maker and may just be out of work, looking to stir up trouble for someone in his ample spare time."

"Hmm, what about the area manager? I hear he isn't your best friend either," Frank said.

"Who told you that?" Jim asked.

"Di. She said he wasn't happy about you calling the cops after that wedding debacle. She also said he behaved very badly to you both."

Frank looked at Jim.

Jim nodded, and cast a glance at Di.

"That's true," said Jim. "And now he's lost his co-manager. Georgeina Bunning was killed in a car accident a few days ago. Apparently, she was on her way home and another vehicle hit her. She died at the scene. Allen was up in Cairns, so we can't blame him for it. They were an item, you know."

Frank kept writing and nodded. Finally, he put his pen away and stood up. "I'm going to check a few things out," he said. "I'll get back to you. Let me know if you see or hear anything suspicious."

"You trust us?" asked Di.

"I consider myself a good judge of character, and in your case, I've got no qualms. Just let me know if you plan to leave town."

"If you'd have asked me that this morning, I would probably have said 'tomorrow' but I guess we can hang in a bit longer," Jim sighed.

"Good man." Frank smiled. "I think you're both doing a great job. I certainly wouldn't want it. Good luck to both of you."

Pekalski made his way out to the entrance then called back over his shoulder. "I'm going to wander round for a bit, might ask a few questions. Don't mind me."

******

At 54 years of age, Allen Sinclaire did not want another management partner. He had always used his area manager's job as a front for his major source of income – dealing drugs. He realised when Georgeina died just how much she interfered with his freedom of movement and personal security. He decided to contact head office and plead his case to work alone.

The company was certainly not against cost cutting and Allen was surprised at how quickly they approved his request. They agreed to give him a three months' trial to see if he could deal with the workload alone. Allen made a decision to get his head down and make sure they had no cause for complaint. He needed to operate unencumbered.

******

The phone in Jack Noonan's reception area rang and his assistant answered.

"Let me speak to Jack, please." Even though Allen had more than one voice, he liked his sharp, direct one best.

The call transferred to Noonan's office. "Yeah?"

"Allen here, mate. Got any news?" He kept the same tone in his voice.

"Hang on a minute." Jack got up and walked slowly to the door to his office. He liked to have privacy with these calls. He also knew that making Allen wait reinforced the power play he so enjoyed inflicting on his underlings.

Allen tapped his fingers. *Not again*, he thought irritably. Allen had figured out Jack's tactic long ago, but it still annoyed him. He could picture his long-standing associate in his office, not that he often went there, and not that he could call him a friend. While he waited, he thought back over his long connection with Jack.

He had been involved with Jack Noonan for more than twenty years. To begin with, they both worked for Jack's uncle, but he was dead now and Jack had built up the multi-faceted business, which included the importation of drugs to Australia, direct from Indonesia or Vietnam. He had distanced himself from a vast syndicate of mainly Asian nationals and illegal immigrants to Australia who had very big operations that ran along similar lines to Jack's. They grew cannabis domestically and used the profits to import heroin. Jack's own syndicate was smaller, older and had links to more big money in Australia and overseas.

As he held the still silent handset to his ear, Allen thought about the several close scrapes he had had with the law over the years. He wanted to get out of the business before he was sixty. He needed one more big deal and he would not be greedy, or so he told himself. *Quit while you're ahead, don't overstay your welcome.* He knew what he had to do.

Jack closed the door and returned to his chair. He put his feet up on the desk and casually took a cigar from a humidor on top of the cabinet beside him. He clipped it with a double-bladed guillotine cutter, toasted the cut edge carefully with his Dunhill Turbo lighter, and then slowly ignited the centre. The ritual never lost its appeal to Jack. He took a long, slow mouthful of the mellow smoke and exhaled smoke rings. He picked up the telephone handpiece, lowered his voice and said, "You there?"

"Oh – yeah," Allen said, as he was jolted back to the present.

They discussed the next big haul, also what might have happened to the parcel that should have come in with Matthew Weatherlee.

"I'm not looking for fuckin' Davo at the moment," said Allen. "I don't think he has the stuff, or Weatherlee either, for that matter. I've got a bad feeling about another operator in Denpasar."

"Aaron's in Bali. If there was another operation there, he'd know," Jack responded.

"Yeah, exactly." Allen knew he had said enough.

He had his suspicions about what had kept Aaron so busy lately, but knew he was on touchy ground. Allen was a pragmatist. Even though he sometimes felt it should have been him sitting in Jack's chair, when he thought about it seriously, he knew he could not handle the stress. Allen was also a realist. He knew that above all else, blood ties were always stronger than other bonds and that was why he never bucked the chain of command. Allen answered directly to his boss, Jack, but was aware that Jack's right-hand man was his brother, Norman Noonan.

Norman was also Jack's man in the government – one of Queensland's leading politicians and someone who enjoyed the support of a powerful faction of the Government. It was common knowledge that Norman had a few less than squeaky-clean friends. There were no other intermediaries and Allen had Jack's respect most of the time, but that could always change, and casting aspersions on a family member was risky business.

Norman's son, Aaron, was also Jack's apprentice, not that Aaron would have called himself that. He now worked mainly in Indonesia and travelled a lot between India and the East. His cover was as an international surfer. He set up drug deals and lived well. He had to be very smart, and he was. Young enough to feel indestructible and quick enough not to get caught, he had trained his whole twenty years for this job. Norman trusted Aaron and never considered the possibility that his son may have already branched out on his own.

Allen thought about the few in the drug organisation who did answer to him, and the responsibility that created. Among those at his beck and call was Davo, as was the ex-resort gardener, Kevin. Matthew Weatherlee had never been involved in the drugs side of the business, apart from the one failed attempt to act as a mule in the Denpasar fiasco. Allen wondered if it was time to introduce him into the organisation at a much deeper level. He needed someone with brains, a person who could be trusted to act independently if need be.

Allen had one big reservation – did Matthew have the guts to take risks? He may need to persuade him.

Allen returned from Cairns and made a trip out to see Matthew as soon as he got the go ahead from Adelaide to continue as sole area manager.

"Heard anything from our old friend, Davo, in my absence?" Allen put his head around the door of Matthew's office.

"Shit, don't bloody do that. I nearly wet myself." Matthew stood up, almost as if to bar Allen's way in.

"Matthew, I know it was you. You're the one Davo trusted to bring that last haul out of Bali, but you buggered up. I could have handed you over to some of the more muscular friends of my acquaintance – the brick shithouses on legs, and with brains to match – but I let Davo take the fall. I've got a pretty good idea neither of you made anything out of that deal, but that's beside the point. The boss is still looking for a culprit. He doesn't care who gets it in the neck, as long as someone suffers – and it won't be me, I can assure you of that." Allen sat down in front of Matthew's desk and started to shuffle through his papers.

Matthew was planning to slide out of all future deals and scams with Allen. He had a sense of doom when he thought about having any kind of connection with him. Hopelessly, he slumped into his chair.

"Not as talkative as usual, eh, my friend?" said Allen. "You may have underestimated me perhaps, but that's okay, I may have underestimated you. I came here to talk about your future. I'm feeling generous and I may consider putting some cash your way."

"I don't want it. I want nothing to do with you or your schemes."

"Correct me if I'm wrong, but I'm pretty sure the cash-for-refurbishment scheme was all yours – so was importing furniture from Thailand for the display units and then issuing your own invoices to the company, with a suitable handling fee added on. What you didn't know, Your Innocence, is that we brought in a very lucrative haul of drugs hidden in that furniture."

Matthew gasped. He was speechless. He stared at the smiling face of Allen Sinclaire.

"Why don't you sit up nicely and we can talk seriously. I'm about to make you an offer, one you may consider refusing – but don't. My advice is to accept it. If you come in with me, I'll make you rich in a couple of years. When I go, you may even take over my job. I don't plan to work forever, you know."

Matthew still could not say a word. He listened. Allen went on. "In time, you'll know who my boss is, but not yet. We have a network of well-established performers; that's why we're still in business after twenty years; if anyone doesn't perform, they're out – right out. I've nothing bad planned for your friend Davo – you can tell him that when you see him. He can come out of hiding. I may even have some more work for him soon."

"I haven't seen him," said Matthew, very quietly.

"Have it your own way. But if you want me to trust you, you'll have to trust me. Works both ways, Matthew. I'll give you until tomorrow to think over what I've just said. I'll call you first thing in the morning to discuss my offer. After that, we're in business. If you decline my very lucrative, generous offer, you may find the job you have here will be the first thing you have to live without. Also, I believe your mother may not be happy about what her little boy has been up to on his overseas holidays – just to name a couple of items of interest to you, eh." Allen stood and looked long and hard at Matthew. "I've a feeling we'll become very useful to one another – don't let me down. I respond badly to disappointment."

******

As Allen got in his car to drive away, the manager, Jim Watersen, looked out the window of his home and said, "What's he doing here? I've never seen an area manager hang around as much as that bloke does. Usually you don't see one from one month to the next – he just about lives here, lately. I can't imagine when he ever sees the other resorts. I bet they can't even remember what he looks like. There he goes. Well, at least he's keeping out of our hair." Di looked up from the kitchen sink in time to see the man her husband was talking about, as he drove out the front gate.

"Hmm. Good riddance," she said, " but it's a bit strange. He really only needs to deal with us – occasionally Matthew. I think it's a bit fishy, considering the amount of strange activity around here. I'm going to wander down to talk to Matthew later, see what he says." Di was stubborn; she had a sharply tuned intuition and rarely resisted using it.

Jim knew that to warn his wife off was never a good idea, always worked in reverse, and maybe she could find out something, after all.

******

Allen had a full day lined up; get rid of odd jobs related to the retirement resort industry, then make contact with Jack.

186

He had to set up a date for a meeting to discuss the next shipment of drugs. No slip ups would be tolerated – there would be no room for mistakes. They were all dependent on Aaron doing his set-up first, and then every link in the chain had to be checked and rechecked. The success of the organisation depended on attention to detail and Allen knew that was the reason they had survived so long. There was little turnover amongst the members of the organisation and rarely did anyone just walk away. Aaron and his cousins were the next generation and they all had a place in the organisation, but Allen's unease about the Denpasar debacle continued.

******

Mikaila, Jack Noonan's assistant, looked down at the two envelopes he dropped in the out-tray on her desk and wondered if there was something she should know. She made it her business to check all her boss's correspondence and she usually copied anything significant for her own file. Jack treated her like one of the family, as many in the organisation were. She had never given him any reason not to trust her and she took his ongoing support for granted.

However, being Jack's personal secretary and Aaron's girlfriend became a conflict of interest and she had made a choice. She gave her loyalty to Aaron, and before he had left on his present sojourn to Jakarta and Bali, he and Mikaila came to a very cosy agreement. They each had a mobile phone that they used exclusively to contact one another. She fed him information as it came her way, certain things that Jack did not think anyone else needed to know, but would assist Aaron to continue working as much for himself as for the family. Mikaila wanted to move on and she knew that

Jack would not protect her from the consequences of her actions when these became known. She picked up the mail and held it below her desk as she quickly slit the envelope and removed the only sheet of paper.

She scanned it quickly then turned and addressed another envelope. It was nothing she did not already know, but she had to check and she did not want to let anything slip by.

Don't overlook small details, don't get lazy. Aaron had impressed on her that it was a complicated web and there was no honour among thieves, or drug runners. She was not going to let him down, or herself either.

******

"Hello Matthew." Di knocked on the salesman's door. "Can I come in?"

"Sure." He walked toward her. "What can I do for you?"

"You seem a bit subdued. I hope that area manager hasn't upset you, too."

"No, why should he?" Matthew did not look his usual bright, happy self at all.

"I saw him leave earlier and wondered why he was here again. He didn't come to see us, which he usually does, and he really should put all business through us."

"He was talking about the refurbishment of a couple of units, actually," said Matthew.

"That's exactly what I mean. He doesn't need to come here to do that. He could call you, or us. It's not something he should be bothered with."

"Don't worry about it, I've known him quiet a long time, and he doesn't concern me at all. I think he may be a bit upset about the loss of his partner, Georgeina, you know, a bit thrown. If I were you, I wouldn't give him another thought. He's not worth it." Matthew started to look a little more cheery. "Forget him; I'm sure you've got better things to think about."

"I guess so." Di started to back off. "As a matter of fact I'm on my way to see a resident who's very unwell. I'd better move. See you later."

Walking away, Di summed up her feelings about the encounter. *I have the distinct impression he didn't want me to say anything derogatory about Allen Sinclaire. I also feel he wanted me to disappear.*

Di continued to think in this vein until she arrived at Carmen Miller's house. "How are you feeling today, Carmen?" Di leaned over the woman in the bed and whispered to her. Glassy eyes fluttered open, and then she frowned.

"Have you got pain?"

Carmen nodded, "Yes."

"I'll go and have a look at your chart. I believe the volunteer has just left, I saw her get into her car. It's a beautiful day outside today."

Di kept up a running, one-sided conversation while she prepared a dose of analgesics. "This will help and I can make you more comfortable. The Blue Nurses will be along soon and later Lillian, and maybe Doctor Morrow." Di sat and held Carmen's hand. It was obvious there was not much time left for this woman. The nurse in Di wondered where Tony was. Surely, he could stay by her side now, with so little time left and so much comfort to be gained by his wife.

Di continued to hold Carmen's hand but her thoughts drifted to the resort and the problems she and Jim had been experiencing. She began to wonder if maybe they should spend more time together. Should she mention retirement to her husband? How would he react to the idea? Maybe travel a bit, have more fun and less long days. They say not all men take to retirement. She would give it some more thought before mentioning it.

Chapter Eighteen

Joy leaned over the man who lay on the path. She looked around and waved to the nearest person she could see.

"Quick, help me, please."

John Turner crossed the grass and bent to see what she was so distressed about; he gasped and momentarily froze.

"Go to the office and tell the manager to ring the ambulance – an emergency – quickly now, I'll stay here with him," said John, a resident, as was Joy, the woman with him. They were both on their way to the community centre to attend the afternoon yoga class.

On the path lay a middle-aged man, his head in a pool of blood and his right leg lying at a very awkward angle. Jim and Di rushed over to the scene. "The ambulance is on the way," said Jim, as they both bent down to look at the body bent up on the path.

Di gasped, "It's Frank Pekalski!" She moved around to get closer to his face. She bent and gently turned his head, "He's breathing." She lifted his wrist. "Pulse is rapid but okay."

Jim helped turn his head to give him a clear airway. Di pulled a handkerchief from her own pocket and wiped his lips then sat back on her heels and turned to Joy. "What happened, do you know?"

"No, this is how I found him and then I called John. Do you know who he is?"

"Yes, he's a detective. We spoke to him a little while ago. I thought he would have left by now. If you want to go we can stay and wait for the ambulance." Di looked at both of them.

"I want to wait," said Joy, as she moved to the seat on the grass nearby.

John stood and shuffled around. "I wonder what happened," he said.

"Maybe this," said Jim, as he pointed to a rock at the edge of the footpath. "And I don't know what that hose is lying here for, but it's a trap for anyone, especially someone with poor eyesight or mobility."

He went to move the hose and roll it up when Di stayed his hand and said softly, "Maybe the police will want to see how this happened. Do you think we shouldn't touch anything?"

"You could be right. I'll go and ring them now." Jim walked back to the centre just as he heard the ambulance come in the front gate.

The paramedics were with Pekalski about ten minutes while they stabilised him, then loaded him into the ambulance. Di stayed at the scene, and waited for the police to arrive. She made sure nothing was disturbed. A crowd had gathered. There was animated discussion about possible scenarios and speculation about whether this was another crime.

A few minutes later, a police car arrived. Two policemen looked at the scene and talked to the managers, then Joy and John. They walked around, asking questions of residents in nearby houses. Those enquiries yielded no useful information.

******

Di followed Jim into their office and watched him stand with his back to her, hands on his hips. She saw him turn to her and shake his head.

"I can't believe this," he said.

Jim had always been tall, slim, and good looking, but looking at him now, Di could see that the events of the past months had taken their toll on him. His hair was visibly greyer and the facial lines had deepened. Di had noticed over this time that he carried an almost permanent worry frown on his face, and she could not remember the last time she had heard him laugh.

"Me either," she said, in a delayed response to Jim's statement. "Surely it was just an accident. Do you think it could be possible that someone has either tripped him up or even hit him on the head?"

"Well, I'm no cop but it looked to me as though that blood came directly from where he landed on the rock, next to the path. Maybe the hose was the cause of the fall. I can't figure out why the hose was even left there. The cops spoke to the gardeners, Lachlan and Tom. I think I'll go and have a chat with them, right now." He made to leave.

"Watch where you walk. We could be next." Di went to laugh but then froze. "Sorry, I didn't mean that, not funny at all. But please be careful."

"I will." Jim disappeared out the door.

Jim looked at his watch; it was almost three-twenty. He walked briskly toward the gardener's shed. He knew Tom and Lachlan would be cleaning up before they left for the day. They started early and usually knocked off at 3.30pm.

"Hi," said Jim, as he gave a knock on the corrugated iron door. "Got a minute, guys?"

"Sure," said Tom. They both turned toward Jim.

"I just wondered what the cops asked you about."

"They asked 'bout the hose, the time we normally water the garden, had we seen that rock there before, stuff like that," Tom answered.

"And what did you say?"

Tom looked at Lachlan, and he spoke next. "As you know, that whole area is supplied by the sprinkler system. We don't hose there and neither of us had put the hose there. We have no idea about the rock; it could have been there forever for all we know."

"I see," said Jim. "Anything else they wanted to know?"

"Not really, we didn't have much to tell them. They took the hose with them, said they'd probably bring it back tomorrow."

"Okay, thanks guys." Jim began to walk away.

"Oh, boss," shouted Lachlan, "they did ask about whether anyone else had access to the shed and we said you guys, and when I told them I was new, they asked about Kevin."

"Kevin?"

"Yeah. We just said he's gone now. Is that okay?"

"Yes, fine. Thanks boys."

Jim immediately wondered about Kevin. *Had he been around when Jessie died? Did he have anything to do with the feud between Miller and White? Why did his name keep popping up?*

Jim was deep in thought as he walked back to the centre. He did not notice a man walk up behind him. A voice in his ear startled him.

"You going deaf, mate?" Tony Miller stood behind him. "I called you, but you just walked on like a zombie."

"Sorry, Tony, I was a million miles away. Did you want me?"

"Yes, I did. Carmen died an hour ago. I'm just stretching my legs and clearing my head."

"Oh, I'm so sorry, Tony. What can I do to help? There must be a pile of things to do now. Have you called Di?"

"Yes. She's with Carmen right now. I'm about to go back and start to ring the family. I didn't really believe it would be this soon. I feel as if I'm not ready, need more time, you know?" Tony looked at the ground, hands behind his back. "I just wanted enough time to tell her how much I loved her. I wanted to express myself properly, say the right words, you know. And now it's too late."

Jim put his arm around Tony's shoulders and the other man began to sob quietly. His shoulders rose and fell as he tried to hold his grief in. He wiped his eyes with the back of his hand and sniffed.

"Just not fair. She's still so young. We planned to go to Tasmania for Christmas, travel for about two weeks. Won't be doing that now."

They walked together to Tony's house.

Di met them at the door. "I've rung the doctor and the nursing service. Tony, do you want to make the calls to your family yourself, or would you like us to help?"

"I'd appreciate if you could help with the calls, if you have time." Tony picked up his diary and sat at the dining room table. Jim and Di joined him while he went through his book and they made a list of all the people to call.

An hour later, Jim was still on the phone when the doctor and nurse arrived. They attended to the final examination. Lillian and Di dressed Carmen, for the last time. Her body was collected within another hour.

Tony stood in his home – bereft.

"Are you sure you'll be alright by yourself?" asked Jim.

Tony nodded. "My son will be here soon. Thanks for everything."

"You're welcome."

Jim walked back to the residence, where Di had started to prepare the evening meal.

"Let the good times begin. It can start any time now as far as I'm concerned," he said as he walked into the kitchen.

Di tried to make light of the moment but it seemed a great cloud had descended on Keeala Resort.

Jim went to the cabinet that housed their sound system. He flipped through a drawer of CDs and selected Mozart's Ave Verum Corpus; it seemed an appropriate choice. They ate in silence and let the music wash over them.

"To Carmen," they said, as they raised the glasses of wine in salute.

Before they retired, Di enquired at the hospital about Detective Pekalski. They told her she was 'satisfactory', despite superficial head injuries and a broken leg.

"I knew that man had a hard head," Di smiled as she turned out the light.

******

When the phone rang at six the next morning, both Di and Jim were jolted awake. Jim put his feet on the floor and Di was already answering. "Of course, darling, bring the kids over, haven't seen them for ages. Ten would be fine. See ya." She hung up, threw the bed covers back, and then went straight to the bathroom.

"Whew, that's all we need today." Jim slowly resigning himself to another terrible, disorganised, completely confused day when he would get got nothing done and everything would go wrong. *But look on the bright side, old son* he said to himself, *Lydia could burn the resort down and then we wouldn't have a job to worry about.* Then he remembered, Lydia had moved to a hostel in a nursing complex about a month ago.

The day began, and progressed pretty much as Jim had envisioned. Di's granddaughters, Jya and Ayla, 7 and 5 respectively, were very active, inquisitive girls with a thirst for knowledge and the speed of gazelles. It seemed they were everywhere, all at the same time. Di introduced them to some of the women at the exercise class.

"We'll look after them, don't worry," said Alexis, the fitness coordinator.

Half an hour later, Di noticed the women filing out of the centre. When she went to investigate, she found Alexis sitting on the floor massaging her ankle. Gym balls were in all parts of the room, knotted skipping ropes and dumbbells were scattered across the exercise mat.

"Has the class broken up early? You okay?" Di asked, hesitantly, because one look at the room had painted a picture all too familiar to her.

Alexis stood up and stretched her legs, then her arms, as if testing to see if they still worked.

"I think so. Maybe the girls are just a bit young for this sort of activity," she said, as she gave the girls a none-too-subtle glare.

In reply came two beaming, butter-wouldn't-melt-in-my-mouth smiles.

"Come on girls, clean this mess up. You can't expect Alexis to tidy up your mess."

"Oh, do we have to?" Ayla asked her grandmother.

"You most certainly do, and when you're finished, we can go and have some lunch."

With very bad grace, the girls helped Di clean up the mess. A couple of times they slackened off, but Di remained firm until the room was back in order.

"Right, let's go." Di said. "Say 'thank you' to Alexis."

The girls waved and yelled their thanks at a shell-shocked Alexis, who stood looking after them, shaking her head slowly from side to side.

The girls skipped behind their grandmother and waved to residents as they made their way back to the manager's residence for lunch.

"We loved that," said Jya, "can we go again?"

"Sure," said Di, "why not?"

The girls jostled each other as they ran ahead of Di.

"Jya, Jya, pants on fire," said Ayla, as she pushed her sister in the back.

"Ayla, Ayla, loves a sailor," Jya said, as she reciprocated the shove.

"Don't!"

"Do!"

"Now that's enough girls. Come on – stop it," said Di, as she reached the front door.

Di knew Jim was hiding, when he did not appear for lunch. *He'll have to come home eventually. I should tell him they're staying for a week. No, I couldn't do that to him.*

Jim's mobile rang. The text message from his wife read, *"Gone for a drive. Back in time to cook dinner."*

Jim thought, *Great, now I can go home and get something to eat,* but it crossed his mind that it could be a trap. Hunger, however, won over caution, and so he slipped in the back door and listened. No sound. He was safe.

Meanwhile, Di listened to the little girls' nonstop chatter as they made their way to the hospital. They took the elevator to the third floor. "Now sit here, don't make a sound, and don't move. I'll be in there for two minutes. Then we can all go home."

The girls both nodded and put their fingers to their lips. Both smiled the smile of an angel.

Di slipped into Frank Pekalski's room. He was asleep and looked terrible. An intravenous drip ran and a bed cradle encased his lower half. His head was swathed in bandages and he had a black eye and puffy lips. She hardly recognised him.

An almighty crash startled Di. She turned quickly and went to the doorway. She looked out to see where the girls were. They were not on their seats. Moments later, they ran back to the spot where she had left them. They sat and put their fingers on their lips when she looked at them, and raised her eyebrows. They both shrugged. Di saw two nurses hurrying toward her in the hallway. *I'm not going to ask – I'm just not going to ask.*

"Let's go," she said. Di grabbed their hands and set off in the opposite direction.

******

"And how were my angels today, while Mummy was making lots of money for lots of Christmas presents?" Alison looked genuinely pleased to see her daughters as they ran up the path to the front door their home.

There were those smiles again. "We had a good time Mummy; can we go to Granny's again?"

Alison looked at her mother with a question on her face.

Di said, "Maybe I'll come to your place next time, girls. You have so many fun things to play with here, and my place is a bit boring, isn't it? I must go, Al, talk to you on the phone later."

Di walked back down the path and heard Ayla say to her mum, "Granny's place isn't boring at all, Mummy."

That evening Di and Jim sat on the veranda. They listened to swing music from the late 1930s and early 1940s. Jim tapped his feet and said, "So how was your day?"

"Great, how was yours?"

"Mine was great too."

Neither made eye contact, nor was in a hurry to elaborate. That seemed to be all that needed to be said, to sum up both their days.

******

"I'm glad we agreed to have Carmen's wake here, but I also had no idea what a big turnout there'd be, there are more than sixty here today." Jim nodded at Di's comment.

Old friends, new friends, and family members were enjoying the facilities at the community centre. One of the benefits of living in a place like Keeala Resort was that drink driving was not really an issue. All the residents lived within walking distance of the clubhouse, though some of the less active used golf carts to get around. The wine and beer flowed freely, then whisky appeared and the singing commenced.

"I hope this doesn't get out of hand, like the wedding," Tony Miller's son said to Jim.

"It had better not. I can assure you I won't tolerate such behaviour again."

"I'm sure you'll find it'll be alright," said the young man, confidently. "Anyhow, Jim, I must find my father – keep a friendly eye on him." He turned and made his way to the other side of the room.

Jim noticed the seemingly endless supply of food coming from the kitchen. *Probably a very good thing, considering how much alcohol is being consumed*, Jim thought. The happy sound of someone starting to play the piano interrupted Jim's musing. The first bars of 'When Irish Eyes are Smiling', stirred the mourners into a sentimental chorus. The song ended, but the piano player immediately launched into 'The Coalminer's Reel'. The dance floor exploded with bodies, the singing and shouting fuelling the enthusiasm of the dancers. Whether the movements of some of them had anything to do with an Irish Jig was debateable, Jim thought, but he felt his body moving up and down as the rhythm of the reel shook the floorboards. *God, I wonder if my send-off will be as happy.*

The food service slowed down and the dancing took its toll on the less fit, but the drinking continued. Jim noticed the crowd had thinned out a bit but the remainder looked like they were settling in for a long night.

Jim beckoned to Di and she joined him a few seconds later. "What do you say we slip back to the house? I'll come back later," he said.

"Suits me, love. I'm exhausted just from watching."

When Jim came back to check on the mourners a few minutes before the midnight deadline, he found Tony Miller's son helping him from the community centre.

"So, you need a hand?" asked Jim.

"Ah, no, but thanks very much Jim. I've brought the buggy down." There was a pause, then he said, "Well, on second thoughts, you could give us a hand to get him on the seat. Thanks, mate."

Jim obliged, and then watched the father and son drive away. He turned around and headed to the front door of the community centre. He dreaded what he was going to face inside.

"Hi, Jim," said a resident, wielding a stick vacuum cleaner, "almost done here – sorry to hold you up."

Jim looked in amazement. The place was spotless. He could see a half dozen or so of the mourners collecting their belongings and heading for the exit.

"All spick and span, Jim," said a woman, coming toward him. "Thought we'd get it all done tonight; some of us might not be too bright in the morning." She gave a hearty laugh as she said it.

Jim waited until the last one had left, then made sure the place was locked securely before heading home.

******

Richard White arrived with a few mates at around 11am. He spotted the manager in his office and stuck his head in.

"Just as well I didn't decide to play snooker at his wife's wake, eh? Not to say I wasn't tempted, when you consider what he did to my daughter's wedding. But I've got more finesse than that, and his wife was a better woman than that bastard deserved."

"Come on now, Richard, let's not use that language and create another disturbance. That's in the past and I won't tolerate any more domestics on my watch. It's over, Richard. Tony is a man in mourning, and I've had enough of your petty dispute – so have the residents. Go and play your game and keep out of my way."

It was very rare that Jim was ever rude to anyone. It just wasn't in his nature, but somehow he knew this occasion called for straight talking.

Richard and his mates moved to the tables and started hitting balls around. They all seemed a bit restless and Jim hoped he had seen an end to the childish behaviour from both White and Miller. He also suspected it would only end when they were dead. They were all too old to change.

******

Harold and Robert walked into the Community centre together. They looked first into the Manager's office, and then spotted Jim coming out of the kitchen with a cup of coffee in his hand.

"Join me in coffee, gents?" Jim asked, as they walked toward him.

"Love to," said Robert, "I'll get it." He continued into the kitchen and Harold made himself comfortable in a lounge chair opposite Jim.

"Never a dull moment around here lately, eh? Have you heard how the detective is going?" asked Harold of Jim, as he accepted the cup of coffee Robert offered.

"Yes, he's going well. If you call a broken leg and concussion and cuts and bruises, well," Jim answered.

"What do you think happened?" asked Harold.

"I really don't know, Harold; maybe just an accident. We've had a few around here lately. You got any ideas?" Jim leaned back in his chair and looked at Harold.

"We walked that way coming over here, and both Robert and I looked at the scene. We're both pretty sure that rock wasn't there before, but anyone could have moved it, maybe kids, the gardeners, even a delivery van, perhaps a resident – anyone. But why? Do you think Pekalski was hit with it?"

"I actually think it was too big to be lifted and used as a weapon. I also think if someone had used it for that reason, they wouldn't have left it there. Don't you agree?" Jim looked at both the other men.

"You're right," said Robert, "it's probably just an accident. We'll know when he's been questioned, I guess. A comment we would like to make though is, we saw Kevin here the day of the detective's fall."

"The former gardener?" Jim was surprised.

"Yep, definitely him,"

"Well, I wonder what he was doing here. More grist for the mill. I don't suppose you spoke to him, did you?" Jim questioned.

"No, we both saw him about lunch time that day. We were driving out the front gate and Harold commented that he wondered if the former gardener was back. I looked to where he pointed and I saw him too. He walked toward the gardener's shed. Maybe it's nothing. Maybe he was visiting a friend."

"Did he have any?" Jim asked.

"Good question," said Robert.

They finished their coffee in silence. Eventually Jim stood and said, "I must get back to work. I appreciate the information gentlemen, and I'll certainly pass it on to the right people. Thank you."

Harold and Robert collected the cups and walked to the kitchen.

Jim went back to his office, picked up the phone and rang the police station to enquire about Pekalski. He spoke to George Farrell, one of the detectives who had interviewed Jim the day of the incident.

"No, sir, we did not plan to come around there again soon. What can I help you with?"

"Well, I wondered if you had discovered yet how the incident occurred. You see, it's my responsibility to ensure the safety of everyone who comes in here and if there is something that should be done I'd like to know what it is," Jim explained.

"Sure, sure. I understand, sir. As far as we're concerned, after interviewing Frank we believe it was an accident. He says he tripped and that's an end to it. You may want to check out the path and make sure the gardeners don't leave that hose lying around in future." George Farrell seemed to have concluded the conversation and Jim rang off. He sat there wondering what, if anything, they all had missed.

Later that day, Jim looked at the whole area again. He had the feeling Frank Pekalski was not a clumsy person, he was alert and perceptive. Jim wondered again how he could trip over a hose. He also observed the native bushes on either side of the path. If someone wanted to hide there, it was possible. Maybe pull the hose tight at the exact moment an unsuspecting foot stepped over it. Jim needed to talk to Pekalski himself – soon.

Chapter Nineteen

Jack strode into his headquarters and asked, "Anything new, Mikaila?"

"There are a couple of email notifications, boss." Mikaila smiled and followed her stepfather into his office.

He threw his hat on the stand and strode to the other side of his desk. He turned to his computer and casually entered his password. Jack opened his email page and saw the two messages in his inbox. "Oh, they're from Aaron," he said. "What's happening with him?" he asked, as he looked up at his personal assistant.

"Don't know, he's said nothing to me. Coffee?" Mikaila walked to the kitchenette and started to fill the jug. *Was that a trick question about Aaron? He knows I don't have access to his emails – well, that's what he believes, anyway.*

Jack regarded Mikaila as his own daughter. She had come to live in his house when he married his second wife, Lauren. Until he met Lauren, Jack had a very poor opinion of women in general, but from the instant they first met, she had been his whole life. She had come into his life when he needed a friend and just at the time when his lifelong luck seemed to have failed him. She had not cared for riches or position and his love and loyalty had been her most valued possession. Equally, Jack always acknowledged that Lauren had stood by him through all the tough times, and when Jack's luck did improve, she was there to reap the benefits, as was Mikaila, her daughter. Jack and Lauren spent fifteen wonderful years together and when Lauren finally died of cancer, Jack once again felt the light go out of his life. Jack was a broken man when she died. No woman had replaced Lauren, and his friends often felt Jack's bitterness – the result of his grief and loneliness for the last two years.

Mikaila had become his trusted right hand. He paid her an excessive salary and was never far away, night and day. She had continued to live in his house after her mother died but his overpowering possessiveness eventually became suffocating for Mikaila. She showed her independence and moved to her own high-rise unit by the Brisbane River. Jack had not wanted her to move out. He had relented grudgingly, but still had the pleasure of seeing her at work every day.

He put on his glasses and picked up the cup of coffee Mikaila handed to him. He looked at the two, thick, buttered slices of banana cake Mikaila put in front of him. He thought how he used to be a trim man, quite handsome, even if he did say so himself. Now, he was overweight and no longer took exercise as a regular part of his day. When Lauren was alive, they had shared their daily routine of swimming, a gym workout, and then a light breakfast. They had little social life that was not business focused, but had both drawn great comfort from the company of each other. Jack had a beautiful smile then, but now, no one saw much of it anymore. Jack worked, ate, slept and worked some more. He had no children of his own and he had no idea why he worked so hard. It kept his mind occupied and most nights he drank himself to sleep. He had lost interest in his appearance – it did not seem to matter anymore.

"Don't like the cake?" asked Mikaila.

"Pig's arse!" Jack grabbed both slices. They were gone in seconds.

Jack wiped the crumbs from his mouth. "Let's see what's wrong now," he said, as he opened his emails.

"Shit, bugger, bloody hell." He stamped his foot and slammed his fist down on the desk. "Sorry love, I know how you feel about that language, I didn't expect this now, sorry."

Actually, Mikaila could not care less about language. She used plenty of it herself, but not in her stepfather's presence. He assumed that since Lauren had never tolerated bad language, her daughter would automatically be the same. Nothing could be further from the truth, but in his mind, Jack had transferred many of Lauren's personal characteristics and idiosyncrasies to his stepdaughter. She had not bothered to disabuse him.

"So much planning has gone into this deal, as you know. Aaron says he's being watched. Call Rod and Marty in please, love." Jack got up and began pacing the room.

"I'm not sure they're here, boss. Let me check." Mikaila went to her desk in the outer office.

"Just call them and tell them to get here, right now," Jack shouted from his office.

An hour and a half later, Jack listened to Aaron on his secure phone.

"I don't know how they got their tipoff," Aaron said, "but they've been on my tail all this week that I know of – I suspect longer. If we move now, they'll close in – I feel it in my guts. One deal is as good as another, as far as I'm concerned. I think I should make my way home quietly and let things cool off. You may need to find another face over here if they've sprung me." Aaron sounded tense.

"Yeah, you may be right. But stay put for now. Let's see what their next move is. You're clean now, aren't you?" Jack sounded worried.

"Yeah, of course. You know me, Unc." Aaron tried to sound light-hearted. "I'll be a tourist, just like thousands of others. I'll wait to hear from you. Bye." Aaron hung up and smiled. *All going well – so far. As a matter of fact, perfect...phase two coming up.*

It turned into a long day for Jack and Mikaila. Jack worried about Aaron's information. He knew he could not afford to make a move if he had any doubts about the security of his consignment. Jack had stayed in business longer than many of his friends simply for that reason. He was meticulous in his planning, cautious to the point of obsession, and had the patience of Job, but he was also unafraid when it came to the moment to strike. This was not the time. He had good reason to trust Aaron's advice. His nephew had never been wrong before and they both had the same instincts. They had to wait.

That was Aaron's advice, and after all, he had trained Aaron himself – he trusted him.

******

Bali was a long way from Aaron and Mikaila's final destination. It was the first leg of a long and convoluted journey leading to a lifetime of riches and happiness. Getting away from Brisbane would be Mikaila's initial challenge, but the pair had planned that first step with precision and great attention to detail.

Aaron put his feet up on his bed. It was a comfortable bed in a very well appointed room in a good hotel, mostly patronised by young travellers and surfers. He had been there before and the owner knew him. The owner always gave him the cover he needed. He was happy to accept Aaron's appreciation in the form of cash payments, well in excess of the usual tariff. It was another small link in the successful web Aaron had created over the past two years, but it was soon to be no more; he and Mikaila were getting out. They had no plans to return to Australia when they completed this job – ever. This big haul of drugs would be their last, and the drugs were already on their way to New Zealand. Aaron stretched and locked his hands behind his head. He leaned back and once again went over the plans he had.

Mikaila would leave Australia, via Sydney, the next day. She had already told Jack she was having a girl's weekend on the Gold Coast, so he would not miss her before Monday. By that time, she would have arrived at Auckland airport, made the contact, and most importantly, collected the money. That would be their part of the deal complete. Mikaila would then fly to Bali where Aaron would be waiting for her. They would travel overland to Jakarta, covering their tracks all the way. Both Aaron and Mikaila had olive complexions and they decided to disguise themselves as Muslims. To make the deception more credible, Aaron had recently grown a full beard and, to the casual onlooker, both their appearances would pass muster. Finally, after a complicated series of broken flights to Toronto, Canada, they would see their journey almost at an end. At Toronto, they would collect new identities and move on again. They had not decided absolutely about their final destination. Mikaila and Aaron had planned their escape weeks before, and believed it stood the best chance of success if they stayed cool and took nothing for granted. They both knew they were sacrificing their homes and loved ones for a chance to alter what they saw as their destiny. They could not turn back now; everything was set in motion and despite any reservations they had, all was going to plan.

******

Monday dawned. Aaron and Mikaila were already on their way to Jakarta. Travelling by train, they slept sitting up and ate from their packs. They were tired, but content with the way things were running, all according to plan. A series of foreign bank accounts in false names held funds in excess of $5,000,000. The money was a fraction of the worth of the haul when it finally reached the streets, but both agreed that there was no point in being greedy. They were confident no one was following them and they had started to relax enough to enjoy the journey.

******

Jack arrived at his office on Monday morning. He noticed Mikaila was not at her desk, nor could he see her in any of the open-plan office spaces. He thought it unusual, as Mikaila had inherited his work ethic and was never late for work. He checked the kitchenette. She was not there. Jack went to his office, but he paused, his hand rested on the doorknob. His brow was furrowed and he stroked his chin slowly. He stayed like that for a minute or so, then a rare smile spread over his face. *Stupid bastard, Jack – of course, she's in the little girl's room.* He turned the handle and went in to his office, sat at his desk, and studied a computer printout of columns of numbers.

Fifteen minutes later, Jack looked up. He realised Mikaila had not appeared to say hello. He got up and went to the rest room. The door was open. There was no one in there.

"Hey, has anybody seen Mikaila?" he asked the other staff members.

"No, boss," they chorused.

"Damn."

Jack rang her home. There was no answer. A feeling of dread clouded Jack's brain. *God, what if something's happened to her and she's lying there, unable to answer the phone? I must go there.*

Twenty-five minutes later, Jack arrived at Mikaila's unit block. He took the lift to her floor and ran to her door. It was locked, as he had expected. He rapped on the door, waited a few seconds, and thumped it again. There was no response. Jack fished in his trouser pocket and pulled out a small leather pouch. He unzipped it and selected a small, thin metal pick. He inserted the tool into the keyhole and jiggled it, feeling for the tumblers. *Not the first time I've done this,* he thought, *and probably won't be the last either.* Twenty seconds later, he pushed the door open and went inside.

"Mikaila! Mikaila!" There was no response.

He quickly checked each room but his stepdaughter was not there. Her unit looked normal; clothes hung in the wardrobe, food was cold in the fridge, but there was no sign of Mikaila and no clue to her whereabouts. He left the unit and locked the door behind him. He took the lift to the basement car park and looked for Mikaila's car. It was gone. By the end of the day he was genuinely worried, and was starting to think she may have met with foul play.

He tried to contact Aaron by phone. He got a 'Service Disconnected' message. He then sent an email but the message bounced back with an 'Undeliverable' notation. Slowly, the unthinkable began to look a possibility. The possibility of a link between Mikaila's disappearance, and Aaron being incommunicado, began to churn Jack's stomach. The search began.

******

Allen Sinclaire waited impatiently for word from his boss about the arrival of the latest drug shipment. He had everything in place to go ahead with his part in the distribution. Matthew Weatherlee had come on board and his participation made things a lot easier for Allen. It freed him up to move around the state, do the drops and collect the money. Allen thought about his new partnership with Matthew and hoped the young man would play his part. They both had a lot to gain and everything to lose.

Allen's mobile phone rang.

"The shipment hasn't arrived." It was Jack. "For the time being, we're buggered. I have no idea where it is. I'm going back along the chain, trying to work out which link has broken."

"Christ, Jack, what's your gut feeling? Surely it's not a repeat of the Denpasar shemozzle?"

"I just don't know. Could be anything – container gone to the wrong destination, bungled paperwork, a strike on the docks over there, the cops – who knows? I'm calling in all the favours I'm owed, inside and outside the organisation. Someone has to know where the stuff is."

"Jeez, I really need this load to come in. I've made commitments. Shit," said Allen.

"You're not the only one with a lot to lose, mate. Get over it." The phone clicked dead.

Allen turned his phone off and returned it to its cradle on the dashboard. He sat still, shook his head slowly from side to side, and tried to imagine what his life would be like if the shipment did not turn up. He knew the next haul like this one could be months, possibly even more than a year away, and frustration ran high in the organisation when this sort of situation occurred. Jack's abrupt end to his phone call left no doubt about that.

One person was happy to hear the news, but Matthew was careful not to show it.

"So what happened?" Matthew asked Allen, when Allen rang to tell him the shipment had not arrived.

Allen did not want Matthew to know how little he knew himself, so he said, "Change of plans at the last minute. You continue as always, and I'll contact you when the next one's in the pipeline."

"Fine," said Matthew. "By the way, do you remember the cop you expressed so much interest in when we last spoke, the one investigating the murder of the old woman?"

"Yeah, what about him? Has he been hanging around again?" Allen responded guardedly.

"No. Well, he was, but not anymore. As a matter of fact, he had an accident here a couple of weeks ago, and now he's in hospital."

"You don't say," was the smug return. "Well, I'll be in touch." Allen hung up.

Matthew stood with the phone in his hand and suddenly thought, *Of course. Why didn't I put that together before now? How could I be so stupid? That cop could have died. Maybe he was supposed to.* Then Matthew remembered seeing Kevin; he had spoken to him the day of the incident. *Shit,* Matthew thought, *What the hell am I doing with these guys? They could be murderers. They're way out of my league.* He sat down slowly, phone still in his hand. He had the feeling he needed to think very seriously about his future, and sooner, rather than later.

******

That night, as Matthew lay in his bed, he thought long and hard about his situation. He could not get to sleep. So far, he had failed to do anything illegal in connection with Allen Sinclaire and his organisation. Through no fault of his own, he had not carried drugs in from Bali. Also through no fault of his own, he was not currently involved in hiding a large shipment of drugs, here on his own property and at his workplace. It might be said that he was very lucky; it might be said also, that he should seriously be doing something positive with all this information before he became caught up in the next job. He knew he did not want to go to prison and ruin his life. Matthew acknowledged his own desire to have money, lots of it, but could see how hard it was to come by legally. Still, he knew it was not too late to make the right decision. He decided he would go and see that cop in hospital. He may well be interested in Matthew's theory about his accident. The cops may be very glad to hear what he could tell them about the drug importing business. He wondered about immunity from prosecution for supplying information that led to the capturing of a big, long established drug business.

Matthew wondered if he should talk to a solicitor first. He knew just the person – Peter Burrows. Burrows had his finger in the unit refurbishment scam. Matthew reasoned that Burrows might decide it would serve his own interests best if he were to advise and represent Matthew pro bono, should Matthew decide to inform on the drug organisation. *Yes, there is still room to manoeuvre,*" thought Matthew, just before he finally drifted into a fitful sleep.

Chapter Twenty

R ena Connelly had to go back to work. She had left her last job and now looked for another. She considered applying for a position in a service similar to the one Daniel presently worked for, home care; a job where she may get to know her clients a little more intimately and perhaps make herself indispensable to someone. Maybe she could ingratiate herself so that she might live-in. She wondered about the possibilities and the advantages. There were times when she and Daniel did not get along at all. Rena was broke, and the thought of living with someone in his or her home, especially someone elderly, had potential. She saw that straight away.

******

Having interviewed Rena Connelly, Toni Johnson left her in the tiny waiting room at the front of her suburban home. Toni managed a busy nursing service and placed nurses with clients, day and night shifts, and often at a moment's notice. The nurses on her books had the qualifications, experience and communication skills she required in her agency. The high standard she demanded was often hard to maintain, but it had earned her an excellent reputation in the nursing agency industry, and she always had more work than she could handle.

"She's charming and comes with several good references," Toni said to her business partner, Roberta Davidson, as she seated herself in front of her workstation. "I think we might find she's the type of person we need. She's about fifty, a widow, and available 24 hours. Heaps of experience, both here and in her home in the Philippines"

"In the Philippines?" Roberta raised an eyebrow.

"Yes, she's a Filipino," Toni said. "She also prefers to work in aged care, and I really can't fault her." She looked again at her friend Roberta, all the time knowing what would be coming next.

"You know what I'm going to say, don't you?" said Roberta.

"Say it anyway."

"We have quite a few clients who don't like Asian nurses, that we know, and there are more who say nothing, but you can tell they're not happy. It's been evident with every satisfaction survey we've done. That's despite the fact that they perform every bit as well as the rest of our staff. And...."

"No, say no more. The fact is we have a swelling supply of staff from Asia and the Islands, and a shrinking supply of Australians willing to do the job. These girls, and some men, as we know, are accepted more than they used to be, and with this present generation of clients dying out, it will eventually not be so much of an issue. So, let's leave it at that shall we?" Toni picked up Rena's application folder and walked out to the waiting room.

Roberta shrugged. She knew it would make no difference if she objected. She turned her attention back to the accounting. At least it dealt with facts and the books did not argue with her.

Toni greeted Rena with a broad smile. She congratulated Rena on becoming part of the team.

******

Rena walked out to her car and felt very pleased. She knew she was good at her job and she liked the recognition she got from her patients, or 'clients', as these new people would be referred to. But, most of all, she loved the thought of being able to get any job she applied for. She knew she must have made a good impression and she thought this would be a better job for her. Happy, she drove home and gave Daniel the news.

"Good," said Daniel, "and don't forget to be on the lookout for a rich widower."

"Yes, yes. I'll remember," responded Rena, as she took out her new uniform to iron. "How could I forget?"

******

"Keeala Resort." Di answered the phone in the manager's office. She smiled as she listened.

"Yes Frank, I did. I called at the hospital to see you, but you were asleep."

At the other end of the line, Frank Pekalski explained to Di that he was now doing a little physio each day and would soon be home to recuperate.

"That's great, I'm so pleased. Do you know when you'll be back at work?"

"Do you have another murder for me to solve, dear lady?" Frank sounded almost happy.

"Of course not. We'd be happy if you just solved the last one." Di laughed, as she entered into the light banter that she and the detective usually fell into. "Actually, I don't think there have been any more enquiries by your guys since you left. I do believe they've dropped the case. Cold case so to speak, if that's really the term you use."

"Not exactly a cold case, but not a number one priority, either; just not enough cops to go round. I do have a few theories emerging from my underactive brain though, and I look forward to testing them." Frank enjoyed the conversation with someone who could relate to his situation.

"What sort of theories?" Di was curious now.

"I certainly can't discuss them at this moment, but perhaps if you were to drop by with some of those delicious pastries of yours, I may be persuaded."

"Of course, I understand, I'll see you tomorrow afternoon. Bye, Frank."

"Bye, Diane." They both hung up.

Di left the community centre office and walked along the path toward the sales office house.

"I'm sorry," she said, as she almost collided with Harold and Robert, "I was in a world of my own and didn't even notice you coming."

"Well, I really would have thought we were a little more outstanding than that, Mrs Manager." Harold nodded and smiled.

"Good morning." Robert gave a small bow.

"We were just walking along chatting about our murder suspect theories, actually," said Harold.

"Really, how strange. I was just talking to the famous Detective Pekalski about just that. It seems he has had an opportunity to create a few theories of his own. You may have to have a meeting."

"Yes, I agree," said Harold. "When?"

"Well, he's still a little way off resuming official duties, but I'll see him soon and I'll tell him you may have something to discuss with him. How about that?"

"Great. We'll develop our ideas a little in the meantime. We have actually thought about writing a book, you know."

"You never! Well that would be terrific. I think I'll wait now and see how it ends." Di reached out to touch Harold's arm.

"Well," said Harold, "we may not be quite there yet, still fleshing out the storyline, but we are getting there. By the way, would you please ask Jim to give us the pleasure of his company at our next musical soiree, and you, of course. We'd love to have both of you. A week from Saturday next?" Harold was transferring his weight from one foot to the other.

"We must be going, I'm sure I'll develop a clot just standing around like this. Surely we all will."

Di said goodbye, and laughed as she walked away. *These fellers could be relied upon to brighten up any day. And Pekalski too of course,* Di reflected.

She knocked on the sales office door.

Matthew Weatherlee was saying goodbye to someone on the phone.

"How's business?" she asked, when he finished.

"A few enquiries this week, but no sales unfortunately. It's that time of the year. How can I help you?"

"I wonder if you've seen anything of our old gardener. Do you remember Kevin?" Di pinned Matthew with her directness.

"Yes, I do remember him and no, I haven't seen him. Why do you ask?"

"I owe him some back pay but don't have his recent address. So I'm just asking around to see if anyone knows." Di managed to make it sound mundane.

"Sorry, I can't help you." Matthew had a way to dismiss a person that was very effective.

"Fine, I'll ask around." Di turned to leave.

"If you find out will you let me know? I may have some gardening jobs for him." Matthew walked her to the door.

"Not around here I hope, he isn't welcome." Di looked directly at the salesman.

"Oh, I see, I didn't know. Why's that?"

"He left with a bad attitude and I have a feeling he was not always strictly honest. I can't prove that of course, just a feeling; I'd rather not deal with him."

"Sure," said Matthew, as he watched Di walk away.

Once again, he mulled over how much other people knew about Kevin or Allen; or himself for that matter. He was very aware of how gossip travelled around a place like Keeala Resort, and he knew no one could have secrets for very long.

He had an appointment to see Peter Burrows the next day. He would put Burrows on notice that he would be prepared to spill the beans on the scams that had gone on at the resort unless Burrows helped him to steer a course through the mess Matthew was in with the Noonans and Allen Sinclaire. Matthew planned to make it clear that he would not mention Peter's name if the solicitor gave him legal assistance – for free. This would be his opportunity to free himself from the illegal organisation and the spectre of jail.

******

"Come in, please." Peter Burrows opened the door and ushered Matthew Weatherlee into his office. He closed the door behind him and they both sat. "I hope this has nothing to do with that resort business. As you know, I won't discuss that here."

"Look, we need to talk. It has to be today," said Matthew.

"Why?"

"Urgent, and it's in your interest as much as mine." Matthew spoke quietly.

The solicitor heaved a sigh and whistled through his teeth. "Go ahead, but make it quick. I have a busy day."

"Thanks to the people you and I have dealt with – on the shady side, I mean – I've been put into an impossible situation." Matthew leaned toward Peter. "Our mutual friend, Allen Sinclaire, has pressured me into working for his drug syndicate."

"What? What drug syndicate? I know nothing about that, and I don't want to know, thank you very much." Peter leaned back from the desk, as if trying to distance himself from what he was hearing.

"You're going to have to listen to me. They're expecting a huge shipment of drugs, and he's forcing me to help him store and distribute the stuff. If I refuse, he'll blow the whistle on the little scams you and I have been involved in."

"That's blackmail."

"Yes, it is."

"Who else is involved beside Allen?" Peter was very interested now.

"That's information I'll keep to myself for the time being. The thing is, I've been used, and I mean used, on more than one occasion when I've imported furniture for the display units. Sinclaire found out where I was sourcing it from, and surprise, surprise, it starts coming in with drugs concealed in it."

"Of course I didn't know anything about that. You can't be serious." Peter stood and walked around the desk. He picked up a glass of water and downed the lot. "So what are you telling me now?"

"In a nutshell, I'm going to need legal advice after I go to the cops and spill the beans on Sinclaire." Matthew was trying to remain patient, though he felt anything but.

"Why would you do that?" Peter's eyes widened.

"If I don't, he'll force me to be directly involved in his next major criminal activity, namely drug dealing, very big time." Matthew was becoming very frustrated.

"Well, why should that involve me?" asked Peter. "You obviously got yourself into this mess, so why should I help you and maybe get myself dragged into it too?" Peter's voice rose.

"For an educated man you're very stupid!" Matthew stood up. "I was in the wrong place at the right time. Can't you see that it could have just as easily been you he called on to help him out in his business?"

"He doesn't know me, not really. We've only talked on the phone briefly, a few times." Peter's eyes were wide. "As far as the refurbishment scheme goes, it's nearly always been you who's been the contact."

"Well, you'd better hope he does forget you. Aside from me, he's the only one who knows what part you played in the refurbishment scheme. It's not crime on a grand scale, I'll grant you, but it's not legal either. We just thought we were getting some nice pocket money, but it's still fraud, whichever way you look at it. You're involved in a deal that we both know is not legal. I mean in relation to sales contracts, false refurbishment costs, etcetera. Am I right?"

"No! You're not." Peter rocked in his chair, head down trying to think about how he may have left himself exposed to all this. He looked up at the salesman. "So now you're blackmailing me. Is that it?"

"Not exactly, but I need help. You're the best free lawyer I know and, if you help me, I'll have no reason to bring up your name at any time when I talk to the cops."

"What about Sinclaire? He knows I'm involved."

"He's going to have so much other stuff on his mind; you'll be the last person he'll be thinking about. What we've been doing is chicken feed compared to what he's up to. Remember, if Allen goes down, it will be for major crime. He's involved in drugs on a huge international scale. His connections here in Australia are big, powerful people; includes politicians and some big end of town businessmen. They stand to gain nothing from you. I'm the one who knows about the filthy business these guys are in. I'm the one who'll be their target."

"So why do it? Clear out. Now."

Matthew shook his head. "Not that easy, mate. I recently saw how a friend of mind tried to escape the mongrels. And he didn't even cross them. They don't care who they hurt; protecting themselves, that's all they care about – and revenge."

There was silence; the air was electrified. Peter got up and started to pace around again. "So you want me to be your criminal lawyer in a big court case?"

"No, I hope it won't come to that. What I hope is that I can direct the police toward an investigation. Maybe they can set up a big sting involving undercover and customs officers, or whatever the hell they do, and they can catch the buggers themselves. Then they'll have all the witnesses they can handle. In exchange for the tipoff, the cops keep me completely out of everything."

Peter nodded and said. "That may be one way to go. Actually, it may be the only way to go. Have you thought how you're going to do this? You don't want to give too much away up front you know – keep in control."

"Sure, but that's why I'm looking at you now for some advice. I could easily make a mistake here and leave myself exposed. I need to know exactly what my legal rights are if I go to the police. I also have to keep Sinclaire sweet until he's out of the way. I can see that our little scam is of no significance in the grand scheme of things, but I have to act fast or Sinclaire will be on to me and he could do me, and maybe you, a lot of damage before they catch him."

Silence reigned again.

Finally, Matthew stood up. "I want to go and see a cop I know, later this afternoon. He's in hospital, had an accident at the Resort. Also, I think the accident in question may have been connected to our friend, Allen. I think this bloke may give me a hearing when I tell him I think it was no accident, and that his presence in the Resort was a bit uncomfortable with all the drug activity coming up. It will certainly be in his interest to keep me as his eyes and ears. He could blow the lid off one of the biggest drug syndicates in this country. Even I only know about the bottom rungs of the ladder."

Both men stood and looked at one another. Finally, the solicitor nodded his head. "I'll think on this for an hour or so, make some calls, and ring you about 1pm." Peter's voice had firmed up again.

"So, you'll help me?" Matthew leaned in toward the other man.

"Do I have a choice?" Peter touched Matthew's shoulder in some sort of comforting gesture. They both exchanged small, resigned looking smiles. Matthew was already making plans in his head as he walked out of the office building. He reached his car around the corner. He patted the roof. "Can't lose you, girl." He pulled his Saab into the traffic.

When Matthew drove back through the Resort gate, he noticed the manager wave to him. He parked his car as Jim walked in his direction.

"How's it going, Matt?" asked Jim, as he strolled up. "You having a busy day?"

"No, not especially. Just had to pop out and see someone. Anything I can do for you?" Matthew knew that he had never really had the trust of the manager – they simply did not rub well together.

"I wanted to let you know that we have a unit going up for sale soon. It's No. 28, belongs to Tony Miller. He's moving out and will leave the unit for you to organise the sale. Maybe refurbish or whatever you think it needs." Jim looked the salesman directly in the eyes.

Matthew almost cringed at the word refurbish. "Yes, that'll be fine. I'll go along and see Tony as soon as I get a moment. I know his wife died recently. Must be still grieving; needs to make a new start, I guess."

"Yes, well, whatever, I'll leave that to you. I'll keep in touch with Tony until he leaves anyway. I think he plans to go and live with his son, hope that works out. I have the impression he's not an easy person to get along with. I'm sure Richard White will be happy anyway, and I won't be sorry to have an end to the ridiculous squabbling," Jim chatted on.

"So, it may be the best thing all round, you think?" suggested Matthew.

"Except for his son, maybe. Well, I'm off to do some bowling, making up the numbers, bit of exercise." Jim walked off looking a little happier than usual. His step had a spring in it and Matthew thought he heard Jim humming to himself.

Matthew stood on the patio at the front of his office and looked around. He so rarely did this; usually his head was down, so full of ideas and plans. He took a moment to take in the gardens. Poinciana trees, spreading their branches and orange flowers over soft green lawns were divided by curving paths with flower borders. Ferns and rain forest leaves bent gracefully to the ground. For a moment, Matthew wondered what it would be like to be retired, free to enjoy all of nature, go wherever he wanted to, relax, and play games with mates, like at school. Life would be one long holiday. Then his mind went out to his mother. When would she be able to retire? She was almost sixty-five now and she had worked hard enough; had no partner in life. He would like to have enough money to see her well set up and able to relax and take things easier as she grew older. Matthew knew money would not buy happiness, but it could make a big difference to his mother's comfort and peace of mind.

Chapter Twenty-One

"Can I come in?" Di knocked and put her head around the hospital room door.

Frank waved her in. "Good to see you again, Di. Please come in and take a seat."

Di walked over to the bed table next to Frank and placed a plate of sweet pastries, covered with plastic film, on the only space she could see. The detective had obviously been doing some reading. There were books, papers and a laptop computer. All of these vying for a place within the man's reach.

"Thank you very much. Would you like to share a cup of coffee and one of your delicious looking sweeties here?"

"No thank you, sir, but by all means, you go ahead." Di pushed the bed table in his direction.

Frank lifted the cover and picked up a fruit-filled pastry. He popped the whole thing into his mouth. His eyes widened when he realised he may have bitten off more than he could chew. His mouth was stuffed and he made small apologetic sounds while he worked his jaw and slowly swallowed the sweet. He almost choked in the process. Finally, red faced, he apologised and coughed and punched his chest gently to clear his airway.

"I had no idea my cooking was that good. For a moment there, I thought I should ring for assistance. I even wondered whether I could be charged with murder if you choked on something I gave you." Di had a great smile on her face as she revelled in the man's discomfort.

"Hmm, that's never happened to me before. Perhaps I've never been so greedy before. Please excuse me. I don't know how I could've so misjudged the size of the thing."

"Well, maybe it was not the size, but the texture that misled you," said Di.

"The texture?" asked Frank. "How do you mean?"

"It may appear to be soft and light, but in reality something else altogether. In your case, both substantial and chewy, so to speak," Di offered.

Frank did not answer for a moment then, he said, "Could this also have been the case with my accident at your resort?"

Di was with him immediately. "Yes, I do believe it could. Both Jim and I hold the theory that you may have been misled into thinking the path that was the scene of your terrible misfortune may have looked safe but was, in fact, sabotaged."

"I wonder, perhaps I should give that theory some thought. The more I think about it, the more I feel I remember something at my ankles, tripping me up and throwing me to the ground. When my mate from work interviewed me a few days after the accident I had doubts, but not enough to voice; now, I wonder if you're right." Frank leaned back against the pillows with a smile of satisfaction.

Suddenly he looked at Di and said, "But why?"

"Well, now we come to the theory that both Jim and I, and Harold and Robert, hold. So far, they've made some pretty astute and even profound observations about what's gone on at the resort, both before we arrived and since. It seems the last managers left under some sort of questionable circumstances. Harold has identified the salesman, Matthew Weatherlee, and our area manager, Allen Sinclaire, as being involved in some sort of activity that they would prefer to keep hidden. There have been times when the area manager has had no reason to be in the resort, and his dealings, when he is there, should mostly be with us. But that's not the case. He comes and goes at strange times and spends much more time at our resort, talking to Matthew, than is reasonable. I have no idea how he gets around to the other resorts he's responsible for."

Di took a deep breath, but before she could say more, Frank said, "Remind me please who Harold and Robert are."

"Oh yes, of course. They are two residents living in unit No. 39. They've been very forthcoming with insight into the other residents and some of the behaviours that would have otherwise left us very confused. Mostly, they've just hinted at things we should look out for. They've told us about things that have happened in the resort that now make sense of our own discoveries. So, what we have is, two gentlemen who make 'people watching' their hobby; they're very observant, and the other day they told me they'd like to meet with you to discuss their ideas. They've even suggested writing a book." Di took a breath.

"Will I have a role to play, do you think?" asked Frank.

"Major," nodded Di.

They both sat back to mull over the possibilities.

"Well anyway, I believe when you meet up with the gentlemen, you may find they've come to the same conclusion as Jim and I have."

"Which is?" Frank bent toward the manager.

"That someone wanted you out of the way – that your accident may have been connected to Jessie Thornton's murder investigation. Maybe you're getting too close to the answers you've been looking for. There's something else going on too; maybe something that involved the previous managers, but definitely involving Allen Sinclaire and the salesman – something fishy seems to be going on, and has been for some time. I think we've walked into the middle of some activity that these guys are trying to keep covered up, and your presence in the resort is liable to uncover." She took another deep breath.

Frank just stared. The clock flicked over the second marks. The sounds in the corridor closed in. They sat in as much silence as a hospital room would afford them.

Eventually Frank spoke, "Well, this is really interesting. I think I will be looking forward to a meeting with Harold and his friend. What else can you tell me?"

Di could sense how eager Frank was to hear more now, so she went over everything she could think of that may paint a picture of the happenings and adventures she and Jim had had since their arrival at Keeala Resort.

Frank knew some of the events and people would be unrelated to his interests, but others would. It would be up to him now to sift through all the information, and come up with some conclusions. He was pleased to have the luxury of all this time to spend thinking about one case only, but without legs to walk around on and pursue any research, or interview anyone, he was also very frustrated.

"I do believe I may be upsetting your recovery with all of my fanciful ideas and you must be feeling like a rest now," said Di.

"On the contrary, I haven't felt this alive since I arrived here. I need to pursue the idea now that I may have just been in the wrong place at the wrong time, that is to say, that I may have stumbled close to some activity that certain individuals found uncomfortable. I'm going to do some background checking on the people you mentioned. At least there are a few things I can instigate with a phone and a computer, not to mention my contacts at work."

"By the way, you may want to factor in the ex-gardener, Kevin," Di said, as she stood and pushed her chair aside.

"Yes, I know who you mean, and I agree. You've given me a great deal to think about and go on with. Thank you. Do have a safe trip home, Diane."

He reached out and shook Di's hand. She rewarded him with her happiest smile and tripped off down the corridor, loathe to let go of the smirk her smile had just become. She headed thoughtfully for the elevator.

Frank closed his eyes when he had the room to himself. Once again, he methodically went through all the pieces of information Di had given him. He picked up the phone and made contact with George Farrell at the police station. Initially, George was reluctant to acknowledge that Frank was in any fit state to be worrying about work while he was still recuperating, but Frank kept talking, and was nothing, if not convincing.

"Okay. I accept your premise and I agree there is plenty we could take a look at, but nothing seems so urgent it can't wait until you come back to work." George seemed adamant.

"I do think we could do a little check on the people I've mentioned in the meantime, though. When you think of me sitting here thinking up work for later on, I might just as well do what I can from here now," Frank bargained.

"Okay, why not? I'll hand you over to Ella. She can be your link with us and then you won't have to interrupt me. How does that sound?" George was already thinking about another job he had that afternoon.

"Great, wonderful. Is she available now?" he said hopefully.

"Hello, Pekalski," were the next words he heard. "It's Ella here, what can I do for you? I can't believe you're still in hospital, malingering, while the rest of us are slaving our guts out filling in for you."

"It's lovely to hear your voice, Ella. Got a bit of free time to do some leg work for me?"

"Certainly, sir. Where do you want to start?"

"Write these names down." Frank gave Ella a list of names and addresses, places of work and other relevant material to keep her busy for hours. "Talk to you soon, and thanks." He rang off and put his head back on the pillow. He wondered what to do next. Usually he moved through an investigation with systematic steps that led him to where he hoped to end up. This time, he moved with unsure feet through a process that could lead him anywhere. He finally dropped off to sleep and fell into dreams that were a maze of alleys and streets that led nowhere, peopled with faces, most of whom he could not recognise. He missed lunch and did not wake until a footfall at his bedside heralded the approach of the nurse attempting to do his observations.

"Good afternoon, Mr. Pekalski," said the nurse. Her name badge said, Kerryn Jones R.N. "You missed lunch, sir, and I see you have a visitor outside. I think he's been waiting for you to wake up."

"That so?" Frank looked behind Kerryn Jones RN, to the door. "Well, perhaps when you've finished you could show him in. We can't keep our fans waiting now, can we?"

The nurse handed Frank his medication and watched as he tossed the tablets into his mouth and washed them down with a full glass of water. Satisfied, she walked to the door, looked up the corridor, and said, "He's awake now. You can go in."

Matthew Weatherlee seemed to fill the door opening. He was not a big man, but being someone Frank had talked about, and then dreamt about within the last hour, he appeared quite larger than life.

Matthew took a few hesitant steps into the policeman's room. "You probably don't remember me, Detective, but...."

Before he could say more, Frank answered, "Yes, I know who you are, Matthew. Come in. This is certainly unexpected."

A sudden adrenalin surge shocked Frank into an awareness of how vulnerable he was. *Could this be the man who so recently tried to kill me?* With a seemingly casual movement, Frank placed his hand on the nurse call buzzer and reminded himself that three quick buzzes was an emergency signal. He closed his fingers around the buzzer.

"Take a seat."

"Thank you."

Matthew moved to the chair that Di had recently vacated. He looked around the room and then back at the cop. He had no idea where to begin.

"I'm here to talk to you about the accident you had at the retirement resort. I may be able to shed some light on what happened."

Frank nodded, "Go on, I'm all ears." He sensed his fear might be unfounded. He relaxed slightly and eased his grip on the buzzer. "Anything you tell me, Matthew, I'll take seriously." He reached for his notebook and pen.

"No, please don't write anything down until I've had my say. I have a proposition to put to you. In a way, all of this is off the record; unofficial, you might say. No, it's definitely unofficial. Do you agree that we aren't having this conversation?"

"Okay, I'll hear you out and what's said in this room will go no further. I'll also agree that I won't act on anything you say unless you give me the OK. What do you want to tell me?"

Pekalski could hear the nervousness in the young man's voice as he said, "Before I go any further, I only want to deal with you. I want you to be my contact, and my co-operation is conditional on you agreeing to my terms. I have some information about your so-called accident and I know that'll be important to you on a personal level, but the matter of your injuries is chicken feed compared to what I can tell you about the major criminal activity behind the attack." Matthew grew more confident. "I'm not exaggerating about the scale of this – this will be a huge boost to your career if you agree to my terms, but there's one thing I must have your word on this before I say anymore. If I'm going to tell you what I know, even though I may implicate myself in a minor way, I want protection from prosecution."

Peter Burrows had emphasised to Matthew not to let his advantage go, and to stand firm about his need to remain anonymous.

"Look, son, despite what you see on television or the movies, I can't promise that. Before you decide whether to continue, let me tell you where I stand. What I can promise is that I'll put your proposition to my superiors. I'll keep your name out of it if I can, but I'll give them an outline of the facts as you tell them to me. What they decide will be their call but I can guarantee you that, if for justice to be seen to be done, you are charged with an offence, I'll do everything in my power to get you a fair hearing with the best possible outcome the system will allow. I won't bull-shit you, Matthew, you may not avoid a prison sentence entirely but that's going to depend on the type and extent of your involvement. Look, let's be honest here, and you need to read between the lines, if you get my drift. Theoretically, you could be in for a long prison sentence if you are part of a serious criminal activity. But, if what you say is true, that is, you've only played a minor role in whatever activity you're going to tell me about, and if what you're proposing to tell me is as big a deal as you're intimating, then we'll obviously be interested in landing the big fish – the top of the food chain. That being so, then there are ways and means of minimising any penalties that may be unavoidable on your part. Sometimes, Matthew, someone's cooperation is appreciated so much that it hardly seems worth our while to do the paperwork for a small offence. Do you understand where I'm coming from?"

"Yeah, as you say, I get your drift."

"You realise that I too will deny this conversation? Do you still want to go ahead?"

"Let's do it. I trust you."

They shook hands.

"Just before you go any further, son, tell me why you're here today. Has something happened, or do you think something is going to happen, that's encouraged you to bring this information to me? Have you been threatened?" Frank adjusted his position in bed.

Matthew bit his lip, "Yes."

The floodgates opened and Matthew poured out everything that related to his situation with Allen Sinclaire.

Matthew told Pekalski how he had commenced work for the Keeala Resort and how he had met Allen. He then gave a brief history of his employment, all very sanitised, but basically correct. Next, he explained his involvement with the unsuccessful attempt to bring drugs in from Bali. He had to go over much of information a couple of times, so that Frank could get a clear picture of all the players. He spoke for several minutes, seemingly not pausing for breath. When he had finished, he sank back in his chair, visibly drained, tears in his eyes.

Frank offered him a drink of water and Matthew accepted. There was a long silence as they looked at one another.

Frank broke the lull in the proceedings with, "So, Matthew, I can understand now why you've come to see me. I can see you have concern for your safety, legitimately so in my opinion. I think you're quite right to be uneasy. Would you be prepared to stay at Keeala Resort long enough for us to nail this bunch?"

"I guess so, but if I feel they suspect something's going on, I'm out of there!"

"Fair enough, but I have to be honest with you. I have a lot of this information already. You're simply filling in the gaps." Pekalski knew that was untrue, but he wanted to make the salesman feel that maybe he had nothing to sell.

Matthew could see the game that was unfolding. *Two can play at this,* he thought. He hesitated before playing his trump card – the information he had so far held back.

"Would you be interested in knowing when the next shipment is coming in? Wouldn't it be worthwhile for me to be your link with the organisation?" Matthew suggested quietly.

"Possibly," Pekalski nodded, "and what would your price be?"

"Nothing, apart from staying out of jail – and of course, your protection."

"I can't add to what I've just told you, but I can assure you that I am a man of my word."

"OK, fine, I guess I can't ask for more than that." Matthew became very nervous. He stood and paced around the small room. "So, where do we go from here?"

"I have some idea what it's cost you to come here and speak to me like this, but if I were in your position, Matthew, I hope I would have made the same decision. However, you can leave this to me now, and I'll let you know what my boss has to say. I'll be in touch with him this afternoon. Any deal will depend on a decision from the hierarchy; you do understand that, don't you?"

"Yeah, I can understand why, I guess."

"And while I'll do as much as I can, Matthew, I am going to be handicapped for a while yet so I do believe you will have to talk to someone else beside me. Now's the time to say no, if you're not happy with that." Frank waited.

"No, it's okay. I can see it'll be a while before you're literally back on your feet, and frankly, I reckon the quicker this is over, the happier I'll be, so yeah, let's do it."

"Great. Give me your contact details. I'll ring you tonight and let you know what our next move will be."

Matthew pulled a notebook from his pocket and wrote the information. As he handed it to Frank, he said, "Is there anything else you need to know?"

"Nah, that's about as much as I can chew for now, believe me. I'll be in touch. Oh, there is one thing though – don't communicate with me by email, don't keep hard copies of any sensitive stuff around, even at home, and get yourself a new mobile phone. You can give me the number tonight. Here's my card. Call me any time. I mean it."

"Thanks."

As Matthew walked toward the door, Frank said, "You are doing the right thing now, boy, you can be sure of that."

Matthew drove home and went over in his mind, once again, everything he had told Pekalski. He began to feel a slight sense of relief. Some of the fear he had been carrying around in his chest had eased. When he parked his car and walked into his home, he had a smile for Myra. "Hi Mum, how's your day been?"

"Nice to see you with a smile on your face for a change, son," said his mother.

Chapter Twenty-Two

Your address please, Mr. Milou?" Roberta sat in front of her computer and typed in the information given to her by Daniel Milou. He had decided to apply to the same employment agency as Rena, so that between them they may find the right target for her.

Roberta pursed her lips and sucked her tongue; she wondered what Toni could possibly be thinking of, employing so many Asian nurses. The different values, religions, and attitudes were, in the true sense of the word, foreign to most of the agency's clients. Roberta had always expressed her reservations about them to Toni. She had even gone so far as to say   some might even be terrorists, for all she knew. She did not know whether to be offended or not when Toni had simply laughed at that comment.

"So here's your I.D." Roberta pushed a name badge across the desk to him. She could not help thinking that this one was a bit too good-looking for his own good.

Daniel picked it up the badge and examined it to see if his name was spelt correctly. For a change, it was. "Thank you. So I will start tomorrow?" he asked.

"Yes, here's the address. Be punctual. There'll be a nurse waiting to be relieved and it's considered courteous to be a few minutes early to facilitate the handover. Remember to fill in your time record." Roberta was brisk.

"Certainly, thank you." Daniel turned to leave then looked back at Roberta, "You have beautiful hair, Miss Roberta," he smiled.

The woman put her hand to her head, and with wide eyes, whispered, "Really? Thank you."

That evening, Rena and Daniel talked about their new employer. They discussed where they had to go the next day. Rena said she had a woman to attend at the resort where Stan's sister had died. She made no other comment about Jessie's death.

******

"You seem to have beaten us to the post then, Di," said Robert, as the manager sat at a small table.

Robert and Harold sat drinking coffee on a little deck that overlooked the front gate and surrounding gardens.

"I wish we could have been a couple of flies on the wall when you expounded your theories to the detective."

"Yes, well, I was a bit reluctant to suggest such wildly fanciful ideas, but he took it all in. Didn't once laugh at me, and said he would look forward to talking to you guys."

"Really, do you mean you credited us with contributing to your story?" Robert sat up.

"Naturally. Most of it I would never have guessed if you hadn't painted such a believable picture. You are my major source and will be getting the credit accordingly."

"Really?" the men said together.

"I can't wait until the book comes out," smiled Di.

"Us either," said Robert. The pair exchanged a knowing smile. "If you'll excuse us then, Madame, we have a hot date with the computer about now. Collaboration is our forte."

＊＊＊＊＊＊

That same day, Rena went to see her new client in the resort. The house was in the group of three-bedroom units not far from Jessie's; Unit 30, the home of George and Letitia Kawalski. A Polish couple, they were both in their eighties and very happy to see Rena arrive to assist Letitia. George had struggled to do the necessities for his wife who was now wheelchair bound. He was happy to turn this chore over to a young woman. It would allow him to read his newspaper in peace for a few hours.

Rena chatted away to Letitia while she attended to her ablutions. Letitia was soon in a discussion about their emigration to Australia. Letitia told how she and George had emigrated in 1950. They had brought up their two daughters and were now in a comfortable retirement; that is, until crippling arthritis had taken hold in all of her joints and made it almost impossible for her to get out anymore. It was hard for George as well, she said, because he remained active, but her illness increasingly restricted his lifestyle, and at least now, he would get half a day, every second day, to himself.

＊＊＊＊＊＊

When Matthew arrived at his office the next day, he immediately picked up the phone and rang Peter Burrows. He explained everything that had transpired when he visited the detective. He said Pekalski had promised to ring him back last night but so far had not. Peter assured him that a lengthy process would commence once the police were in possession of that sort of information. Matthew was content with the solicitor's explanation and was able to get on with his usual work, reassured.

He turned to his email. "Salutations, Old Buddy", the email from Davo began.

Darralyn and Davo were getting married. He was going to change his name. He was already working for her father in the earth moving business and he loved it.

"Well, how about that!" Matthew sat back in his chair and wondered about the luck of some people. A broad grin split his face.

"Congratulations, my friend," he said to the computer screen. He really was pleased for his old school friend; perhaps there were such things as happy endings.

******

Jim called to Di to join him for breakfast. "I've made the tea," he shouted.

When they sat down together, they picked up their conversation from the previous night, discussing Di's visit to Frank Pekalski.

"So you really think he believed you when you said we think there's some sort of criminal activity being conducted by the area manager and so on?"

Di nodded, and continued to chew the mouthful of toast that stopped her speaking.

"Well, we can't do more than tell him what we know for a fact, and what we think is an educated guess," she said, as she patted some crumbs from her lips. "It's in his hands now."

"Guess who's getting married?" Jim asked suddenly.

Di shrugged, "Tell me".

"Margaret Robilliard and Ethan Dougherty. You know the pair living in the bed sitters, 96 and 110."

"Sure do. I guess they'll have to sell up now and move to a one or two-bedder," Di said. "Shame about that nice new awning we just had installed. Still, it adds value and they'll need whatever they can get for the sale."

"Guess so," answered her husband.

"By the way," said Di, "I've considered taking Ben down to Unit 27 for a little holiday. The new resident there has been very kind to him every time he turns up on his old doorstep. He's like a homing pigeon and he just sits in the sun on her front patio. I spoke to her yesterday and we both agreed to see if he would like to live there with her. I think it's the best possible outcome. What do you think?"

"I agree," said Jim. "It isn't always easy to find someone to look after a dog when you want to go away. As long as Ben's happy, I'm happy."

They turned their attention to resort business, but the ringing of the telephone interrupted the conversation.

"Good morning, Mrs Watersen." It was the voice of Frank Pekalski. "I may have some very interesting news for you soon, but I wanted to thank you for sticking your neck out and coming to me with your suspicions yesterday."

"You're welcome, but don't keep me in suspenders – what's the news?" She hit the speakerphone button on the cordless phone to let Jim in on the conversation.

"Unfortunately, I can't tell you right now, but rest assured, as soon as I can, I will. In the meantime, keep your eyes and ears open. I'm doing some background checks on the people you mentioned and they've proven to be of great interest. All this is between your husband, yourself, and me. Please say nothing of what you told me to anyone else. Also, if you give me the number of your friends who are writing the novel, I'd like to remind them also to keep silent for the time being." Pekalski spoke quickly, almost as if his batteries had recharged overnight.

"Well, I'm sure they'd love to have a call from you, Detective. You're like a celebrity around here, you know."

"Really, well I'll try to live up to everyone's expectations. They may be able to help as well. That phone number?" ... "Thanks, bye now."

Di looked up at Jim and felt the tension, or was it excitement between them, as they both considered the possibilities.

"Come on, Ben," called Di as she waved the lead. She walked off with him to the new resident in Unit 27.

******

Jim unlocked the doors to the community centre and strode through to his office. As he sat down, he heard the front door open and looked up to see Martin Judd.

"Good morning, Mr. Watersen, remember me?" Martin Judd put out his hand.

Jim nodded, "Call me Jim, please. Take a seat." Jim pointed to the seat opposite his desk.

"I was wondering how the police investigation was going in the matter of Jessie Thornton. Do you remember we had a conversation about this subject one night on the path, when I was jogging and you were returning from a visit to Mrs. Dern?" Martin looked steadily at Jim.

"Yes, I remember," Jim smiled. "How's the late night workout going?"

"Good, always good, thanks. I dread the day I'll no longer be able to keep fit."

"Well, it's my experience that some of us do fall down before we wind down, and some of us just die in our sleep and don't actually deteriorate." Jim said knowledgably.

"Like Jessie, do you mean?" asked Martin.

"No, not like Jessie. I think we will eventually get to the bottom of what happened to her. It's still under investigation by the way. It hasn't been shelved yet."

"Oh, good, good. That's what I wanted to talk to you about really"

"Sure," said Jim. "As a matter of fact, my wife was talking to the police investigator yesterday. He will be out of hospital soon and back on the job."

"I'm not sure whether to talk to you about this or wait to see the detective. How long before he's out of hospital, do you think?"

"I'm really not sure but if you think it's important you could ring his station or perhaps talk to him on the phone at the hospital." Jim suggested.

Martin nodded and thought for a moment. "Perhaps if I run it past you we could decide between us?"

"Shoot," said Jim, not one to mince words; nor was he one of the world's most patient men.

"Yes, yes, of course." Again, Martin hesitated, while he formed the words in his head. "I saw a lady the other day and I believe she may have been the person I saw leaving Jessie Thornton's unit the night she died." Martin was visibly thinking of his next words.

"You saw what?" Jim stood and leaned on his desk.

"As I just said, I saw a lady ... "

"Yes, I heard that part. How come you never mentioned this before when the questions were being asked?" Jim was incredulous.

"I considered it. That I did, but I wasn't sure – until I saw the same person again the other day. I always felt it would be the worst thing to be accused of something you weren't guilty of. The responsibility was quite overwhelming. I decided they would soon enough figure it all out without any help from me. But they haven't and when I saw the woman the other day I began to wonder if she was the killer and what if she were to kill someone else? And what if I could have prevented it?" Martin's face was flushed and beads of sweat emerged on his top lip.

Jim thought to himself that this man was physically fit but emotionally extremely fragile. He stood and poured a glass of water from the jug.

"Thank you. I'm afraid I've stewed about this for far too long. I should have said something long ago, I realise that now."

"Don't worry," said Jim. "You've spoken up now and that's all that matters."

"Yes," said Martin, "What next?"

"Is it someone who lives here?" asked Jim.

"No. A visitor. I think I may know who she is, but not her name."

Jim picked up the phone and looked at Martin. "Is it okay if I speak to the detective about this now?"

The other man nodded and Jim dialled a number. It was Di's mobile and she answered straight away. "Can you come back to the office now please, love, it's important."

"I'm walking back now,"

"Wow," was the best she could come up with, when they told her the same story. "Let's get a hold of the detective now. I think this would be quite important to him," she said.

"Do you really think so?" asked Martin. "I don't know whether I'm glad or not that I spoke up. I'm going to look pretty stupid if I had this important info all the time, aren't I?"

"Stop worrying." Jim came around and put his hand on the other man's shoulder. "You are doing the right thing now, that's what's important."

Chapter Twenty-Three

Jack looked around his crowded office. He was a reclusive man and avoided all social get-togethers and gatherings. Noise worried him and he liked to focus on one person at a time. Today, he had Rod and Marty with him, his most trusted 'dog's bodies', his accountant, Paul, and his stand-in assistant/secretary, Julie. Every time he looked at Julie, she reminded him of Mikaila's absence and pain seared his heart. He had slept fitfully over the past week and surprised himself at how strong his feelings were for both his nephew and stepdaughter. He was in a bad mood every day when he arrived at work and even worse when he left, after another day without a word from either Mikaila or Aaron. No one double-crossed Jack, least of all the people he loved or trusted. No one ever had – until now. Jack had been told his last shipment had turned up in New Zealand and, by now, would already have been swallowed by the competition.

There had been no trace of Aaron or Mikaila. No trail to follow. It had ended in Bali. Whatever they had done to cover their tracks, they had done it well, and with each passing day, the chances of tracing them were becoming slimmer. Jack and his brother, Norman, sat at the window behind the desk in Jack's office, their heads together and trying to go over where they thought the runaways may reappear. Neither of them considered the possibility that the pair may never come back to Australia.

"Jesus, Jack, I reckon if we wait long enough, sooner or later, they'll crawl out of a hole," said Norman, "and I'll tell you what, I'll be ready to smash their bloody heads in as soon as they stick their necks out." Norman and Jack were shocked, disappointed, angry. They had groomed Aaron and Mikaila to be the future of the organisation; all the recent plans included them. Now, if they returned, there would be no place for the young couple to hide. They had betrayed the trust of the family; retribution would surely await them. They were finished.

"Boss, you have a call from Mr. Sinclaire." Julie leaned past Norman to speak quietly to Jack. She had a cordless phone in her hand.

"Tell him to fuck off. Don't interrupt me, you nit-wit. You can see I'm busy." Jack growled at Julie.

Julie moved away.

"No, don't say that," Norman called to Julie. "I'll talk to him."

Julie returned with the cordless phone and was about to hand it to Norman, when Jack snatched it.

"Whadda ya want, Sinclaire?" He barked aggressively.

"I've got something I need to discuss with you."

"Tomorrow, come in tomorrow." He handed the phone back to Julie and she disappeared.

"Why don't you send him to replace Aaron for the next lot? By what you tell me, he can be trusted and he knows the whole set up," Norman suggested.

"Not a bad idea. I'll think about it. We need to get the next shipment in the pipeline pretty quick or I can guarantee our customers will go elsewhere." Jack frowned and rubbed his forehead. "Hey, Paul, can you bring those figures over here, we need to get some work done." Suddenly Jack looked a little brighter; the wheels began to turn again. Paul stood up and manoeuvred his way over to the two brothers.

"Will you lot all get out of here? I'll call you if I need you. Marty and Rod, you keep free for tonight. I have a little job for you." Everyone made his way to the door. Jack looked at Norman, "You too, mate, we can talk again later." Jack abruptly dismissed his brother. Everything had changed since the young ones had disappeared and Jack felt he could no longer trust anyone. He began to think about retirement – not to have to come in to work every day – not worry about everybody else. To maybe just cut his throat. He smiled at the thought – might be the best idea so far – guaranteed peaceful retirement!

******

Di rang Detective Pekalski with some important news about the murder inquiry. He was immediately interested.

"I'm being discharged tomorrow. It is a bit premature, but I can't stand this place another day. Can you meet me at my home about 3pm?"

Di agreed. She said she would bring a friend to talk to him.

The next day was Monday. Pekalski spent the early part of the day with the physiotherapist, learning to use his crutches. The surgeon agreed he was improved enough to go home under limited conditions. Remembering exactly what those limited conditions were became his challenge once he set his foot on home ground. He had not told the physio that he would be getting a cab home.

Martin and Di drove to the detective's stately old Queenslander home in Hamilton, a leafy suburb on the northern bank of the Brisbane River.

"Please, come in." Pekalski stepped aside awkwardly, while he held back the leadlight front door.

Leaning on his right crutch, he pointed with the left down the hallway to the veranda at the back of the house. Di's head was on a swivel, taking in all the old furniture and accessories that made the house a collector's dream.

"My goodness! My friends Harold and Robert would love this place," said Di smiling. "I love it."

"Well, it's a bit beyond me. I inherited it from my mum and she spent years restoring it, as did my late wife. I was about to put it on the market when I had my accident. I'm better suited to a smaller place, maybe a unit. I can see myself with a bachelor pad."

"Me too," said Di.

They all made themselves comfortable on the old cane lounge and the detective pointed to a tray on the table.

"My niece is staying with me until I get rid of these crutches. She said we should grab the glass jug from the refrigerator before we sit down."

They all sipped in silence until Pekalski put his glass on the table and turned to Martin.

"So I hear you may have something of interest to tell me."

"Yes," said Martin, shuffling his feet, he put his glass back on the tray. "I realise now I should have spoken up sooner, but as I explained to the managers, I wasn't sure what I had seen until I saw it again, if that makes sense. In the meantime, I had convinced myself that I should say nothing rather than point a finger at the wrong person. I simply can't imagine what it would be like to be falsely accused. On top of that, I felt sure you would've found a culprit by now. But I see I must now speak up before something happens to someone else."

"Rest assured we'll check whatever information you give us. We have a system of law to protect the innocent, so don't take the responsibility on your own shoulders, okay?"

"Yes, I do accept that," Martin nodded. "Jim said to tell you what I saw and leave it at that, not to try to analyse what it may mean."

"Right, go ahead, I'm listening."

"On the night of ... " He looked down at his notebook to check the date, and watched as Pekalski noted the date in his own leather-bound folder, " ... I was walking toward the front gate where I start my warm-up. I exercise at night. It was about ten-thirty and the gate is not far from the three-bed units where Jessie's is. I walked out of my unit, turned left, and strode briskly to the gate where I turned, and would normally start to jog. On this occasion, I saw a woman leaving the front door of unit No.27. I looked at her and realised I had seen her before. I went to wave to her but she was looking away from me. She walked out of the resort by the pedestrian gate, as the vehicle gate was closed, so she never saw me standing there. I think I was in the shadow cast by the Jacaranda tree, which partially overhangs the entrance. The light cast by the entrance lamps is diffused by the branches for the first few metres. I heard her get into her car out the front and she drove off. I never thought of it again until I found out Jessie was dead."

"Go on." Pekalski encouraged.

"As I said, I decided to keep what I thought I saw to myself. Until the other day when I saw the woman at the resort again, and it all came back to me. Do you know what I mean?" Martin leaned toward the detective.

"Yes, I know exactly what you mean. What else can you tell me about this woman?"

"She was Jessie's sister-in law."

"I see," was the detective's cool response, a slight smile appeared on his lips.

"I should have known it!" Di jumped up "I did know it. It had to be her. We eliminated the Clarkes, it only left Kevin with a revenge motive and Rena with a motive of..." She looked at Pekalski.

"I gather she was expecting an inheritance," said Frank. "She had no idea the lady's money had already been redirected to the Clarkes." Pekalski attempted to stand and, wobbling on the spot, he took a few steps to stretch his legs.

"How do you think she did it?" asked Di.

"Well, if I may speculate, I do believe the method will be the easy part. Jessie would have welcomed her in and then perhaps they shared a drink and a discussion, after which they had another drink, possibly one laced with barbiturates, which either Rena had in her possession, or perhaps she used Jessie's supply. Both Stanley Connelly and Jessie Thornton had such drugs prescribed to them. I've seen the containers. Rena Connelly had knowledge about drugs and managed to disguise the taste until Jessie consumed enough for her frail heart to fail." The detective took a breath. "That will be for the prosecution to prove. I also can't help but wonder what may've been the cause of death of her husband, Stanley. But he's been cremated now, so we'll probably never know."

Pekalski sat propping his chin on his locked fingers, which curled over the handle of one crutch. "Well, Martin, you realise this is the beginning. You'll have to answer more questions and be a witness in court?"

"I've thought about that. But I've seen this woman going into Letitia and George's home. What if she kills someone else? Maybe she has even done this before. I know I'm doing the right thing."

"Good man!" Pekalski put his hand on Martin's shoulder. "I have no doubt you will do a great job. But, for now, all this is absolutely secret. We must catch the culprit and then we must convict her. Huh?"

"You can rely on me to keep my mouth shut. A bit too much sometimes," he laughed.

Di stood. "And me, I know we can't say anything about this yet. I'll brief Jim on all this. No problems. We had better get going so you can swing into action." Di turned to leave.

"I'm not too sure about any swinging into action, but we can set the wheels in motion, thanks to you." He gave them both a smile and escorted them to the front door.

Chapter Twenty-Four

"I'm gonna give you a shot at this one. Don't fuck up," Jack said to Allen, as they sat facing one another in Jack's office. "You know the whole process better than anyone. Of course, the greater the effort, the greater the compensation."

"How much compensation are we looking at here?" Allen was interested now.

"Aaron's ten percent – maybe half a mill. The haul is expected to bring in excess of $5,000,000."

"Does this mean your nephew is out? Forever?" Allen pushed.

"That's my concern." Jack did not intend discussing his family with Sinclaire. He planned to deal with them in his own time.

"I guess this is as good a time as any to bring up my retirement. If I can get a decent haul, I want to quit. Disappear for good." Allen knew what a chance he took, throwing this in now. But there would never be a better time, especially when the boss actually needed him.

The silence hung thickly in the room. Jack reached for the remote control and turned the temperature down on the air-conditioner. He could never get cool enough these days. Both men recognised the absolute ruthlessness in each other.

"You know no one ever quits, not absolutely," said Jack. "We're a family, and as long as we live, we all know too much about each other. I can't see why you shouldn't take it easy for a while though, sort of look at it as an extended period of long service leave, eh? You never know when one of us has a need, later in life, and the organisation is there for support."

Allen had dreaded hearing this, but always knew it was probable. "Yeah," he said, "I gather by that you mean I can stop work but you'll continue to keep tabs on me – like, don't leave town".

"Well, let's put it this way, mate. We'll put you on the bench, one of our reserve players, you might say, but always available, and willing, I would hope, to replace a player on the field. But don't be put off, Allen." Jack leaned toward him. "You'll be well cared for. Take as many holidays as you can afford. If you run out of money, we may be able to help out. You'll be a hard man to replace. We'll miss you. Anyway, you might find a need for a little excitement in your old age."

Jack was looking smug. He rocked on his swivel chair, looking comfortable in his soft, rayon, open-neck shirt. He loved his Indonesian clothes; his light slacks and slip on shoes.

"Do you have anyone to replace me?" asked Allen.

"Why?"

"I might be able to suggest someone. Young, hungry, smart. A new recruit."

"How new?" demanded Jack.

"Well, he set a few scams in motion when he started work as a salesman for one of the resorts in the chain I oversee. I flagged him straight away as an operator and allowed him to continue. It took him a while to wake up to the fact we used him on several occasions to bring drugs in via his furniture importing. Just recently he was set to do a pickup in Bali, you may remember?"

"Yeah, yeah," said Jack.

"I'm pretty sure it was Aaron who organised to relieve him of that lot in the airport. He came home empty handed and we were after either him or his mate, Davo, who, incidentally, has disappeared without a trace." Allen sat back, he felt more relaxed. This was probably the longest session he had ever had with the boss.

"What's the kid's name? How old?"

"Matthew Weatherlee, about 32 or 33 I think. I haven't really tested him yet but this job may suit him well. You would need to decide about him yourself."

"Yeah," Jack grunted.

They talked for another hour without interruption and finally came to an agreement.

Jack said, "I'll meet this bloke and then, if all goes well, you can go on extended sick leave from your regular position with the Sleighmen Group. You go to Bali and pick up the threads of Aaron's network. I have someone in mind to take over from you there, but not immediately. You can't go just yet."

This could be Allen's swan song and he was ready to give it his best shot. In a way, he had prepared for this job for twenty years.

******

"Organise a men's group dinner," Jack said to Marty.

Before joining Jack and Norman's organisation, all potential employees had to be scrutinised for the purpose of security. A dinner would be arranged, known as 'The Men's Group'. Rod and Marty, as well as several of Norman's most trusted employees, would make up the numbers. The Men's Group could uncover a great deal of information about someone in a very short time. Matthew would have no idea he was going under the microscope.

******

"Leave next Friday night free from about 8pm," Allen said to Matthew, when he dropped by that same afternoon. "You may be invited to join our men's group. The boss likes us to keep fit and be sociable. He wants you to suss out some of the blokes you may be working with in the future. Make a few contacts, relax, have a drink and get to know a few people. I'll come by and pick you up."

"Does this mean I'll meet the boss? Am I in now?"

"No, and maybe. Depends on how you perform. No one meets the boss. You'll always be contacted by him on the phone, or by one of his assistants. It's for your protection as well as his. Can't talk about what you don't know about."

Allen was his usual abrupt self. "So after Friday night, if I'm accepted, what happens?"

"I might be going for a holiday and you can fill in for me for a while. If you do okay, great, you may stay in the job and I'll move on, but that's all to be tested. You've gotta measure up. Remember, all you have to do is play your part." Allen locked eyes with Matthew, keen to pick up on his reaction.

Matthew shifted about restlessly in his chair, "Sure, sure. And what would I do when I was doing your job? I mean, do I have to resign from my job here?" Matthew sounded a lot keener than when Allen spoke to him last time. Allen wondered whether Matthew was having some doubts, and he wanted to be sure of Matthew's commitment.

"This job is your cover, dummy. It gives you access to storage and the freedom to move around. I could recommend to Head Office of the resort group that you fill in for me, but whether you do that or not, you need a cover, of course."

"Right, and just what would I be doing?"

"Whoa! One thing at a time. You'll be fully briefed by me and then by the management, when, and if you're in. Right?"

"Right," said the salesman. "Count me in."

Mattwew's head was full of what he was going to take to Pekalski and he was shaking in his boots as well. He had moved into dangerous territory now. There was no going back.

When Sinclaire left, Matthew picked up the phone to speak to Pekalski in hospital. "Discharged? Can I have his address? I see." He hung up, frustrated, he wondered how he could contact Pekalski now.

His phone rang while he was still staring at it. "Detective Pekalski, Mr. Weatherlee. Can I have a word with you?"

"Yes," said Matthew, as he sat down at his desk and marvelled at the timing of Pekalski's call. "I'd like to have a talk to you." He filled the detective in.

"Wow, well I am impressed." Pekalski had listened without interruption. He asked the same questions Matthew had asked Sinclaire. He got the same answers.

"So, now we wait. After you've been given the once over on Friday night we may be in business. I'm going to have to pass all this over from here on. I've spoken to my boss and he wants to deal directly with you." Pekalski was talking fast.

"No. I only deal with you." Matthew was adamant.

"Can't do that," was Pekalski's reply. "If I was fit and back at work I may have been able to set something up but, officially, I'm not even working. Look, Matthew, I know the guys who'll be on this case and I can assure you there'll be no funny business. I can't say this for all my colleagues in the force, but I'd trust these fellers with my life. Things will move very fast once you get started. A substantial team will be on the alert when you get the go ahead, and they'll have to jump to. We can't afford to have any obstacles or communication breakdown. What I can do for you today is set up a meeting, so you can make your deal and know who you'll be working with. It's in your interest to have someone you can rely on and instantly be there for you. Remember, those guys you're working for are dangerous, and if they feel threatened in any way, you'll be the first one they'll look at.

They'll act first and ask questions later. This won't be like joining the Sunday School choir. Do you understand me?"

Matthew sighed. He was almost overwhelmed. He already wanted out – to escape and have his old, very boring, very quiet life back. A criminal group almost owned him now. The cops knew him, and all that was left was for him to play his part and hang on until the end. Then the most he could hope for would be the freedom to go back to his old job, if his cover had not been blown and he would become front page news.

"Okay, where do I have to go?" Matthew resigned himself to being totally compliant.

"Nowhere. A bloke called Andy will be there this afternoon. You treat him like any client in your office. He can take it from there. Trust him, he's a good cop, and he won't let you down. And another thing, Matthew, and I'm sure you've thought of this, yes, we know some of the higher ups in the department aren't exactly lily-white, but we know who they are, and the way we're going to execute this operation will mean it'll be game over before they can kill it. You'll be looked after, never fear." The detective was more worried than he let on. He knew they could not guarantee Matthew's safety and he was playing with some of the most dangerous men in the State.

"Thank you. When will I be speak to you again?" asked Matthew.

"You won't, not for the time being. Make no attempt to contact me from here on. Your regular phone may be bugged, but Andy will brief you about all that. When this game is over, we'll talk again. I can assure you I'll be watching from the sidelines and looking after your interests. You're gonna be fine! Good luck, son. Goodbye."

Matthew turned off his mobile phone and stared at the wall. He felt as if he had just entered another world.

Chapter Twenty-Five

"What a beautiful change of pace." Di reached out and held Jim's hand as they strolled along the path in the moonlight, following another musical evening with Robert, Harold and friends. "I feel one hundred percent better now than when we walked up here a couple of hours ago."

"So do I, I can't believe what a difference a little musical time-out can make. We absolutely must do this more often."

Since their time at Keeala Resort had turned into a rollercoaster ride, Jim and Di had agreed on several occasions that they really should jump off, but they were still there and something, maybe just stubbornness, kept them holding on and hoping for some successful outcomes. To see a conclusion to the murder investigation and to find out about the drug smuggling operation, both of which had occurred on their watch, had now become their goal.

"Jim, Detective Pekalski said today on the phone that we need to remain clear of interaction with the salesman. He has handed the case to the drug squad and although he didn't say anything, I think they'll be watching. I think they may be setting up something and we have to mind our own business; keep well away and not get involved in any speculation, also he said we aren't to ring him."

"Yeah, okay. I hope they deal with all this pretty soon. It makes me nervous thinking there may be criminals hanging around."

"Me too." They continued their walk home in silence.

Just before she turned the bedroom light out, Di commented, "I think it took a lot of courage for Mr. Judd to talk to Frank about what he'd seen. He felt embarrassed because he'd left it so long and a bit of a fool for not acknowledging the importance of what he saw."

"I feel we should've known as well. It all seems obvious now. Anyway, tomorrow is the big day and I'm sure Harold and Robert will play their part to a 'T'," Jim said, before he rolled over and pulled the sheet up. "Good night, love."

******

On Friday night, Matthew went home and changed. He was getting very nervous. "Mum, I won't be home early, just leave the front porch light on, please," he said, as he moved to the door and picked up his car keys.

"Got a new girlfriend?" asked Myra.

"No, as a matter of fact I'm thinking of joining a men's group, you know, to keep fit and discuss politics and the state of the world – and women. That sort of thing."

Myra laughed, "Sounds very interesting, I'm glad to see you taking an interest in your personal development and not just always focusing on earning money. I'm sure it'll do you good. Enjoy your night."

She leaned forward to kiss her son on the cheek. He was gone a moment later.

Allen and Matthew met at the Wild Orchid Club in The Valley. At the front, it looked like a restaurant, which it was, but in the rear a stairway led up to several noisy and smoky rooms where men sat around drinking – some were playing cards. They were directed to a round table at the side with about twelve chairs, most of them already occupied. Matthew immediately wondered if they were late.

He and Allen approached "Are we late?" Matthew worried.

"No, not at all. This lot can't wait to start checking out the menu. Come and sit down."

Matthew took a chair between Allen and another bloke. Matthew thought the guy did not look as though he spent much time in the gym. Allen began introductions, pointing first to the man next to Matthew. "That's John – Jerry – Marty – Rod – Laurie – James – Simmo – Dicky – Carlos – Paulie – and Geoff." Most of them nodded and a couple reached across the table to shake hands.

Jerry seemed to be the leader. He said "Shush now. Can you blokes just order, and then we can all get down to making Matthew here feel welcome."

They waved a harassed waiter over and there was finally an agreement to order the banquet meal with a few additions, and all manner of beer and spirits to wash it down. The noisy talk and laughter started up again immediately. Matthew began to relax.

"So what sort of an occupation are you in?" was the first question thrown at Matthew from Rod, whose hands were busy toying with a couple of dice, tossing and catching them on the back of his hand, not letting the dice hit the table. Matthew had his eyes on the dice and had to think what his answer was.

Many questions followed. Jerry seemed to have plenty to say, and they were interested in what sort of a car Matthew drove and how he could afford it and what football team he followed and what he did in his spare time. The food came and John, next to Matthew, asked about his love life and who his current girlfriend was.

"I don't have anyone in my life right now, John," he answered.

"Best way to keep it too, son, they'll have you undone every time. Give 'em enough rope and they'll hang you with it."

John was a morose-looking bloke, not exactly the life of the party, and a little after 10pm, he left. Matthew could not see how he fitted in with the group. He thought as he drove home, maybe they just need one of every kind and he was the token dickhead.

******

That same day had been very exciting for Jim and Di, also Harold and Robert. At about 8am, the four gathered in the manager's office where two of Frank Pekalski's colleagues briefed them. They had a plan. Their inspector had agreed they would like a little more evidence against Rena to be sure their case would hold up in court. Having an eyewitness to her presence at the scene, and the fact that she had lied on several occasions, made the case against her looked reasonable. Added to that, she had motive, opportunity, and no alibi for the time of her sister-in-law's death. She also had knowledge of a means of causing death that would not be open to everyone; to know the possible outcome of using certain drugs was, in her case, incriminating. Much of this would be seen as circumstantial, – what the police prosecutor would like was a confession, naturally – that is what they were all hoping to achieve.

******

Rena arrived at Letitia's unit to assist her with her personal care. The bedroom window opened on to the little front porch, where George sat, reading the paper. They greeted one another as usual and then Rena went in to help Letitia out of bed.

"Good morning, Robert," said George, when the other man walked up with his dog on a leash. "How's your little friend today?"

"Oh, very well, thank you. Dogs are such good company, don't you think?" Robert answered.

"True, but more trouble than I want now. I spend so much time looking after my wife."

"I understand. And how is she?"

"Not too bad, especially now we have assistance with her care. It gives me a little time to myself."

Robert released Gypsy's lead slightly and the little dog trotted up to George for a pat.

"I used to have a daily visit from the little poodle down the road. Do you remember Ben?" asked George.

"Yes, as a matter of fact I believe he now lives there again with the new lady. Such a shame what happened to dear Jessie. I miss seeing her around and she was always into everything."

"True, true," answered George. "I'm glad to hear Ben is back anyway. I do wish they could've found out what happened to her."

"Well, I think they have. Haven't you heard?" Robert walked up to the other chair next to the table and sat down. He leaned forward in a very conspiratorial attitude. "Yes, yes indeed. You know the police detective that was doing the investigation into the murder?"

"Yes," nodded George.

"Well, I'm a friend of his you know, and I visited him in the hospital the other day and he let slip a few very interesting facts." Robert leaned closer to George and the window. "Apparently, until recently they had little to go on, but now an eyewitness has come forward to say he saw a person on the night in question, and on top of that they have now uncovered the murder weapon so to speak."

"But I thought she was poisoned with drugs," George exclaimed.

"She was. But the drugs were in little brown bottles that have now come to light. And, I hear, covered in the murderer's fingerprints!" Robert slapped his leg with delight. He rocked back in the chair looking very smug.

"And who do the fingerprints belong to, do they know that?" was George's next question.

Both men heard a mighty crash. They turned and saw the curtains come down to the sill, closely followed by Rena, falling on to the insect screen.

Rena regained her composure and waved. "Just adjusting the blinds, so sorry."

"Are you okay?" asked George.

"Yes, thank you." She went back to the darkness of Letitia's room.

Once again, George and Robert put their heads together. "Well, that's what they're now investigating. I believe, as of today!"

"Dear? Rena, are you listening to me? Could you please push my slippers over a little?" It was Letitia's voice. "Oh Rena, could you please pass me my slippers?"

Letitia looked up to see a mask of panic on the face of her helper; then she was gone.

Rena paused at the front door and said, "I'm sorry, sir, I don't feel well and have to leave. You will have to attend your wife today." She was gone in a flash to her car, and away out the front gate.

"Good heavens, what was that all about?" said George. They both stood. "Excuse me," George said, as he disappeared inside to check on his wife.

With Gypsy's lead in hand, Robert took the steps to the pathway.

"I'll see you later, old friend!" He threw the comment over his shoulder as he turned toward the community centre to join the meeting in the manager's office. As he knocked and opened the door, he had a grin from ear to ear.

"I do believe we may have started something," he said.

Jim fetched another chair from the waiting area outside his office and made room for Robert beside the two detectives. Di, Jim, Harold and the two detectives listened intently as Robert recounted his story. An undercover police vehicle was already heading down the road in pursuit of Rena's car.

******

"It seems you must have impressed the boss, then," said Allen to Matthew, when he arrived on his doorstep at the resort sales office on Monday morning.

"Really? So what happens now?"

The salesman leaned back in his easy chair but was not as impatient to hear the answer to that question as Allen presumed. Thrusting both hands into his pockets, Allen walked around looking at his shoes.

"I've already told head office in Adelaide that I'm going to be on sick leave for a couple of months. Needless to say, they weren't happy, but stuff them, that's their problem. I've got two days to bring you up to speed, then I'm outa here and off overseas."

Allen plonked himself down on the office chair at Matthew's desk. He pushed Matthew's computer aside and lifted a laptop into its place. "Take a seat, Matthew. We've got some work to do. Pull up here." He pointed to the space next to him and then he turned his attention to the computer.

"Put the Out to Lunch sign on the door – we don't want any interruptions."

Matthew did as ordered, knowing his absence could attract the manager's attention.

"Tough," he said to himself.

The day rolled on, and by two-thirty, both men were starving. They closed the computer and drove down the road for a burger. They sat opposite one another and devoured their lunch. Matthew came up for air and said, 'so you say I'll have a direct line to Marty or Rod, or both, and that all my inquiries go through them?"

"Yes, and don't make a habit of ringing up for any petty little thing you can sort out yourself. Your mummy won't be holding your hand in this job, Matthew, and remember, you can't share with anybody. There is absolutely no one you can trust – no one! Understand? If you talk to anyone, you put the whole organisation at risk. Do that, and you're history."

"I understand. When do I get paid?"

"I was wondering when you were going to get round to that. The answer is, when I do. That's when the job is done. Right?"

"Sure."

Once back to work in front of the computer, Allen continued to force-feed information into his associate's head. Allen gave the laptop to Matthew, also a mobile phone.

"Ever owned a gun?" asked Allen.

"No." Matthew looked stricken for a moment.

"That's okay. There's plenty of time for that. First, we have to get this next job over. You and I are both on probation, so don't fuck up, hear me?"

Matthew was beginning to feel numb. He would take over from Allen as 'Mr. Fix It' in the drug running business. He would be hanging out with murderers and big-time criminals. *Bloody hell. What am I doing?*

The next day was more of the same, and by seven that night they had both had enough.

"Let's call it quits, son, I have the feeling you've got a handle on the main issues and I believe you're just smart enough to wing the rest. You'll be hearing from Rod in a couple o' days. He'll let you know what to expect, and if you have any queries you can ask him then."

Allen went on his way, nervous, but excited too; this next job would be the culmination of all his plans.

That evening, Matthew sidetracked to a quiet bar in a tavern not far from his home. The undercover officer, Andy, made contact and they sat at a small table discussing everything that Matthew knew so far.

"It's good mate, all is going to plan, rest assured no one can do any more. Keeping your nerve is what's called for now; remember we're right behind you, you're not alone."

They set their next contact date. Matthew slept little that night.

Chapter Twenty-Six

“What are you doing?” asked Jim, when he walked into his office on Monday morning.

Di looked up from her computer. “Making a list. Then I’m going to order caterers, for Margaret and Ethan’s wedding.”

“Really, when do they plan that?” Jim looked over his wife’s shoulder at the screen.

“As a matter of fact, they don’t yet, but I’m organising a surprise for them. Yesterday I talked to some of their friends, and we’ve agreed to put a few things in motion; maybe include their wedding in the annual dinner dance. That way they get a free reception and we all get something to celebrate.” Di was looking pleased with herself.

“You don’t mean you’re going to suddenly spring it on them at the last minute, surely?” said Jim.

“No, I realise that may be a mistake, especially if one of them changes their mind or something. No, what we plan is to organise everything, then, before we press the 'Go' button, we'll consult the lovers. That way we take the worry out of organising the celebrant and the reception and we plan to make a joint gift to the happy couple for a weekend away, all expenses paid at a five star hotel on the Gold Coast," Di finished with a flourish.

"Sounds good to me."

The phone rang and Jim picked it up. "Yes, it is. Hello, Frank." Jim listened intently for a couple of minutes. "Great, bye." He hung up. For a moment he stood staring straight ahead as if unable to digest what he had just heard "Well, good news. After Rena left here, she was followed, then arrested when she left her place with a packed bag. She was held on suspicion over the weekend and finally, on interview, she confessed. Frank said she cried, sulked, became aggressive, and clammed up. Then she became confused, and started to talk about Stanley and admitted to killing him and finally, Jessie. She'd forgotten she'd left the incriminating medication bottles in Jessie's kitchen.

"My God!" gasped Di, as her hand flew to her mouth and her eyes widened. "Unbelievable."

"Anyway, the story is, she came to ask Jessie for an advance on her inheritance, and Jessie refused her. Jessie hadn't told Rena she'd changed her Will. Then Rena decided to give her a laced drink, and finally, pretty much force-fed the last lethal doses. It sounds as though she did the same to Stanley but over a longer period. She wasn't aware it would all be for nothing. Despite the presence of her attorney, she confessed, but then withdrew her confession, saying she was forced by the police. They put her in a line-up and Martin

Judd picked her. She's now been charged with murder. Frank doesn't know what they'll do about Stanley's death, but they have her confession of Jessie's murder."

"Well done." Di smiled as she put her hand out to Jim. "Congratulations on assisting in solving a major crime, sir."

"You first, my dear. You've contributed your brilliant mind once again to maintaining law and order in the battle against crime – in the name of truth and justice ..." They both burst into raucous laughter and fell together in combined relief.

Di pushed Jim away. "Oh, shut up. Let's go and share a coffee with Harold and Robert." They collided in their rush to get through the front door.

Harold, Robert, Jim and Di, laughed as they congratulated themselves yet again, and tossed around snatches of quoted conversation and anecdotes from the events leading up to the arrest of Rena Connelly.

"You know, we're definitely writing that book now," said Harold, as he looked at his dearest friend. "We have our conclusion and, if all goes well, we may even get to interview the lady herself."

"You mean Rena?" Di asked.

"The lady herself. I have a feeling she may be interested in being immortalised in print. And she can paint her image anyway she likes."

******

Both Allen and Jack underestimated Aaron's abilities. When Allen arrived in Bali, he made his way to Aaron's known haunts and contacts, but he found that information had dried up.

"We have so many young people staying here, especially in the peak surfing season, sir. I can only check my records."

The manager of the hotel where Aaron stayed could not remember him at first, then only vaguely. He addressed the computer on the desk, nodding as though he was trying to remember Aaron. Finally, he looked up at Allen.

"He checked out several weeks ago, sir, no forwarding address."

Allen knew he was lying and, in his usual aggressive manner, he followed the man to his office door and lodged his foot in the crack before it was closed in his face.

"You know exactly who I'm looking for."

He leaned forward and grabbed the front of the manager's shirt, their faces inches apart, their breath mixing.

"You aren't the only one with influence in this town mate. Where the fuck is he?"

Intimidation tactics were nothing new to the manager, he smiled and stepped back to allow Allen to enter the room. He adjusted his shirt and ran his finger through his thick dark hair.

"Perhaps I can make some enquiries for you? Please sit down."

Hesitantly, Allen sat in the chair in front of the small desk and watched the other man pick up the phone, dial, and then talk in his own language to another party. After making several calls, he finally turned back to the impatient Aussie, staring daggers at him from across the desk.

"Sorry, we have no more information about your friend, sir, however there are some business associates of his who are anxious to meet up with you." He pushed a small piece of paper across the desk and Allen noted a name and address and two phone numbers. He grabbed the note and plunged it into his shirt pocket, stood, and walked out without another word.

Sitting in his small hotel room for the next two days did nothing to improve Allen's temper. He had made his call and was told he would be contacted. He waited, watched television, paced around the room, kicked the wall, and became increasingly anxious.

On the morning of the third day, there was a knock on Allen's hotel room door. He opened it to two small, young, but tough-looking, Indonesian men. They strolled into the room and looked around then, unintimidated by Allen, the slightly taller of the two said, "We believe you wish to make a deal with us?"

"No. Incorrect. We already have a deal, as you know. I'm here merely to see it is carried out as arranged. We see no need to change a thing. Our previous contact has left and now you deal with me."

He attempted to establish a new deal, however Allen was hoping to continue with the agreement they already had with Aaron.

"No," continued the taller one, "We have many more expenses, and security must be maintained. It is hoped you can be trusted more than your associate." He demanded a new deal.

Allen refused.

"Please yourself, sir, we have many more people we can do business with; you may take our offer or walk away."

It was obvious to Allen they held the upper hand. He was not a man who liked to back down but, with a sigh, he realised he had no bargaining power and it was all unfamiliar territory to him. He cursed Aaron and the little bastards who stood in front of him. He cursed his lack of local knowledge and language. He turned his back on the pair and began to pace around the room.

They took this as a sign that he would not agree and they too turned toward the door.

"Where the bloody hell are you going?" he shouted to their backs and they both turned with a grin that only infuriated him more.

Allen tried to show some resistance to their demands, but he knew they had the upper hand in the negotiations. He did the best he could do in the circumstances, but he knew he was being done over. The pair agreed to the same plan as usual, but the split was different, and no matter how much pressure Allen tried to exert, they would not be moved. They had more options than he did, and the only reason they went ahead with him was because previous dealings with Jack's syndicate had been trouble-free and time was running out. They needed their shipment out of town within the next two days. They all finally shook hands.

Allen had lost weight. He had barely eaten since his arrival in Bali. So that night he treated himself to a banquet in the hotel dining room.

"Hello, you must be an Australian. I heard you ordering. I'm Marko. Would you like some company?" A stranger stood hesitantly looking down at Allen.

Allen looked up at the man; he rarely wanted company, and least of all now that he had so much to think about. But, maybe he could use some conversation, and just maybe, this guy could fill in a few gaps about local customs. He stared, and then said, "Yeah, sure, mate. Pull up a pew. My name is... Tom," after a moment's hesitation and the two shook hands.

"You on holidays?" asked Allen, as he continued to tuck into his meal.

"No, I'm doing business, as usual. I import leather goods for my distribution warehouse at home in Brisbane. What are you doing here?"

"I import furniture. But it's all new to me; I'm just filling in for someone else in our organisation. I'm going home day after tomorrow – a bit empty-handed."

"That so? What a shame. You really gotta know your way round this town to make a good deal," said Marko.

"Yeah," grunted Allen, They finished their meal over a couple of bottles of not very good wine. They said their goodbyes and parted company. Allen realised he had given more information than he had gotten.

Marko returned to his room and made contact with his superior.

Allen had no idea he had eaten dinner with an undercover cop from Australia. He was also very surprised to find himself sitting next to Marko on the flight back to Brisbane.

Chapter Twenty-Seven

The salesman studied his reflection in the bathroom mirror as he absent-mindedly ran the razor over his face. Matthew looked at his own dark eyes and tight mouth and wondered how this face would be looking back tomorrow. For a moment, he saw an image of his body lying on the ground in a pool of blood. He heard gun shots and police sirens in the background, his eyes widened. He shook himself and the image cleared. He stood still, wondering if it was a vision of the events to come later that morning, or just an overactive imagination coupled with fear and guilt.

Matthew's mobile rang. It was his undercover cop, Andy.

"Everything's set to go and you'll be okay. Now listen to me. You'll drive into the car park at Chermside, the one I told you about before, at precisely 9.30am. When you're out of sight behind the air-conditioning tower on the south side, we'll do the swap. You out, me into the driver's seat and change caps. I'll drive out. You walk around the shopping centre for half an hour and then make your own way home. Got that?"

Matthew nodded into the phone, almost overwhelmed with relief that he would not be the one to drive into the wharves.

"Did you get that, mate?"

"Yeah, yes I did, and I'll have the soft-top up, as you said before."

"Right, all set. See ya." Andy hung up the phone and Matthew heaved a great sigh of relief.

The plan had been for Matthew to drive to the wharves to meet up with Allen and the other gang members and help unload the shipment that came in, hidden in furniture destined for Keeala Resort.

The door slammed behind him as he left the empty house and made for the car that sat in the garage, his Saab convertible with its soft-top up. He glanced at his watch for the tenth time in the past few minutes. Matthew saw that he was precisely on time for his role in this next-to-last leg of the drug journey. From Indonesia and Vietnam, to the streets and back rooms of Brisbane, the illegal cargo would be exchanged for cash and passed from hand to hand, emptying many pockets, filling others, before it wreaked its final havoc. The thoughts of the destruction it brought to so many lives gave Matthew the courage he needed to carry out his role in the events planned for the next few hours. He fastened his seat belt and headed toward his rendezvous.

Like many other mornings for the previous few days, the sun shone and the breeze rustled the trees on the roadside as

Matthew drove through the traffic. He imagined the drug squad moving into position at the wharves where the imported furniture stood packed, ready to be claimed. Everything had to happen according to the precise plan laid out by the two leaders of the squad. His hands shook on the steering wheel as he entered the shopping centre car park. Whether he was being watched at this point, Matthew was not sure, but as he pulled up out of sight behind the air-conditioning tower, he jumped out of the driver's seat. Andy materialised from behind a concrete pillar and replaced Matthew. Matthew had worn a red Broncos cap. He gave it to Andy, who pulled it low on his forehead. Matthew took Andy's plain white cap and tossed it onto his head. He watched his Saab disappear on the down ramp, on its way to the warehouse.

******

"Things are pretty quiet around here this morning, eh," said the brawny dock worker.

"Yeah, mate, just this half a container to go," said his offsider. "What time's the pick-up for this stuff?"

"Should be here in about half an hour. We'd better get a move on, get those crates out of there. We'll stack 'em on Loading Bay 3."

The two men each got into a 3.5 tonne forklift and started toward the shipping container. The lead operator lined up the tines and slipped them under a pallet He reversed slowly, turned 180 degrees, and came back the few metres to the loading dock in Bay 3. His mate executed the same manoeuvre a few seconds behind him. Their timing was impeccable; their practised skill was evident. They were unaware of the dozen pairs of eyes watching their every move.

Twenty minutes later, the crates were stacked on the dock. The drivers were about to park their machines in a bay inside the building, when a shrill buzzing sound from a remote phone bell ringer alerted the forklift drivers that the office phone was ringing. The lead hand stopped his machine and ran up the steps to the office.

He emerged after a few seconds and shouted to his offsider, "Perfect timing. They'll be at the gate in a couple of minutes."

Hidden behind a stack of boxes at the rear of the dock, the police officer in charge of the operation whispered into his radio, "Couple of minutes, guys. Wait for my signal."

Three short horn blasts signalled the arrival. Pigeons, startled by the disturbance, flew out of the rafters. The offsider walked twenty metres to the gates at the front of the compound. He unlocked the padlock that secured a heavy chain, wound through both sides of the gates. The gates squealed as he spread them open.

Scattered around the compound, concealed in their hiding places, the police team members heard the sound. They tensed, their breathing quickened, hearts thumped, guns were checked. It was about to happen.

"Where to, mate?" asked the driver of a three tonne pantechnicon. Ash fell from the cigarette in his mouth, as he spoke. He did not look like he had been to finishing school.

The offsider yelled, "Number three – around to the right. You back in first – the fourbys can go either side of you."

Two four-wheel drive off-roaders waited behind the pantec as it moved forward. "Follow him and slot in either side of him, boys," he yelled at the drivers. They looked like they might have gone to the same university as the pantec driver.

From vantage points scattered around the compound and within the warehouse, the police team watched every move. Hidden at the side of the warehouse, but with an unimpeded view of the loading docks, a camera operator slowly raised a video camera and focused on Loading Bay 3. He started recording. The team leader held a hand up, palm out. The signal to wait passed from man to man.

The pantec driver backed in toward the edge of the dock. The cabin filled with sound, as long, high-pitched beeps gradually increased in urgency as the reversing camera did its job. The truck jerked to a stop. The driver and two passengers alighted and jumped up to the waist-high loading floor. They swung the doors open.

The two four-wheel drives stopped short of the edge of the loading dock. Both drivers jumped out and flipped up the rear doors. They climbed back in, reversed again, and stopped just short of the lip of the dock. The cargo floor in each vehicle was thirty centimetres below the lip of the dock, but there was still sufficient room to load the smaller crates. The drivers each had four passengers. They all got out and hauled themselves up onto the loading bay floor.

The pantec driver shouted at the other twelve, "Righto, boys, small cartons and crates in the fourbys, the rest in the truck. Be quick about it now, we don't want to hang around."

"Hey," someone yelled, "Where's the new guy?"

"Ah, shit, I dunno," said the pantec driver. "Bloody hell! Look, can't be worried about him now – just get this stuff loaded. We'll sort the stupid bastard out later."

The four-wheel drives were loaded. The drivers and passengers got back in. The driver of the pantechnicon shoved the last crate in the back of the truck and slammed the doors shut.

"Right, we're off," he said to his passengers, "Get in." He climbed into the cabin and gave a thumbs-up to the drivers of the other vehicles. He went to turn the ignition key.

Right on cue, Matthew's Saab drove in. The tyres squealed in protest as Andy slammed his brakes on and skidded to a halt, side on, in front of the pantec and the fourbys.

The pantec driver stuck his head out the window and yelled, "What the bloody hell are you doing, Matthew? Get that piece of shit out of the way, or ..."

A shrill whistle blast pierced the air. Bodies brandished handguns and appeared from behind doors, partitions, piles of cartons, underneath the loading bay.

"Stay where you are! Put your hands where we can see them! Don't fuck with us!"

Mr. Brainiac in the pantec raised one hand, but grabbed his mobile phone from the door pocket with the other. He deftly hit the speed button for Allen Sinclaire's number and raised it to his ear.

"Toss it out – now!" screamed the detective closest to him.

The driver hesitated for a few seconds. He saw the end of a pistol a hand's breadth away from his forehead. He tossed the phone out the window. It remained connected to Sinclaire. Brainiac proved he was not completely stupid – he held up both his hands in surrender as he yelled, "Don't shoot – it's a fair cop."

His passengers threw their hands up, as did the others in the fourbys. As they stared at the guns pointing at them, they knew there was no point resisting.

It was all over in less than thirty seconds, and not a shot fired. It was a good result, or was it?

******

Allen stood in the shower with his hands flat against the tiles. He had not moved for a couple of minutes; he just let the steaming water cascade over his head as he pondered what to say to his wife before he left. He planned to meet with the other gang members at a self-storage facility in a nearby suburb. He had an hour to kill before he needed to leave. In the meantime, he let the water wash his cares away. He fantasised about his future. He smiled and let the water fall into his mouth and down his chin. His mobile phone rang. The sound shook him from his reverie. He slid the glass door open, reached clumsily from the shower, and grabbed it from the top of the vanity basin. He fumbled with wet hands to find the talk button and then set it to speakerphone. He heard shouting and someone yelling, "Toss it out – now!" He pulled a towel from the rail and his eyes widened as he heard a familiar voice shout, "Don't shoot – it's a fair cop."

"Oh, shit," Allen blurted, "I've got to get out ... ." He never finished the sentence.

"Police! Police!"

The bathroom door burst open. Two guns pointed at his chest. He gasped and stumbled backward. He could see more police officers behind the two in the bathroom, guns held at their sides.

He saw his future disappear before his eyes, as the cold, hard embrace of handcuffs crunched on his wrists. He thought of his wife, his money. He thought of jail.

He knew it was all over.

Chapter Twenty-Eight

From the solitude of his prison cell, Allen mulled over the botched operation. He presumed Matthew had been arrested, and taken in at the same time. Strangely, he had not considered it could be Matthew who had betrayed him. Instead, he guessed it was Marko who was the Judas, and that Marko was Aaron's accomplice. Allen, however, had no intention of going to prison for the rest of his life. He had a plan.

Knowing he was on his own, he could not look for support from the Noonans, or anyone else. He had to get in first if he wanted to benefit from a deal.

That afternoon, his solicitor, Eddie Jostovich, saw him in the interview room.

"Eddie, I'm willing to turn State's evidence if you think it will help get me a reduction in my sentence. What do you think?"

"Mate, it's worth a go, definitely. Let me see what I can suss out".

Two hours later, following Jostovich's confirmation that a deal had been struck, Allen told the arresting officer everything he knew about the organisation. He gave details of Jack and Norman Noonan's involvement, and named another dozen links in the chain. He was assured he would receive a reduced sentence in return for his cooperation.

Thinking about his accomplices, Allen wondered for the first time if he would meet up with the resort salesman in jail. He had named him in his confession, so he could expect no support from Matthew. Allen began to wonder whom else he might see during his stay at the government's expense. He became very aware of his own vulnerability. He feared for his survival. Jack still had too many friends on the outside. Allen's stay, whatever it amounted to, would be a very testing time for him and there were those in the know that predicted the ex-area manager would not come out alive. Allen knew that when he got out, if he got out, he would have to disappear very quickly.

******

Frank Pekalski stood in the wings and watched as Allen gave enough evidence to put the entire syndicate away for many years.

The next day, the state prosecutor informed Matthew he would not have to appear in court, as there was enough incriminating evidence from Allen's testimony to ensure a successful outcome to the case. He also said that there was insufficient evidence to charge Matthew with any offence.

Matthew took a week off work after the arrests.

Di and Jim were the only ones who had any idea that Matthew had been involved with the ex-area manager. Harold and Robert's novel would have to be rounded out by their own imagination.

******

The guests celebrated at Margaret and Ethan's wedding. Apart from celebrating the couple's happy event, the big topic was the end of Jessie Thornton's murder mystery. Of course, being wise after the event, everyone said they knew it had to be Rena Connelly, the ex-sister-in-law.

"Hindsight is a wonderful thing, isn't it, darling? said Jim.

"Yes, Jim, it certainly is," Di replied.

******

"Relax; put your seat back and your feet up." The handsome man reached over and fluffed a cushion behind Roberta's head, as he made her comfortable in the luxurious passenger seat of the new, $120,000 motorhome.

Roberta flashed her beautiful new diamond wedding ring in the sunlight. Her husband put the automatic gear stick into 'D'. He was in the driver's seat of the most amazing home-on-wheels he had ever laid eyes on. Both ring and motorhome were compliments of Roberta's long-saved, and hard-earned, superannuation payout.

As the motorhome eased into the traffic, a cultured female voice purred from the six speakers in the cabin, "In four hundred metres, roundabout ahead, take the second exit." Roberta's husband glanced at the GPS screen ahead of him and smiled. In the top, right-hand corner it said, 'Distance to Destination – 4,343 kilometres'.

"Let's go," said Daniel Milou, with a smile on his face.

The End

Author Kumari and husband John live in an Over 50's resort in Queensland.

In their past careers, John was a business manager and Kumari, a registered nurse.

After their marriage in 1992, they combined their skills to manage retirement resorts in N.S.W. and Queensland. They used to joke that the many interesting characters and unusual situations they encountered would one day provide a wealth of material for a book.

When Kumari became wheelchair bound following foot surgery in 2010, she realised the period of physical inactivity presented her with a golden opportunity. She decided to weave her memories of those management years into a fictionalised story. The result was not one novel, but a series.

The series follow the trials and tribulations of the residents, employees and diverse characters of Keeala Resort. Kumari also introduces social comment about ageing issues and some of her characters draw her readers into a dialogue about the social and practical questions encountered in people's mature years.

Sixteen grandchildren fill in the spaces when she is not writing.

www.ingramcontent.com/pod-product-compliance
Lightning Source LLC
Chambersburg PA
CBHW070216030726
47505CB00006B/1700